The Champion's

Torment

By M. Francis Lamont

Thank you for your support ♡ m Lamont

First thanks go, as always, to my daughter Morgan. Keep on writing your dreams, little one. Next to the person that this book would have been impossible without, Tanya. I owe you beer and wings as soon as I see you. You were there for me when I needed you most, thank you doesn't cover it. Jessa, Wendy, Diane, Analyn and my great work family your support has meant the world. Amanda, Dillon and Laurel and the crew at Longriders, you all jumped on board and made every little success feel so much greater. To my fellow Captains, Barbossa and Jack, your prayers held me up, thank you.

To my cast of heroes; Barry, Dan, Dustin, Gwen, Liam, Manu, Simon, Todd and Viva. You continue to inspire me with your words and works. I'll never forget your advice and will be forever in your debt. Eternal gratitude to you all.

A huge and unforgettable thank you to everyone who bought a copy, shared a post or posted a review. Each of those things make such a difference for any author, especially a new one like me. A special shout out to the man, the face of the series, Will Taylor. You're amazing and I can't wait to see what your future holds.

Last but never least, to the people I wouldn't have made it through the drama of book 1 without, my 'team': Christine, Erin, Heather, Karla, Lara, Laura, Lila and Steffany. Thank you for the 'red pen' opinions.

"Live with Passion, Live with Purpose, and Never Lose."

This is a work of fiction. Names, characters, businesses, places, events, locales, and incidents are either the products of the author's imagination or used in a fictitious manner. Any resemblance to other works of fiction, actual persons, living or dead, or actual events is purely coincidental.

Preface:

Cassian, 'The Celt', is the Champion of Velletri who recently regained his title after an intense battle in the arena. A battle that had been fueled, and almost ended, by a dose of opium given to ease the lingering pain of the wound that he had received in an attempt to win that same title back. The inspiration and drive for his return to glory was not coin or the promise of eventual freedom but the heart of a young woman who had been sent to his bed as a gift of esteem by her Dominus, Felix Census. Her innocence and demure beauty touched something long buried in the heart of the rough and violent man causing him to name her his personal priestess: Violetta. Through trials of spirit and physical agony the lovers had persevered, oblivious to the manipulations of their masters for financial and societal gain, all they desired was to be in each other's arms.

The purchase of a disgraced champion of Rome brought a chance for Cassian and Violetta to be together after a night of painful revelations in the house of Census. Commanded by the lanista who owned him, Tiberius Tertius, to let Proximus, the recruit from Rome, earn the mark of gladiatory brotherhood Cassian was filled with anger at the blow to his pride and doubt in his own standing with his master by the fight's end. He could not know that the Romans had come to the agreement that Violetta would be sent to his arms upon each victory, but should he lose she would face punishment meant to inspire him to constant victory.

Violetta had witnessed the match from the side of her master and his preferred body slave, Meridius, who she held to heart like a father despite the recent revelation of his own secret desire to hold a different place in her heart. She had feared Cassian's death in the match and that worry grew when he took a blow to the head that robbed him of consciousness. Respite had come when the lanista had sent her to ease the gladiator's foul mood. Soothing his soul had turned to the verbal and physical expression of the love that had grown between them. Before being parted by guards he had spoken to her of a gift he would see to her hands before she left the villa but there had been no time for him to explain before they were separated with only the gods knowing when they would see each other again.

CHAPTER 1

Cassian's fists clenched at his side as the guards led Violetta away from him and towards the stairs to the villa. There had barely been time for her to dress after their passionate lovemaking upon the table that he ate at daily with the men he called his brothers. If, by the betrayal of the gods, this was the last time he saw her then he would enjoy this secreted memory each time he sat down to eat. His mind was still focused on her and what they had shared as he left the dining area with a smile on his face that would not leave despite the pain starting to throb once again in his leg.

It was not likely to be chance that his path crossed that of the druidic medic, Arturo, who put up his hand to stop his following of the Romans that had his woman. "I would see that wound tended before you do anything else to aggravate it this night."

Cassian attempted to protest but his friend was firm and left little choice when he directed the gladiator down the hall to his infirmary.

"Proximus has fallen then?" He asked quietly while heating the needle to apply the stitches needed to close the wound from the big German's blade that he had received during the match meant to bring Proximus into the fold as a member of the brotherhood. Both Cassian and Arturo knew that the gladiator hated to take a life outside the arena which was why for years he had not participated in the test, but this time he had found no way to avoid the command.

"No, the man yet lives. I took a blow to the head and Proximus now stands a brother." Said Cassian darkly. The reminder of his forced loss souring the bliss that had lingered with him. "I must return to Dominus' office to break words or so I assume." He hissed at the pull of the needle but shook his head when his friend offered him something for the pain of it.

"You know how I feel about your drugs Arturo." He said with a forced smile. He had no desire to insult the man, but he would never again willingly take such a thing without dire need. Sighing deeply the champion could not help the rise of his spirits when the shake of his head wafted the scent of Violetta across his nose. He looked up and noted the curious look on Arturo's face and a smile spread across his lips. "I found love, my friend. It is more than I thought I could feel and yet does not feel like enough."

The druid laughed softly and nodded. "Cassian, my dear friend, I could have told you that you loved her that first morning when she left your arms." He shook his head. "But you would not have heard it for you had to find it for yourself." His hand gently gripped Cassian's shoulder. "I am happy for you. This is a thing you have deserved for years and now it is yours. If I can help you with this all you have to do is break words to the way it can be done." He stepped away, cleaning his tools and Cassian sighed. The guards would be back in a moment to take him to Tertius.

Cassian rubbed his hand across his jaw and laughed a little to himself. "You break words of the very thing I would ask of you." He glanced down the hall to ensure that the guards were not so close that they could hear every word they spoke. "The drug you would have given to me, put it within a vial for I know of one who is likely to have a greater need of it than either of us." He beckoned his friend closer and spoke quietly of the horror that his woman faced and the pain she was in.

"Can it be done Arturo? I'll instruct Jovian to see it to her hand. He can get closer than I will be allowed again this night."

His eyes pleaded with his friend to consider his request and to do so quickly before the chance was lost and she was gone from the house. He knew that the lanista's boy would do anything for him and it would be easier for him than anyone else. Though there was the concern he would tell Tertius of what had passed between them instead of staying loyal to his friend. "Arturo? What say you to this?"

Arturo turned to look at Cassian, surprise in his eyes. The Celt knew that what he was asking could put every one of them in danger if they were caught. Jovian was a likeable youth but his loyalty to the lanista was unquestionable.

"You would have to convince the boy that there is no harm to Dominus if he does as you ask. You know that I cannot stand idly by at the thought of any being suffering abuse such as you say she is. I will do my part, but you must find a way to do yours." Arturo handed him a small vial and whispered. "It is the lightest dosage that I have now, without knowing her or how she would handle the drug I cannot give anything more powerful." The druid pressed Cassian's fingers closed around the vial and then said in a louder voice for the benefit of the guards. "That should see you to Dominus in better condition to break words with him. You are not likely to fall now."

The gladiator laughed and stood, nodding his thanks to the medic as the guards returned to take him to the lanista's office. He followed them with his head held high, the epitome of gladiatory pride as they crossed the floor of the celebration that continued. He forced himself not to notice that the voices of some of the Romans stilled at his passing; he would not let them distract him from his task.

Waiting at the wall outside the lanista's office he saw Jovian approach and took a single step to block his path. "I would make request of you, if you stand able to aid me and if you can form words in the presence of a woman of great beauty without attempting to bed her?" His tone was teasing but it was obvious that his request was serious. "Will you aid me in the delivery of a gift Jovian?"

The boy looked at him and leaned against the hand that held him in place, his voice a breathless whisper that played at seduction, irritating Cassian that he had to tolerate the unwanted flirtation.

"What reward would you give me if I do? Long have you denied my touch though you are the man that taught me to use it. Would you allow it now, Champion?" Jovian licked his lips in anticipation.

Cassian guessed the boy had seen in the looks passing between him and Violetta, which would give away that he would do just about anything to see the gift to her hands.

"I am not so foolish as to think that one equates the other boy. You can do it as a favor or not at all. I will not be treated as the whore I once was, for you or anyone else. Understand?" His voice was a tense growl that was met by the youth's flirtatious laughter and raised hands of surrender. Too long had the boy been the pet of Tertius, it was beginning to show in his character.

Jovian shook his head at Cassian's reaction to his teasing jest. "Oh Cassian, you do break my heart with such refusal, but I would not see yours to the same pain." He held out his hand and batted his dark lashes. "I know whom you would see it to. Simply see it to my grasp and I will see it to her person."

Cassian bit back the snarled reply that was rising in his throat. The boy was willing to help and that was what was needed. He pressed the vial into the soft brown palm and whispered. "Tell her who sends it and she will not make a scene that draws attention. You have my gratitude for this Jovian." With a nod of his head Cassian stepped back to the wall and took his expected stance to wait for Tertius to appear while Jovian sashayed towards the party.

He watched the guard notify Tiberius Tertius that his champion was ready for him. The lanista excused himself from his conversation and made his way to the office. Snapping his fingers as he passed Cassian, Tiberius stepped to his desk and turned to face the freshly bandaged man who bowed his head in uncommon submission.

"Have you lost mind?" Tertius snarled. "To defy your Dominus' direct command? To defy Doctore for giving same instruction that I would have in the same place?" Cassian tensed as Tertius circled then came to a stop just in front of him. "Find tongue and break words of explanation."

He was cleanly shaven and smelled of whatever herbs it was that Arturo had used to sooth his wound after stitching the edges together. He had insisted that they were not jagged, and the scarring would be minimal and yet Cassian felt as if he was an abused dog, waiting for the next strike. Shifting his weight from the damaged leg he considered how to answer the question without increasing the man's wrath. There would be a punishment regardless of what he said, but if he worded this right it might be lessened. Finally squaring his shoulders, he replied calmly. "Apologies Dominus, Forfeit clouded my mind with contempt."

"Forfeit?" The lanista's eyes blazed with rage. Reaching out he gripped Cassian's hair at the roots and twisted his head until their eyes met. "Explain how it was you forfeit when I saw you cut and felled to your knees?" He released the hair and stood glaring at the man who knew that he would have been lashed already had he stood any less skilled in the arena.

"I did as was commanded, Dominus." He said in a low growl. "You did not break words as to how it was to be done." He fought the instinct to ball his fists, the action would be seen as aggressive and the man would be justified in seeing him beaten for it.

"Then I would have thought my command enough to see temper stayed." Tertius cuffed Cassian on the back of his head. "Tell me, oh proud man, what was lost today besides your pride? Was title ripped from grasp by the allowing of Proximus to earn the mark of the brotherhood?" Turning he raised his hand to silence Cassian's protest.

Sitting behind his desk he leveled the man with his glare. "You are done with training until I see that you have learned that pride is not taken by any fall, but only surrendered by your own foolishness. I would also see mop to your hands in the stead of a sword for a time until patience is relearned." He smiled just as Cassian felt a glare of indignation flash across his face at the outrageous insult commanded by his Dominus. "Go now before mind changes and the pits greet your insolent attitude with blood."

Cassian could not believe his ears. The lanista could not be serious; a mop instead of swords? To clean his villa instead of fighting alongside his brothers? This was cruelty beyond what was warranted. He had done as commanded yet stood punished for his dislike of the task, as he had suspected would happen. As Julius and Auctus led him from the office he took a small measure of peace in the nod from Jovian as he ducked back to the celebration. Violetta would have the gift and so pain would be eased and, thank what gods there might be, she would never know what went on in the office and the base position her champion would fill until Tertius' mood improved.

Violetta turned as she heard a second set of footsteps on the balcony moments after she had stepped out into the cool evening breeze to calm the flush on her cheeks. Looking out across the training yard she was startled to hear her name whispered from behind her. She was surprised to see who was standing in the doorway staring at her. The bronze skinned boy that she had seen at the lanista's side was so beautiful he could have almost been a girl. His jet-black hair fell to his shoulders and his deep brown eyes were lined with kohl and sparkled with mischief and flirtation.

"Dreaming of him upon the sands? He is of a form that lingers in the mind. It is the champion that fills your thoughts is it not?" He said with a teasing smile. "Do not think that I did not note your eyes upon him all evening and how you followed him from the room after the test."

When he rested his hip against the rail and smirked at her Violetta blushed, unable to argue the point since he obviously already knew. Raising her eyes to meet his with a soft smile she said quietly. "He is glorious beyond measure." She then whispered more to herself than to him. "And I love him." She did not think he would be able to hear her whisper over the noise of the Romans but when a carefully groomed eyebrow arched, and a look of shock washed over his face she knew that he had, and she looked away to the sands again.

"Love? You love him? How is that possible? The man is a whore turned to gladiator." He smirked slyly. "Though he is a most pleasurable fuck. When he and I…" His voice trailed off dreamily and she felt a look of shocked dismay come across her face. "He taught me everything I know about fucking." The boy said, sliding towards her until he planted a hand on the railing on either side of her, trapping her within his arms while he pressed close against her in a subtle invitation to explore what he had learned. He was living, breathing sensuality as he tried to distract and envelop her with his nearness and the press of his sex against her through the fine linen he wore around his waist. Leaning to whisper in her ear, the heat of his breath on her neck, he said. "Oh, and I learned many, many things." His lips brushed the skin just below her ear as a smile spread across his lips when she shivered. "Perhaps I should show you."

"You and he have…you were lovers?" She asked in confusion. For some reason, it did not seem possible and the thought of her Cassian making love to a man as he had to her was all but unfathomable in her mind. "What do you mean by naming him a whore?" Her voice carried a note of indignance at the insult thrown not only at the man she loved but at one who was not present to defend or deny it. There was a familiarity in how the boy moved and that she could not deny but still there was a doubt in her mind that his words were as he meant them. "How is it that he taught you? Who commanded such lessons or were they freely given?"

Jovian pulled back from his lean with a pout upon his plump lips. "With words instead of touch though it seems you will learn by his hands." He sighed a little and shook his head. "I admit that I stand jealous of you. It is laughable that I, Jovian who stands the right hand of my Dominus, highly favored above all others, should be jealous of a girl who seems afraid of her own shadow, but it is true." He turned his head as the curtains parted once more and Meridius stood to watch them disapproval in his expression.

With a look in his eyes daring the big man to do something the youth leaned closer to Violetta and pressed his lips to the rapidly beating pulse at the base of her throat. He pulled her close against him, every defined line of the muscles on his stomach were pressed into the softness of her flesh making it easy to slip his slender fingers into her dress pocket. Raising his head to bury his nose into her hair, Jovian muttered. "One day I promise you that I shall taste those sweet lips. The Celt will not mind over much that it is me that does but I swear to you that it shall be so."

Violetta was frozen at his words, trying to understand all that he said and all that he had implied with his cryptic words. Her eyes found Meridius' and when he took a step towards them her whole body sagged briefly in relief but then his name was called from within the room and he had to leave the balcony to attend Tertius. Closing her eyes, she whispered a prayer to the heavens that it would end, and this confusing youth would leave her be. She was so intent in not feeling anything, in distancing her mind from him that she almost forgot that his hands had deposited something in the inner pocket of her dress. Sliding her hands to examine it, he caught her wrists with teasing laughter sparkling in his dark eyes. "What is…" A finger pressed to her lips stopped the question before she could finish asking it.

Jovian shook his head. "Do not look now. It is a gift from the champion, a drug prepared by the medicus, and sent to you by me. It will help with pain." He leaned forward and kissed his finger across her lips, chuckling again when her body stiffened. Stepping back, he shook his head. "You and I will be friends, little girl. I am Jovian, and we will see each other again soon." He said with a wink before stepping back inside the villa. She wondered if he would now find Cassian and inform him that his gift was given and safely received, if he did, she doubted he would reveal the details of its giving.

CHAPTER 2

It had only seemed that a moment had passed after Jovian had finally left her when Violetta heard the familiar click of Meridius' fingers summoning her to return. With a sigh, she gave a final glance to the sands and wondered if he was down there watching her from one of the barred doors that lined the perimeter of the yard. Joining the man waiting for her, she smiled slightly. "I am alright Padre. He did not hurt me though I admit he did frighten a little with regard to his intent." She fingered the vial in the pocket of her dress, wondering what it was and what it was meant for. Stepping into the room the lights dazzled her and forced her to blink rapidly to adjust to them as she scanned the room looking for Cassian. All she saw was Jovian glaring at Meridius and Proximus, the giant of a man that had defeated her champion to earn his place and send the man she loved into a valley of self doubt, watching her for some reason. "Is it time to depart Dominus?" She asked Felix softly, taking her place behind him on his left.

"Indeed, it is Violetta, before too great advantage is taken of good Tertius' hospitality." Felix said with a tired smile. As they walked to the door, their host still chattering about the games in a few weeks' time, how Cassian and now Proximus would certainly feature prominently in them for his enjoyment. He must have noted that she was craning her neck, searching for the champion.

"You will not see him." Felix said with a whisper. "The gladiators were all returned to the ludus so stop looking. Pay attention to tasks at hand." Then in a louder voice he added.

"Meridius shall attend me tonight and you will need your rest after the events awaiting our return."

She blinked in confusion as a sudden chill took her; Cassian had lost. Did that mean there would be some punishment exacted upon her by Felix? Or even worse, by Vitus? Her distraction was deep enough that she did not notice that she shared an expression with the lanista that walked them to the door.

"Events waiting upon her return?" Tertius asked. "Is she no longer the prize of Cassian? I would ask that she not be abused so that his rage is not increased by it. She needs to be lovely and available when it is needed for her to be." He glanced at her. "Bruises do not appeal to many men Felix." He glanced nervously over his shoulder to where, perhaps, her gladiator was waiting.

Watching Meridius escort Selenia outside to their cart, where she began to tease him by dragging the sharp point of her nail around his neck. Felix turned to lock eyes to the lanista. "You agreed to the terms that his loss would be felt by her and there is no going back now." He bowed his head in farewell to Lycithia and snapped his fingers to summon Violetta to follow him. "Come girl, I am sure Vitus has something in mind for just such an event as this."

Sitting beside her the merchant turned and ran a finger down Violetta's neck while addressing his daughter who seemed amused at Meridius' discomfort. "Stop tormenting the man Selenia. Tell me of this new gladiator and his stamina? Do you think he has what it takes to defeat Cassian in the arena? Should I change which man I back in the games after tonight?" He glanced at Violetta, who sat nervously beside him, "Should he be offered a glorious prize for further victory?"

Violetta paled at the suggestion combined with Selenia's devious grin as she stopped toying with the dark hair at the back of Meridius' neck. "Well, he has the stamina of a bull, but from what I hear the champion is a god, though perhaps there are others here that are better suited to that answer." She shook her head. "He is good, but I truly think Cassian is the better fighter and should remain the favored of the house of Census. He has proven himself worthy of it in the past and I would think, now that he is motivated properly, that he will rise once again to the height of former glories."

Felix nodded and closed his eyes, his silence commanding the rest of the party to the same as they drove the distance of the hill and the dark streets of the city. Through the most elite section of town towards his isolated Villa.

Violetta's mind raced as they moved; what was waiting upon her return? Surely Felix would not send her to the bed of Vitus after such a night? Selenia eyed her curiously but did not say a word as they moved towards the destination, it was as if she knew that something worse waited for her at the villa with her brother who had been deliberately left behind.

It was with a sense of dread that she was the last to depart the cart as it stopped. She watched father and daughter bid each other good night and then took a sharp breath when Felix turned to her and Meridius to utter his command. "Meridius, see to my room and bed. I have papers to see to in my office and Violetta, you will attend me there before returning to your own bed." His voice left no room for question or protest and so with a long look between them she followed the Roman wishing that the man left behind was able to protect or comfort her against what was to happen.

She was so absorbed in her own thoughts that Violetta did not notice that Vitus was in the office until he came upon her from behind and gripped her arm tight, twisting it behind her until she cried out from the pain. "I see the little whore returns with you tonight father. What happened? The gladiator has had her and no longer desires her?" He pulled her flush against him and slid his free hand down her side and gripped her hip. He growled viciously in her ear. "Though perhaps his roughness makes my touch more appealing?" He continued to keep her arm twisted and held tight behind her until the whimper slipping loose from her throat brought his father's attention up from the papers before him with a disturbed frown.

"Vitus, cease. You forget, again, that she stands my property and not your own." Felix said in a voice that bordered on bored before he stood and curled his finger, beckoning Violetta to approach his desk as he stepped around it to meet her. "You tend to break delicate things my son and this, trembling girl is delicate indeed and must not be shattered upon your desire until all other uses have been exhausted. Understood?" His eyes met his sons with unmistakable firmness and Violetta shuddered.

"You have my apologies father, but you did say that I could administer the punishments upon her after a loss and he did lose did he not? Or why else is she here instead of your bed or his?" He stepped up behind her again, he refrained from touching her skin that was beading with sweat from the fear.

"Administer, not decide Vitus. As usual you jump ahead of yourself and forget that there is a proper way such things are done." Felix shook his head with what looked like sadness until he looked up and made sure that Violetta was meeting his eyes. "You do know, of course, that you are to be punished for the champion's loss?" He asked, tracing the tips of his fingers down her throat as she nodded.

"Yes Dominus." She whispered, her lips shaking as she stood between the two of them not knowing which evil was worse: the father or the son.

"Good." He said with a slow smile. "Now since there was no loss of coin the punishment will not be too severe just enough to upset him when he hears of it." He paused his speech, as if he wanted to make sure she was listening and understanding the weight of his words. "And he will hear of it, that you can be very certain of." When she nodded, he continued. "Your pains will serve as much as inspiration as the parting of your legs; he will not wish for any further loss to occur, especially of value, to ensure the safety of his favored prize."

She waited with closed eyes as she tried to ignore the touch of Vitus up and down her spine. She straightened her shoulders and took a deep breath; if it was to be pain, she would bear it as Cassian did. He could be her strength to draw on in this too, though from afar. Violetta could almost feel Vitus' anticipation in the delivering whatever punishment his father decreed suitable for the loss of a champion in the test of a new man. Her heart thundered in her chest, anticipating the moment when the first blow would fall. She barely saw the Roman pause on his return to the desk. She pressed her lips together when he turned to watch her. Did he note the air of detachment she had found so that this did not affect her the way he had intended?

Sitting down with tented fingers, Felix watched her and Vitus, a war of wills that she seemed likely to win if he let her. "Violetta." His voice snapped her attention back to the moment and she opened her eyes to look at him with resigned fear. "I think, since this is the first instance where you will be punished, for him, that you should be allowed the choice, this one time." Her eyes widened and he continued with a smile. "Your choices, to pay for Cassian's loss tonight; are to either lay in submission to Vitus and all he demands of you for this night or five strokes of the lash by his hand." His grin spread broadly as did his son's. Both men seemed certain of her response as she stood, puzzling out her choice for the first time in years.

The true depth of the choice was playing in her mind. If she allowed Vitus free reign over her then it would be the word of the Roman against her own as to what happened, but the lash would leave marks and perhaps even scars that would be impossible to hide though it would mean that her body was Cassian's alone for now. There was no true way to win for either choice held its own horror. She feared the pain of the lash wielded by a man she rejected but that fear paled when compared to giving herself to the demands of Vitus. One would mark her body and the other her soul. She weighed the options circling them in her mind and trying to find the right answer, the knowledge that the man she loved would learn of it either way caused the greatest concern of all.

Vitus inched his fingers to the bruises he had put upon her side. He must have felt smug in the certainty that she would be his for the night for he pressed his rigid arousal to the crease of her backside as he dug his fingertips into the purpled flesh on her ribs with deliberate intent.

Gasping in pain and fear Violetta cried out. "The lash Dominus, the lash."

Which caused both men to raise their heads in surprise, Felix had obviously thought as Vitus that she was certain to be in his bed that night and thus appease his son's anger while making good on the deal with the lanista. "The lash? You are sure of that girl?" He asked calmly.

When she answered with a brief nod he gestured with an open hand towards the small whip on a table by the wall. "As you choose. Five only Vitus. I will not have her utterly ruined for use." He then returned to his papers as if her decision held no more weight upon his mind than his choice in meals.

Vitus gripped her hair with a snarl and dragged her to the wall, placing her hands upon it before ripping the top of her dress from around her neck to bare her back and upper body completely. "Do not move." He barked, turning from her to take up the braided leather and cracking it in the air to make her jump.

Bringing the lash down in the first blow across her back Vitus was rewarded with a sharp scream as Violetta's back bowed at the contact. He quickly followed the first blow with a second and a third. Her screams brought a smile of almost orgasmic pleasure to his face. The fourth blow found its mark and the welts began to rise when he paused to lean close, pressing her into the wall as he licked a tear from her cheek before whispering. "Now do you wish for my cock inside you slave? Do you beg for me to fill you or to deliver the last blow?"

She could hardly breath for the pain, it was unlike anything she had ever felt and yet she could not give in, could not let him think that she would ever willingly be in his bed. Drawing the deepest breath she was able, Violetta whispered. "No Dominus." then rested her forehead against the cold stone wall to await the final blow that would see her excused for the rest of the night once it landed. The knowledge of the drug in her possession gave her some strength to face the oncoming agony as did the memory of her lover's lips across the very skin that was now defaced with violence.

With a vicious roar, Vitus brought the lash in a final stroke, not to her back but across the purple bruises on her ribs. The sensitive skin split under the intense abuse and blood began to flow. Violetta felt her knees give out and fell to the floor with an agonized wail. This was unlike any pain she had ever felt, it robbed her of breath as she curled into a ball on the cold stone floor.

If this was the cost of a minor loss that had not taken coin from the hand of either Roman what would happen if it did? They would kill her, that was the plan, it had to be if this was not the worst it would be. Her whimpering sobs filled the silence for a moment until Vitus dropped the whip to the floor and stepped to his father's desk, she vaguely heard him speak of taking the note of thanks to Tertius himself in the morning before he exited the room leaving her half naked, bleeding on the floor.

Once she was sure that Vitus was gone Violetta pulled herself up to stand, gripping the edge of the small table beside her that had held the whip. Each move was a slow torture to the newly broken skin as she tied her dress about her neck again, wincing at each pull of muscle and choking back a cry when the fabric touched the wound of the last blow. Slowly she walked to where Vitus had dropped the whip on the floor and crouched to pick it up, recoiling it to place the weapon back on the table where it had been then she stood silently, awaiting Felix' dismissal as a few tears still streamed down her cheeks.

"Wine." Muttered Felix from the desk, his hand holding a quill, moving quickly across the paper in front of him. When she placed the poured cup beside him, he added. "One for yourself as well girl." Looking up he watched as she struggled to steady her breathing before drinking the rich wine. "The drink will help with the pain." He said, putting down the pen and resting his chin on his fingertips for a moment before continuing "It is unwise to antagonize him Violetta. You know this and yet you knowingly incur his wrath with rejection?"

"Gratitude Dominus." She said softly, sipping the strong wine and closing her eyes as it slipped down her throat, burning slightly but not enough to distract from the pain of her side and back. She could feel the blood from the injury wetting her dress and she worried that it might drip upon the floor. Even though it hurt terribly she pressed a hand to her side to try and slow the bleeding as she tried to finish quickly. She needed to get away to her cell, to see if one of the older women would stitch the wound closed for her before she took the drug from Cassian so that she could find some rest at last. "Is there anything else you require of me Dominus?" She asked carefully, not wanting to assume he was finished with her but unsure what he could want.

Felix shook his head to pull himself from the dark musings that the late hour often brought to his mind. "Go and see wounds tended, if the medicus is required he will be sent for. I would have you willing and able to attend me at breakfast with dry eyes and wounds closed, no longer seeping blood upon dress or floor." He waved his hand in dismissal and watched as she exited the room slowly, the pain obvious in how she moved.

As soon as she left Felix's office Violetta stumbled to the kitchens and then down the hall and stairs to the slave's cells. She found an older woman there that could stitch the wound closed. She applied cold cloths to the raised welts from the lash while a needle gently tugged the skin together at her side where it was darkened from bruises and then the blow of a lash had split it open. The marks upon her back would not scar though it would take some time for them to heal but the final blow across the skin already softened by the bruise had cut deeper than the rest and even the small stitches of the seamstress' hand could not change the fact that it would leave a scar for the rest of her days.

Tears streamed down her cheeks, red with pain and embarrassment, but she simply shook her head when plied with questions regarding the cause for such a strike to be administered.

Trying to distract herself from the pain of the needle Violetta turned her thoughts to Cassian and what would happen if Vitus did, in fact, break words with him of what had happened that night. Would his strained grip on control break and cause his temper to flare once more?

As the thread in her side was pulled tight, she whimpered, but when her nurse muttered something about the need for medicinal drugs to be in the house she remembered the 'gift' hidden in her dress. As soon as the woman's back was turned, she drew the small vial out, removed the cap and paused only for a second before downing the contents. Closing her eyes, she waited for the potion to take effect. letting her thoughts wander back to the stolen moments in his arms upon the dining table in the ludus.

As the narcotic took slow influence over her senses every moment was brought back; his hand upon her hips as they moved together, his mouth devouring her body, his voice in her ear making her shake. It took only moments until every voice around her sounded like his and a smile spread across her lips.

The women gently moved Violetta to lay on the mat in her cell, making sure that she was not on her injured side when they covered her to sleep off the pain and the drug. She was murmuring and whispering in her sleep, holding conversations with him in her mind. She spoke of love and wishes to be in his arms again without being pulled from them. All those in earshot could not help but smile at the heartfelt innocence of her words; the affections of a lover spoken aloud. The old woman sat guard outside the room as Meridius would have done, to keep any curious hands from her injured, intoxicated, body. Eventually the girl quieted, passionate musings turned to prayers to any and all gods to see them to each other arms again and for the reporting of her injury to not bring pain to her lover but pride that she was strong enough to choose this over allowing another to take her body, that her love for him was strong enough to choose pain over the touch of any other man in an intimate caress.

CHAPTER 3

Dawn came in the villa above the ludus, but the sunlight found its champion not training upon the sands but with iron at his throat and looped at his wrists. It was not swords or any other weapon that found itself in his grasp but a broom. He stared down at himself and thought that no one would recognize the champion of Velletri now. Bare footed in a tunic that was loosely belted at his hips. He could not ever remember wearing such things even in his childhood freedom. If Tertius sought to humble him then he had achieved his goal for even the rest of the house slaves skirted his presence as though to be seen near him would draw the displeasure of their master.

That he deserved some punishment for attitude and behavior the night before he did not doubt but this was too much, even after arguing with Doctore. He possessed skills in combat beyond any man within the walls, he could deal death without the guilt that plagued some and yet what did it earn him? The anguish of finding love that he could call his own, but having it held beyond his reach?

He let his thoughts wander to the image of the true wish of his heart: Violetta. He longed to hold her close in more than just the momentary embraces they had been allowed so far, to touch her until he knew every inch of her skin as well as he knew his own. He wanted his touch to make her whimper and moan with desire. To watch her come apart in his arms with nothing more than his hands upon her. He had never thought to find love again, without reserve, and yet the gods had seen fit to see her to his heart if not his arms.

There had to be a way to see her more than just after a fight, perhaps once he was returned to the lanista's good graces he could break words on the subject. The corners of his lips lifted in a soft smile at the thought of being able to surprise her with a meeting that had nothing to do with the games. How her face would light up, a beaming smile and the sparkle in her beautiful eyes. She would throw her arms around him and he would carry her to the nearest bed they could use. He wanted to court her, with witty words and the small gifts a slave could afford but it did not seem as though that would be permitted either. His smile broadened until he heard a voice that turned daydreams to nightmares.

"Tell your Dominus that Vitus Census awaits him, at his leisure of course." The Roman called loudly as he stepped inside. Cassian watched his enemy look around the villa as though he were surprised there was no trace of the previous night's celebration. Strolling through the halls as if it were his own house Vitus walked past the man wearing iron collar and shackles, pausing when he recognized the face.

"Well now. I see the champion stands in glory this fine morning." He chuckled as he circled Cassian, taking in the sight of his humiliation with a smirk that could only be described as ecstatic. Stopping before him Vitus tapped a finger to his lips in thought. "I am sure that Violetta would laugh at such a sight." He arched a brow as a corner of his mouth lifted in a mocking smirk. "If she were able to do so without tears."

His entire body tensed; muscles clenched ready to strike as his heart thundered in his chest. Comprehension of the words he spoke sliced through his fog of hatred. "Violetta cries? When? Why?" He asked, eyes narrowing while his voice tightened with sudden anxiety for her safety and the wish that the wood in his hand was steel sharped to a deadly edge so that he could find justice for her if this monster stood the cause.

Vitus smirked as his words found their mark. "As a woman does following the sting of the lash applied to flesh. You should have heard the screams, gladiator, as it cut that sweet flesh." Vitus licked his lips and his eyes glossed slightly. Arching a brow, he baited him further. "It makes the cock hard to think of the sound, wondering what other ways she could be brought to such fevered state. She has that effect does she not. With her innocent eyes and soft lips made for pleasuring her masters."

Closing his eyes for a moment Cassian swallowed back the bitter bile that rose to the back of his throat at the thought of Vitus' hands upon his woman. The collar seemed to tighten with the unspoken command that he stay silent and still as a proper slave would even under such offence. A darkness covered his eyes and the world itself stopped turning as he weighed the truth in the Roman's words. "You," He paused for a breath. "You laid the lash to her innocent flesh absent cause? She has done nothing to warrant such a thing. Nothing that transpired here last night was her doing or fault."

Grinning at the second victim of his actions, Vitus was practically purring. "You would know better than me her lack of innocence, would you not?" He chuckled and leaned closer. "Her punishment is of course part of the agreement between my father and your own Dominus. Did she not tell you of it? Or was her mouth filled with things other than words when last you saw each other?" He grinned deviously and continued with a careful eye on his clenched fists. "The lash was her choice and I was only too happy to apply it. She had another option." He shrugged, visibly savoring the distress he was causing. "You must be as good as you are reputed to be Cassian, if she would rather take the lash than willingly bed the son of her Dominus." His hand reached to grasp Cassian's chin and wrenched it, so their gazes were forced to meet, both men with unmasked hatred for the other blazing brightly.

Their eyes still locked together Cassian let the broom fall from his grasp. The fact that this pathetic excuse of a man had lifted a whip to the tender flesh of his woman was beyond what he could allow himself to comprehend. It could not be true and yet it was impossible to deny the look of triumph in the eyes of Vitus, there was a satisfaction too deep to be a lie shining in them. He did not fight the grip upon his chin but glared in deadly rebuttal. "Your effect must be small to bring her preference to pain over your cock." Had his words been too much? Would they be the cause of more pain for her? Perhaps the man's jealousy was the true drive to this insane torment, but he could not now give her up, not after knowing her touch and seeing her love for him shining in those bright blue eyes. Guilt would be a heavy weight upon his soul until he had her safe in his arms and away from this madman.

Vitus brought the back of his hand across Cassian's mouth. "You forget position slave!" He snarled viciously before gripping his hair to pull him closer. "Trust that I affect her. When I buried my cock deep inside her she cried like a virgin plucked for the first time." He took a step back and smiled slowly at Cassian's tormented demeanor. The Roman monster was reveling in the anguish he caused by sharing the knowledge of Violetta's pain. "Perhaps one night I should borrow you from Tertius. To have your hands hold her in place while I take her so that you can see with your own eyes the effect that I have upon her." He hissed as the lanista approached at last.

Cassian did not flinch, did not blink, when the blow landed but instead kept his eyes locked to those of Vitus so that the sole sign of any pain was the bead of sweat glistening across his brow. They could try to break him, to break them both, but it was something he would not allow. They would find his spirit unbreakable and if it was his heart that they chose to use against him then he had only two options; return to glacial coldness and let no one, man or woman, close enough to warm him, or fortify the bond so that there was nothing and no one who could influence their feelings for one another. The choice was obvious, he fought a smirk at the certainty he felt. He would offer no missio in his pursuit of her now, she was the light in his darkness, and no one would leave him in the shadows again.

Tertius' timely appearance to lead the fool away to conduct whatever business lay between them was a gift, allowing the gladiator a moment to breathe and collect himself. He retrieved the mop he had dropped so that he could continue the foolish task given to a champion who should have been training that very moment, but he was determined to take advantage of the menial task to give freedom to his mind and focus upon the solace of her and the memory of the moment he realized it was not just a physical connection between them but something so much more precious; love. He would see her again so that he could find a way to make up for the suffering and cruelty he had caused without knowing. He would fortify her against the Roman games and find a way to assure her that he wanted to keep her safe and as close to him as possible. "Play your games Dominus." He muttered to the retreating men. "For I stand champion of her safety as well the sands."

"Good Vitus." Tiberius Tertius, closing his hand over his countryman's shoulder he smiled broadly, masking the warning glare that he gave his own man to still his tongue before further offence was offered.

Vitus forced a smile to his lips as he guided him away from the gladiator. "A pleasure to see you this fine day within my villa, one that was not expected after your father breaking words of you feeling unwell last night so that you could not join us." There was no doubt that the lanista would try to discover the reason for the tension between them, but he had to know the longer their interaction the greater chance it would become worse and so he drew Vitus away. "Come, let us break words over wine in the solar where there is greater sun and more pleasing sights to look upon than a mulish gladiator atoning for his faults."

Turning to face his host Vitus plastered a wide smile to his face that made Cassian want to smash his fist across it even if he would be punished more. "Tiberius, the pleasure is mine to be within your walls once again." Following at a discreet distance to the solar the gladiator hid and watched his enemy hand a parchment to the lanista before taking a seat and the glass of wine that a docile slave held out to him. "I come bearing a note of gratitude from my father for last nights' entertainments. I would add my own with it in person." The lanista's expression was puzzled and so he added. "Though I was unable to attend myself I was more than pleased at the results of your test and to fulfill my father's side of your agreement regarding your man's loss, any loss." He smiled with a serenity that turned the hidden gladiator's stomach and sipped the wine, his lips puckering to say that it was grossly inferior to his pallet.

Tiberius stepped to the small table holding the wine and poured himself a glass, a thing that would normally have been left to Jovian, but the boy had been sent to the ludus to fetch a tonic from the Druid in the infirmary only moments earlier. Returning to Vitus he sat down, rubbing a hand across his chin. "Any loss? I had thought it was the arena matches that we had been speaking of. Did you mention this to him, to Cassian? I had given no thought to her being punished for loss during the test."

Cassian could not believe what he was hearing; that he had agreed to a contract that brought harm to her but there was nothing to be done now except to contain the damage done and use it to inspire himself to constant victory. He brought his attention back to the words of the Romans as Tertius asked. "Is that what brought you to the need to strike him? Did he bring offence upon hearing the news?"

Vitus set the cup aside and shook his head. "I assure you that it was my father's decree not my own that saw it done. I was happy enough, of course, to please my noble father by seeing his will done." He smiled and took up the cup again. "I only broke words with the man to inform him of her state since he does seem to have some care for her well being. I was not bothered though his words demanded retribution. Apologies if the strike brought you offence, I fear my temper got the better of me in the moment." He swirled the contents of his cup before taking another sip of the sharp liquid. "The test was an enormous success, I hope. I was surprised to hear of the outcome upon my father's return."

Tiberius lowered the glass with a reassuring smile and shook his head. "There was no offence taken Vitus, I assure you. I carry greater concern that the slave bought you defiance and stood curious as to the cause of it." His expression grew serious as he continued. "Trust that he will be seen to further reprisal for his actions, my hand will be as heavy as though it was the magistrate himself that was accosted."

Cassian held back a scoff at the pathetic ass-kissing his master engaged in when he should have defended the man who earned the very coin that had paid for the wine they drank.

Turning his eyes from Vitus, Tertius picked up the parchment that had been brought and removed the seal. "The champion has not been informed of the details of the bargain with your father. The idea that each loss will bring the girl to pain or peril is something I had hoped he would learn over time as he discovered that each victory brought her to his arms." He stood slowly and rubbed a hand across his jaw. "Your visit today, while an honor of course, has altered the plan as far as his knowledge of the deal but it may yet work to mutual favor if it brings him to obedience and a greater concentration in training and the arena." He looked out the window and down to the sands. "No offence was taken for your words could see an even greater fortune brought to both our houses."

CHAPTER 4

Jovian crept the halls of the ludus after retrieving the tonic to ease the aching head of Tertius' wife, it would be at least a few minutes before it was noticed that he had not returned immediately and there was someone he wanted to see, even if they did not break words. The Syrian boy made his way to peer into the shadowed cell holding Argus, the German beast of a man that was said to be training with Cassian if the Celt ever returned to the sands. His blood surged at the idea of the man's gloriously sculpted body but there was little chance Argus had ever seen him as anything more than Tertius' devoted lapdog. Was there a chance that he could see him as something more? Something beautiful? He did not know if he even held desire for men, but he had been told it had been some time since whores had been sent to his cell. It was easy to hide in the shadows, watching the object of his fascination pacing back and forth across the small space.

He froze when Argus looked over towards him, the small form crouched in the shadows, and smiled softly. Jovian often stared at the older man, desire in his heart, but anything between them would be incredibly dangerous. The lanista hoarded the affections of his body-slave with a deadly jealousy. He must have decided that the youth was not going to leave and so the gladiator would take the risk as he looked down to unfasten his sandals while he sat on his cot.

"Jovian. You linger in shadows instead of approaching to break words? Why? Do I frighten you?" Argus asked, without looking up and with a note of laughter in his voice.

Stepping from the shadows towards the bars, Jovian smiled. "You know my name? I was not sure that you did. We have not yet broken words before this." He could not help staring at the chiseled form smiling at him from the other side of the bars, he wanted to reach out and run his fingers down the sculpted chest but if he did that it would reveal his want for the man. Instead of giving in he turned the talk towards safer things. "Will you be upon the sands during the next games? You have been training hard. You must be ready to face anyone they could pair you with." He nervously ran his fingers through the inky length of his own hair, trying to draw Argus' attention in the hopes that he would want to touch it. "I think that you would stand victorious at day's end, especially with Cassian not upon the sands until Dominus releases him from the villa."

The simple flattery from pouting lips must have affected him for Jovian found Argus smiling when he asked. "You think I would have the victory? Perhaps I will if you yourself finally attend the games to see what it is that we gladiators do there. Why do you never accompany Tertius to the games?" Pausing the gladiator frowned before continuing. "He truly holds the champion back from training? What is in his mind?" Argus raked a hand through his hair, spiking it absentmindedly. He looked over at Jovian "What do you know?" He asked, not demand but concern in his voice.

He had felt as though his heart was soaring just to have Argus looking at him but to have him speak and have a true conversation with him as though they were friends was something else, something precious. "I would come but Dominus refuses to take me, though I have begged, to come and see you fight. I mean, to see the games, where you fight." He flushed, not usually at such a loss for words but there was something about this man that was not like anyone else in his life. "He told me that it was a promise he had made to a dying man; that I was not to ever become a gladiator or become close with their life." Staring up into his eyes he wished for another life, one that brought him into this world of men, violence and death. "He tells me it was a promise, but I truly think it is something more than that."

Argus cupped the Jovian's chin and stroked his thumb across it, sending a thrill to the young heart, and asked with a raised brow. "What more is there it could be? Does our Dominus stand jealous of your reaction to gladiators? Does the sight of our savagery stir your blood?"

He grinned and ran his tongue across his teeth with a near predatory gaze making Jovian wonder what he was doing down here in the depths of the ludus. No one could hear him, no one could save him if one of the more brutish men managed to get their hands on his soft flesh.

"Tell me, does the danger of this place, of me, excite you Jovian?" The gladiator asked with a teasing note in his voice.

Instead of answering Jovian pulled his chin from the hand holding it still and shook his head. "Argus, you ask questions to which the answers could bring us both great pain, depending upon how they were received. Do not ask such things of me." How could he tell the gladiator that it was not as much the danger that excited him but Argus himself? It hardly seemed possible but whenever he was not consumed by the passion between him and their Dominus, he found himself thinking of this giant of a man and wondering what kind of lover he would want? Did he like women or men? Would he be rough and brutish or was he secretly tender and gentle? There were so many questions that burned in his throat, screaming to be asked and yet he could not bring even one to voice. "Please do not ask."

"Of course. Apologies." The German said, stepping back from the bars. Maybe he had not needed Jovian to point it out but had been willing to take the risk. Perhaps it might be worth it to him as well? "I would not want you to risk yourself breaking words with me, even though it is you who sought me out to do so. Is this a game for you?"

The colour drained from Jovian's face and he stepped up to the bars, clasping his hand around the iron as he shook his head in denial of the gladiator's words. "No, please Agrus, you misunderstand me. You misunderstand my intent." He was desperate to make amends and ensure that things were moving forward between them if it was possible. "I think Dominus knows of my preference and he is concerned that I will find joy and satisfaction in the arms of another man…in the love of a gladiator." He wanted to say that he thought the lanista would know that he held affection for him specifically if he even caught them speaking. Jovian knew that to tell him would end any chance of even friendship between them with the risk. "Please believe this is the truth."

The gladiator shook his head with a gentle smile teasing his lips at the sound of the desperation in the Jovian's voice. "If only truth were but allowed the light of day instead of being forced to stolen moments hidden in the shadows." He took a deep breath and stepped back from the bars again. "You should not linger too long, or someone will be looking for you." He nodded towards the hall. "Dominus will come for you, you know this. He cannot find you in my company, breaking words, and we both know that to be true." The German seemed to be forcing himself to be the responsible one between them, putting flirtation aside for serious warnings.

Daring a soft smile back Jovian could not help but ask. "What meaning is there behind these words you speak?" He could not tell if the gladiator was teasing him or if he was sincere in his concern for his safety. If he could hold onto the hope that there was a chance for something more between them then his heart would soar to the very heavens. "Do you hold feelings of friendship for me?"

Their eyes locked together, and Argus stepped back to the edge of his cell. Reaching through the bars he put a calloused hand to Jovian's shoulder. "I would not wish for you to have to hide truth for fear of reprimand from our Dominus so perhaps it is better if certain words are left unsaid between us now."

"I would not hide the truth between us when I stand before you Argus." Jovian said softly, his voice a gentle seduction while he reached a hand to trace lightly over the broad muscled line of the gladiator's shoulder. He wanted this man so badly that it ached throughout his body but now was not the time to tell him. "What words of truth do you hold thinking that the secret keeps me safe instead of in agony to know your heart?"

"I hide what I do to keep you safe, little man." He said with a grin. "You cannot tell me that you will not break words in its regard and then expect me to break the silence that protects you simply because you stand curious." He chuckled for a moment then stepped away from the bars to lean against the wall. "Return to Dominus if that is what you need to do but trust me, little man, that I hold you in regard. Hurry away before we are caught in words and I stand punished for it."

At the mention of the man before him being punished because he sought words with him absent invitation Jovian shook his head adamantly. "No. I would never allow such to happen. Apologies for putting you at risk though I admit I found words worth the risk to my own person." A seductive grin spread across his face. "I think you would find I am not so little, not in all things, gladiator." He stroked the bars in a demonstration of what he would do given the chance to do what he was all but certain now that they both yearned for. When Argus' brow arched in curiosity he added. "I must return to Dominus, who waits for my touch and company but know that I have thoughts that linger here with you and I pray that some of yours can be spared to linger upon me as well."

Argus smirked and shook his head. "You can trust that more than a few of my thoughts will be upon you until we speak again." They both knew it was dangerous to want what they did, but Jovian was still drawn to him in a way he could not explain.

"Perhaps one day you will prove to me that the name 'little man' should not be the name I think of with you. Now go before we are both in more trouble than we know how to handle. Go." Argus shook his head and grinned; a broad warm spreading of his lips that had sent a flush to the cheeks of many women within the city and a twinkle in the deep green of his eyes that caught the gaze of any who happened to see them.

Returning the smile, though somewhat dazed by it as well, Jovian turned to leave the cells the way he had come.

Watching the pair of would-be lovers Proximus knew that Argus had no idea that he had just taken Jovian's breath away.

The sound of the flattery from the boy's lips had alerted him to their intimate conversation and he had become the not-so-secret observer to the meeting.

The eyes of both gladiators locked before Argus said. "Run along and see that Dominus is well tended and in a better mood so that he might actually allow our champion to train me. If I am to be ready for the next games, I need a partner that will challenge me and teach me, that is Cassian. Without him I am not going to be as ready as I need to be." He looked at Proximus "You are not skilled enough to help with what I need."

Proximus laughed and shook his head. "No, I do not have the skills to teach you what you need to know, and you are certainly not to my tastes." When a shadow of rage flashed across Argus's face Proximus shook his head again. "I have no care for your preference Argus except the one that might get us all killed or mistreated." He took a deep breath and watched the boy from the villa quickly scamper down the hall towards the stairs. Thoughts of another young slave who had snuck through halls and streets to see a gladiator not so very long ago flooded back to him so swiftly that it felt as though he could not breathe. It was with a voice filled with emotion that he turned to Argus and said softly. "You are taking the first steps upon a very dangerous path brother, one that could be your doom as it was almost mine. Be cautious and step lightly."

"What would you know about the path I may or may not step upon? You have been here days and now think to know the inner workings of the ludus and those within its walls?" Argus shook his head, his expression annoyed. "You know nothing and are still nothing even if you bear the mark. How you bested Cassian is a mystery to us all but do not think that you now take his place as leader among us." Argus raised venomous eyes to meet Proximus' calm face and snarled. "You are still the new man, whatever your life was before does not matter."

"You think that because I am new to this place that I have not stood inside the arena a hundred times? That I was not a champion in my own right?" Proximus said angrily. "I do not seek to take the place of the man who tested me, perhaps one day in the arena but not now. I am trying to help you avoid the very thing that saw me fall from glory." The man was testing his patience but if he was to become as one of them then he could not give up just because the other German proved more thick-headed than most. "I was at the height of glory when it was discovered that the body slave, and lover of my Dominus, had become my lover as well." The big man sighed. "It was bad enough that he knew that his wife called me to her bed when she wanted a certain kind of pleasure but he would not have his slave shared and so I am here in this shit hole of a town trying to prove myself once again when only months ago my name was upon every tongue in Rome."

Argus regarded him carefully, with narrowed eyes. "You stood Rome's champion and because of a woman you fell to disgrace?" He chuckled and clapped his hands. "Then you stand the greatest of fools. To fall for a woman is the biggest mistake any gladiator could make for none want to own the heart of the beast, merely his cock for a time." Argus shook his head and paced the small cell with an obvious frustration. "Who stood your Dominus before you came to the fabled house of Tertius? Some merchant turned lanista? Or did the man at least have some knowledge of gladiators and their skills, fighting and how to win?" He sat on the mat upon the floor and took a drink of the cheap wine that was served to the men in the evenings. "What then is your advice? Oh great man who fell from glory because of a woman? Still my heart against its desire? Be careful of the secret or simply deny myself because you were fool enough to be caught in the biggest tangle of cock and cunt in all of Rome this season?"

"You would be better served paying attention than yapping like a small dog in heat at the heels of a boy you can never have, even if you can make up your mind that he is what you want." Proximus growled slightly before sighing in frustration, the man was a fool and an undecided one at that. If this was how he behaved it would take no time at all for word to reach the lanista of his intent and soon it would be impossible to piss without someone taking note of it. He had seen it happen before and lived through it while his former Dominus had been searching for the man who was bedding his body slave, Maya. "In answer to your question my former master was no mere merchant or even a lowly lanista who must bow and scrape for every coin in his purse. I was owned and fought for the name of no other than Titus Claudius himself, so hold tongue if you would offer insult to his knowledge or the coin he afforded to the training of the men who fought in his name."

"You were owned by Titus Claudius?" Argus was paying attention now. The wealth of the family was legendary, and some of his slaves lived almost as if they were free. "It is said that some of his slaves have their own small houses on his property. Is it true? Were you also trained by captains of the legions?" The German's questions revealed his curiosity to know the man who had truly been with the elite of the Republic and not just those of a small provincial city. There were more things he could teach than they realized, even if he was no true match for their own champion upon the sands it seemed that he was not entirely without worth and use to his brothers. "You have balls to rival Jupiter himself if you would bed Titus' wife." Argus said with a teasing smile.

Proximus almost laughed at the new tone of voice that had so swiftly changed from mocking to admiration. Argus plied him with questions about the life of privilege that his foolish thoughts of deceiving his Dominus had seen forever taken from his grasp, but even here in the dank cells of the ludus he could not hold regret, for the brief time in Maya's arms was worth all that he had lost and more.

"It does not take balls to obey a command though it was not easy to work up the nerve the first few times. I held concern that it was a trap to see me to the cross." He did not add how it had been months before he had relaxed enough to truly realize the Roman woman desired him and was not attempting to break the ties between Dominus and gladiator which would see him to his death or how hard it was to go to the bed of one woman while his heart and soul belonged to another, who was not permitted the chance to even speak of it.

Proximus thought of her often and wondered if she had survived the wrath of Titus. Her life had been made difficult enough with the hatred of Titus' wife who had full knowledge of the choice her husband had made for a bedmate, but this could have put her to death and there was no one to bring word of her to him. There was a rumor among the men that Tertius was trying to curry the family's favor and entice the great man to visit from Rome. He could not decide if the idea excited him or terrified him. What if he refused to come and named Proximus as the reason? The lanista would be furious and see him as a liability to be killed or sold. The more terrifying thought was that he would come and that she would not be with him, that one of them the slaves would tell him what had happened to the woman he loved. What would he do if she was dead? If her life was taken because of his affections he would spend the rest of his life, however short it may or may not be, fighting in her name. He would paint the heavens red for her.

"But what of the luxury?" Argus asked with the impatience of a small child who had no desire to hear about women, let alone of a Roman one commanding gladiators to her bed. "I heard that he had indoor training sands for his best men. You were one of them? At least until he found out you were fucking his wife." He grinned, likely at the thought of being the favored gladiator of a man of power and wealth like Titus Claudius but he could not know the fullness of it. The weapons that he held in his hands would be worth more coin than most would likely earn in all his lifetime. There were soft beds, delicious food and all the pleasure he could take after each victory.

"I don't see how any woman could be worth risking all of that plus your title." He grinned at Proximus, but the older man was shaking his head, the boy knew nothing about what he was speaking of. "You think differently? Was she worth it all?"

"She was worth everything I had and everything I ever dreamed that I wanted." Proximus said, stepping away from the bars to sit in the darker corner of the cell. "And unless your little Syrian is worth the same you had best be careful, for you do not have the standing that I did and the only thing that can be taken from you is your life and his."

He rested his head back against the walls and sighed at the painful memories flooding his mind, the clearest being the look on his woman's face as they were parted for the last time. He could still remember the agony in her eyes and the sound of her screaming his name while guards pulled them apart, never to lay eyes upon each other again in this lifetime, or so it seemed.

"Be aware Argus, you can never know what price the gods will exact from you for accepting the gift of another's heart. It may be more than you are willing to pay." He let the silence settle between them, neither man noticing the eyes watching from the shadows; one pair as dark as cinnamon and flashing with the joy of discovery and the other a brown so deep they were almost black with a warm sadness at the pain of good men used for the pleasure of others.

CHAPTER 5

Arturo, the druid medicus, had been trying to catch Jovian who had left behind the list of herbs that he needed replenished in the infirmary but when he had heard him laying as much of his heart bare as the boy was able, he had paused his footsteps. It was unusual for Jovian to trust anyone in the ludus beside Cassian and himself. He had so few friends due to holding the favor of Tertius, it made the house slaves envy him and the gladiators distrustful. The fact that he had reached out to one of them and not been rebuffed or molested was a good sign but as soon as he saw the look between Argus and Jovian he knew that there was more between them, on the boy's side at least, which was dangerous for both.

He was going to pause to speak to Argus about the risks when he heard Proximus begin and he caught sight of Astrix, another Syrian slave that was older, far more cunning and far less liked than Jovian. With a deep breath, he sped up his pace to catch the man by his shoulder. "Where is it that you rush to Astrix? Something needing your attention with urgency?" He narrowed his eyes, the usually peaceful brown turned to a smouldering fire as he hissed. "You would not be thinking of spreading rumors to ear of your Dominus that would cause him anger and distress? Surely not. You must know how dangerous that could be for everyone involved, everyone." His tone ensured that there was no room for misunderstanding. He would gladly see this man to some pain if it kept Jovian safe from the disaster that the rumor would bring.

"Arturo. It is odd to see you so far from the safety of your little nest. What brings you so far afield?" Arturo could see Astrix was trying to calm him with words that would turn to lies but it would not work. "I only go to give the nightly report to Dominus. He likes to know what happens within the walls beneath his house. Is there something you would have me tell him? Perhaps I can deliver that paper clenched within soft fist?" He pointed to the rolled parchment Arturo held tightly.

Arturo smiled but it was more vicious than his usual pleasant expression. "No. You can take yourself elsewhere and I will speak to Tertius myself. This night and what you think you might have heard did not happen; do you understand me Astrix?"

The Syrian smiled and shook his head slowly. "You want to protect him? Is he in your arms as well Arturo? Is that why you want to speak to Dominus yourself?" He chuckled trying to remove the vice like grip Arturo had on him. "You cannot save him from his own foolishness druid. This will be the end of him, either tonight or another, but it will happen." Slowly Astrix stepped away with a smirk on his lips despite the dangerous glare Arturo shot him in the shadows. "So, save him tonight if that is your wish but it will only make the anger at his betrayal more dangerous. For all of us, as you said." He slowly stepped away, not turning his back, since Arturo had revealed himself to be far more dangerous than anyone suspected. "Remember that Arturo, your words, not mine."

Arturo let him walk away because he could not deny the truth in his words. Jovian had started something that could not be undone, and it was going to have the capability to destroy the happiness of each of them. With a sigh, he turned and headed up the steep stone cut stairs to the villa, moving through the halls silently until he was before the doorway to Tertius' office.

Collecting himself for just a moment, forcing his face and body to relax before he stepped inside with the serene expression that always grated on the lanista's nerves. Though he seemed unbreakable, unflappable, but in truth he was more on edge that night than most. More and more often in the last few years he had found himself near to breaking and praying to his gods for release or solace in some form or another. He had a brotherhood with Cassian, but they were not the same sort of men. The druid was learned and devout while the gladiator was wild and unpredictable. More than he missed his freedom he missed the conversations and communion with his fellow priests and would give much for such a thing once again.

"Good evening Dominus. I am afraid in his hurry to return to you Jovian forgot the list of herbs and other ingredients that I need for the infirmary." He set the paper on the desk and smiled as he sat in the chair and plucked a cherry from the bowl sitting on the table beside him. "Where is he? I assumed that he was rushing back to your arms, as he usually does at night, does he not?" He knew that he might be baiting the lanista's anger, but it was better than having him suspect Jovian of infidelity which would lead to questions and punishments. Having heard Proximus talk to Argus of what he had gone through and what could happen with Tertius it was better for everyone if his rage had another target that distracted him from the things that he should not see. "I made sure that the tonic requested for your wife was sent and certainly the youth has seen it delivered, I am sure that he will have yours with him as well."

Tiberius stared at him, the expression on his face telling how he wished to see the druid on the cross or to the mines. "You are bolder than usual this night. What brings such to my door with the thought that it will be tolerated?" Drinking from the cup of wine in his hand he watched Arturo closely.

He guessed that Tiberius was trying to figure out the way his mind worked, it was something that he had not been able to discover in ten years of possession. If, somehow, he was able to discover the secret to his serenity the lanista would be merciless in the attempt to break him and have him at whatever mercy he possessed.

"Find tongue and give answer or take self from my sight. There are other things to occupy my time than a slave who thinks himself his master's equal simply because he once stood a man of importance to his own gods." Tiberius snipped.

Arturo smiled calmly; he was determined to use his full advantage over the Roman. "There is no boldness, simply the desire to ensure that your men have the best care when they come to me for aid. For that to happen I need the things written in that list and since your boy forgot it, I thought that it would be best that I bring it to you myself."

He straightened and flicked a random fluff of dust from the cuff of the robe he wore instead of the subligaria or wrap that the other men of the household wore to mark their status as slave. "I did not want to set it in Astrix's hand in case he took it upon himself to…edit the contents as he has done in the past." Arturo tilted his head and added carefully. "I would not want to see him hurt by those he angers with such slights of hand when he is in the ludus. It may be wise to keep him from journeying there for some time. There is talk of an unfavorable nature in his regard of late."

"Unfavorable talk? What does that mean?" Tertius sipped his wine and arched a brow. "If you mean that his life is in danger then I would have the names of the men that would dare to threaten the man who stands at my side?"

According to the fighting men Arturo knew that Astrix had once been a recruit gladiator. Instead of receiving the mark he had proven to be of greater worth to the lanista transporting secret messages and carrying out certain deeds that he could not stain his own hands with. Though even Tiberius did not 'like' Astrix he was a valuable servant and he would not want the men of the ludus accosting him.

"Loose tongue and spill names of those that would bring him harm."

Arturo hid his smile but shook his head. "I would not see a man punished for mere words though the intent behind them is still the same." He could see the protest rising in Tertius' eyes and held up a hand. "I came to offer council that you keep the man from the ludus, for his own well being and your peace of mind." Slowly the Druid rose to his feet and pushed the parchment he had placed on the desk in front of him. "The sooner this is filled the better, just as it would be better to see Cassian back to training, sooner instead of later, the men need to see their champion on the sands." It had not been his intent to bring up Cassian with the lanista tonight, but he knew better than most what being forced to serve inside the house would do to the man. Treated like a houseslave would slowly drive Cassian out of his mind.

Setting down his cup the lanista laughed. "Now we get to the heart of what you are truly here for, do we not? It is no secret the closeness between you two Celts, but I did not think he would ask you to beg for him."

If this was what had happened, Arturo would have begun with the request and not bothered with the agitation. The man was a fool not to see that.

"I am not of a mind to see him to the sands yet. I ask the heavier question; his wounds from the past two matches, how much do they trouble him?" Tiberius asked with a casual tone.

It was difficult to get around the lanista, but if he was going to help his friend then he had to be willing to dance with the lesser mind. "I have not broken words with the man since I mended his leg, but I know him as I know the gladiators downstairs. He needs to fight, needs a blade in his hand as he faces down death itself under the heat of the beating sun." He leveled his eyes at the Roman, determined not to back down until he had made his point; it was an insult to the man who was supposed to stand tall for his house to be merely cleaning it.

"I do not need you to tell me what a gladiator needs Arturo. You forget yourself as easily as you forget my heritage. I stand the third son to hold title of lanista beneath this roof and if the gods will it then I will be the last when I elevate this house, at last, beyond this piss hole, provincial city." Tertius snarled with a glare, slamming down his cup. "Perhaps living among animals has dulled your once fabled instinct for tactics and battle for once again you have chosen a fight you cannot hope to win and spread your resources too far apart." Tertius grinned at what he thought was brilliance;

throwing the reason that he had been captured as a slave in battle back in his face: the small pack of Celts against the might of a Roman legion had been doomed from the beginning, which had been Arturo's intent when he pursued his errant prince's folly.

Arturo took a short breath then released it with the anger the insult brought and shook his head. This little man seemed to thrill at throwing his status and what he thought of as a glorious lineage in the faces of his slaves. If he knew that in his ludus he had a high priest who still had devoted acolytes, the lost prince of a Celtic tribe and the son of a Germanic warlord he would either preen and brag to the point where it got him killed or use the information to taunt Cassian and make his life harder. If the man had any sense at all, he might find himself holding a little more respect for those under his roof.

When the lanista crossed his arms in self declared triumph Arturo took one more calming breath. "I think, if you looked, you would see that I forget very little and that I am simply doing the task that you set me to; seeing the men you call your slaves to the best medical care that I am capable of." Letting that statement settle into his mind he continued. "Cassian is a champion and all within the city know it. To have him shackled within your villa, whatever it is that you have him doing, breaks at the image that has been achieved by his blood and sweat. The one built at your express command: the glorious golden god upon the sands. Even the other men are affected by it and not in the ways that I think you desire. There is no concern that it could happen to them or words of never crossing your wrath. You have given your gladiators a dangerous distraction, one that could prove very costly to you."

"You wax about the virtues of men that think less of you than they do of the whores that service them after the games." Tertius said with a smug laugh though they both knew his words were a lie, the men held him in high esteem almost like a father to many of the fighters even those that were well seasoned and near to him in age. "Tell me of Cassian's injuries and I will tell you what I shall do with the man and spare me your thoughts upon the effect his absence has on his brothers for he will be returned to them soon enough." Arturo could read in Tertius' eyes that he was trying to hide the worry that his medicus might be right about the mental state of his men and that such distraction could see his best men put to grass if games came too soon.

Arturo nodded "The wound in his leg bothers him still and I would not put him in the arena for at least seven days more though he is well enough to train." He wanted to add that there was more benefit than loss to having him train even if he could not fight for it would prepare Argus for the arena and upcoming games, but he was interrupted by Tertius' dismissive voice beginning once again.

"Then it is settled. He will not start training just yet, he has not been requested for any games just now and there has been a request for his use by Felix Census for a week, perhaps two, and I had thought him too close to training strength to allow it but now, after hearing your report, I think that it would be a good thing if I did allow him to leave these walls." He grinned darkly and held up the opened parchment from Felix. "It may remind him of what he has put behind him and bring back to us a more grateful champion." He laughed and locked eyes with the man sitting before him. "You will break no word of anyone about this or I may yet find a way to see that tongue severed at last."

The druid stood and frowned as he left the office without further words. The man was outside his mind to threaten to go against the edict set down by the senate at the time of his delivery to Tertius. The man who captured him held his articles of slavery but did not wish to keep the 'dangerous druid' inside the city of Rome and so he was sent to Velletri under the watch of the lanista. The lanista and druid hated each other but Tertius had been promised the favor of his captor for the inconvenience. By the order of the senate itself he could not bring harm to the holy man who had been a leader in the Celtic army and might one day be wanted for a ransom. Slavery kept him in one place, and it kept him a prisoner and most likely in better condition than if he had been in a prison without light or good food.

Arturo leaned against the wall deep in thought. How could he sleep that night without telling the man that was his closest friend that he was to be sent to another house for a week, perhaps more? It would not matter that it was the house of the woman he cared for, it would remind him of the days in his youth where he was handed about as a beautiful toy to be played with by any with enough coin to pay the price until he fought his way out and to the sands.

Arturo was still deep in his musing when a friendly hand touched his shoulder and the very man who had consumed his thoughts appeared beside him, his face filled with deep concern. "Druid? What brings you here at this late hour? Is this not your usual time for prayers?" Cassian seemed concerned about his unexpected appearance in the villa. It was well known that he rarely, if ever, attended the lanista in the villa since they both preferred to keep their interactions confined to the infirmary and therefore as brief as possible.

"Do not tell me the man is now ill. I do not want to think about what this place will be like if he is. It is bad enough in the ludus where they search for any excuse to drink more wine and get injured in foolish quarrels. If he is ill now, when I am here, there is going to be blood shed and we know that there are going to be more injuries than you can handle so do not tell me that he is ill." Lowering his voice to a gentle growl Cassian asked the question that must have stopped him and make him disturb what had looked like prayers to their shared gods. "Did he lay a hand upon you? Hurt you?" There was precious little he would have been able to do if Tiberius had violated the edict, but he, as a friend, would have offered support if needed.

"No, the man is not such a fool as that, not yet." Arturo said with a sigh as he forced a smile at his friend. "The holy ones protect me as they do you, though you should be at rest by now should you not? That leg needs it." He tried to avoid eye contact, worried that the man would be able to see that he was hiding something in his expression. "If you are going to retake the sands in the next day or so you have to be smart and rest your injuries when you can. Do not make things worse just to boost your pride." His eyes danced teasingly. "You'll never make it to her arms again if you put pride before wisdom." When a smirk crossed the handsome face that had been filled with worry and concern only moments before Arturo knew that he had distracted him from the lanista and given him something to fight for.

"There is skill enough my friend, do not worry about that." He said with a soft chuckle and shake of his head. "You should know me better than that by now and if it is your order as medicus then I will go find what rest I can in this place." He sighed and looked around at the decorated walls. "All this finery, these things, bought with coin earned by the blood and sweat of my brothers and I yet there is nothing for us, no good will or even time to hear desires and concerns? Tell me Arturo where is the gods' justice now? Why is it that you, their faithful priest, must live this way when they could save you? You speak of their protection where all I see is their failure."

Before Arturo could speak Cassian shook his head dismissively. "Keep your faith in your gods I hold more belief in your skill as medicus to keep me and those I hold to heart safe." His eyes lit as though an idea had just sparked in his memory and he lowered his voice to a whisper. "Did Jovian tell you if he got the gift to her?" There was no chance of mistaking who 'her' meant, when he nodded Cassian smiled "For that I am grateful. The sadistic son of her dominus claims to have taken a whip to her flesh this past night and it eases my mind slightly to know that at least she did not need to feel that pain for long. You have my gratitude for that dear friend."

"It was a thing easily done. If it helps her and you to have some peace, then I am glad of it." Arturo said with a smile and a bow of his head. He recalled the slender girl that had caught the champion's attention and wondered what she could have done to deserve a whipping by a man like Vitus Census but there was little else that he could do besides to pray for her safety. He knew that if her life was taken Cassian would be a broken man that would not recover from his agony a second time. Her death would be shortly followed by that of the man whose heart she had taken possession of.

His sigh was heavy as he stood straight to look Cassian in the eye. "I will offer prayers for her safety and add them to those for your swift return to training and the victory that will bring you your heart's great desire. Be safe my friend and we will break words again soon." He clasped his forearm tightly and nodded before departing to the ludus once again, seeking out his secret sanctuary to offer prayers to the hallowed names of his homeland.

CHAPTER 6

The main street of the city and most of the smaller ones leading up to it were humming with activity that made Cassian smile despite himself. The merchant stalls lining the square bustled with a roaring trade that spoke of the vitality of the city. If one was of a mind there were everything from candles to perfumes, slaves and weapons available for the right price. Money changed hands at a rapid rate and created an air of infectiously good humor among all those present. Some of the vendors knew Tertius by sight and waved, calling out for him to inspect their wares and make them a gift to his wife whose luxurious tastes were well known to any man who wished to make coin in Velletri. The lanista returned the friendly gestures but it was not purchasing a gift for his wife, Lycithia, that had brought him to the market today; Felix Census was sure to make his regular trip to the market to drink wine with the other more affluent merchants who had enough wealth that they no longer needed to stand shop keep at their own stalls. Tertius had stated that he wanted to break words with the merchant, but Cassian suspected there was more to this than he was willing to say.

Cassian kept his footsteps behind his Dominus steady while he tried to ignore the heavy chain linking the shackles that bound his wrists but the noise of them, slight to any other, sounded like trumpets in his ears making them impossible to forget. This was not the way that the champion of the city should be seen in the market upon the busiest day of the week. Instead of keeping his head lowered beneath the tattered hood of a cast-off woolen cloak he should have entered the square as though it was the arena and he its possessor, its lord and master. Someday that would be his right again but not today.

The small mercy of the cloak keeping his identity secreted from those that pressed through the narrow aisles was the only thing that kept him from ripping the warm fabric from his head and tossing it to the ground. It had been mockery enough of his status to face Vitus' ridicule holding only a broom and not even a training sword to make him feel like the man he was, if he was noticed here by the press of the mob looking like a chastised body slave it would be more than his pride could bear. He did not even know the purpose of his being brought into the heart of the city for Tertius had responded to his query with the words. "You will know when it is my desire that you do and until then you will keep silent upon the subject." The Celt had wanted to laugh at the man's arrogance and his pathetic need to attempt to show dominance over a man he could never hope to equal but that would have resulted in a show of temper making the day worse and so he had left well enough alone with a squaring of his shoulders.

The champion gladiator stood silent and still while Tertius spoke about him to the owner of a stall next to the one belonging to Census as if he was not standing just behind him. He waxed on about the prowess of his champion and how the man would send any who opposed him in the arena to a speedy death, though not too speedy as to risk the displeasure of the crowd. It was disgusting to listen to him sell his life as though it were a bolt of silk on the table before them.

As an appealing youth, Cassian had often accompanied his Domina, Tiberius' mother, to the daily markets. It had seemed a marvel to his eyes and ears then, the wonder and excitement almost overwhelming to the young Celt who had never seen many of the strange foods and traditions of the south. The smells of sweetmeats and fruit accompanied that of oils and perfumes to create a heady mixture that tantalized his curiosity. In those days if he had pleased the older woman, or she was feeling affectionate, she might buy him a small jug of wine or fruit crystalized in honey. It had taken over a year before he realized the true reason for those excursions, she had been parading him to her friends that held curiosity for the beautiful young Celt with hair cascading down his back in a style so unlike the Romans of the city.

The memories brought to him by this place were not even remotely pleasurable anymore, so he pushed them aside and reached out to touch a thick coil of rope resting on a table next to him. He had not had his hand on it a second when the stall owner's hand flashed out to grip his wrist with a near bruising force. Had he been free he would have taken the man down in seconds but since it was a slave facing a free man, he waited for his wrist to be released before withdrawing away from the table in passive silence.

Taking a deep breath, he glanced up to the sky, noting that in the last hour it had darkened, the sun slipping behind dark billowing clouds. With a shake of his head he returned his eyes to the crowd only to have his eyes land upon the face of a woman who he would have recognized from any angle, in any light. When she smiled, at something he could not see, his heart skipped a beat in his chest and a soft smile of longing played across his lips for that moment of brief joy. The ominous skies threatened rain and though he would have welcomed the cool relief it would turn the linen of her dress to clinging translucence. She glanced across the square to look directly at his hooded form with curiosity in her eyes. Even though he knew she would be unable to discern his face beneath the wool he wondered if she could feel his eyes upon her. Was he the one she wished to see beyond all others?

He had his answer when a strong gust of rain scented wind caught the edge of the hood and lifted it, just for a few seconds before he yanked it quickly back in pace. Glancing back at her Cassian saw the lovey face of his woman light up with recognition and he could not help but return her eager smile. Felix glanced casually across the square in that moment and happened to lay eyes upon the lanista. Raising his hand in salute he called to him. "Tertius, how do you fare this hour? I pray you spare a moment to break words over a glass of wine." He cut through the crowd, Violetta falling behind him as the men met and clasped arms with broad grins.

"Census." Tiberius extended his hand when his co-conspirator approached, and Cassian wondered what plan the pair had made now. "I fare well, and I hope the same can be said for yourself." His eyes wandered over the girl at his side briefly, the look in his eyes causing the heart of the slave behind him to thunder dangerously in his chest. If the Roman touched her it would not be easily forgiven.

Looking up at the sky before meeting the merchants gaze, Tiberius tilted his head towards the building beside them. "The sky will soon fall in torrents, or so it seems. Your thoughts towards seeking shelter and drink for its duration is one of wisest consideration. Shall we?" He motioned in a broad sweep towards the tavern.

It was impossible for Cassian to take his eyes away from her as she followed the old man towards the house of drink.

His gaze lingered hungrily from behind the safety of the hood, his eyes narrowed to focus on her unassuming beauty. Amid the boisterous sounds of the market and those rushing to finish their tasks before the inevitable rainfall she was a beacon of peace for his soul. A bright flash of lightning lit the sky and was quickly followed by a roar of thunder that shook the ground as a warning of the strength of the approaching storm. Cold winds wound their way through the streets whipping the edges of tents and threatening to clear the tables full of wares.

Their masters would be deep in wine and conversation which might allow for them to have the chance to break words of their own though it would have to wait until their safety was made certain by the Romans attention in their own talks. His heart raced as they entered the lamp-lit confines of the tavern. There were so many words that were threatening to spill out but the proximity of those that kept them enslaved stilled his tongue. To be so close and still be forced to silence was a new kind of torture but it would only last a few minutes more and his body vibrated with the anticipation of it while she tightened the shawl around her shoulders only a quick pace ahead of him, close enough to touch but forbidden to do so.

She seemed so small, vulnerable and fragile, as if she could break at the slightest touch and yet he could sense a quiet strength in her that kept her standing tall when so many others would have broken, shattered by the horrors of the lives they led. He was close enough to her now to see the fluttering pulse at the base of her neck and inhale the soft, intoxicating floral scent that surrounded her. Every muscle in his body grew tight and hard with the desire to have that softness wash over him, to have her writhing and sweating beneath him. She was so close, but it would be impossible to have her here and no matter how much his body screamed to possess her she was not his, not yet.

"Sit." The command barked from Tertius was like a splash of water to his possessive musings while watching the woman who held his heart see her Dominus settled before she was dismissed to stand at the wall by the stool he had been assigned to. "Stay until summoned. I will leave you absent guards, give me no reason to regret the decision." The lanista growled before turning back to face Felix with his usual jovial façade. "Let us raise cups to celebrate the plans towards future endeavors.

Felix clapped a hand to the lanista's shoulder before he sat down so that they could pour each other wine. Violetta followed Cassian to the shadowed corner and stood silently next to the wall. Watching her fidget with her dress Cassian could tell that she was nervous but at last she found the courage to whisper softly, barely audible over the din of the tavern. "Gratitude for the gift. It was well received and put to effective use." She glanced to the side to meet his eyes with pain written on her face as she braved further words. "Does your wound still cause grief? The one on your leg?"

He heard the fear ringing in her voice, sensed the scrutiny as she waited for him to respond to her seemingly innocent question. All he desired was to take her in his arms and wipe away her terror with his strength. He cherished her affection and wanted to take care of her, protect her and still he stood helpless against the lust of Romans. If she had found need for the opium, then Vitus' words had been more than a mere taunt to torment. Ignoring the sound of the chain as it clanked when he moved, heedless of who might be watching and the possible reprimand, he reached up to cup her chin in his hand and stroke her cheek tenderly with the tips of his fingers.

He wanted nothing more that to cover her mouth with his and to taste the sweetness of her mouth once again. "Give no concern to the scratch delivered by the German, wound and fall were both taken by command. Had I known the price would be paid by someone other than myself..." He found himself suddenly at a loss for proper words to express himself and so he offered his apology in the way he knew best. Drawing her down to him he pressed a soft kiss to her lips for a moment before moving his mouth over hers in a possessive caress.

As his lips made contact, he rose to his feet and Violetta pressed her lips back against his for a moment before pulling back just enough for questions to slip from her divine mouth with rapid succession. "Dominus' command? He would command his champion to take a wound? Did he order the defeat knowing what would happen as a result?"

Even though the spark between them beckoned to pull her tight to his chest and wrap his arms around her small frame he allowed her room to take a step back to look up at him, her eyes searching for answers to understand what was going on. He wondered how he was to answer such questions without causing her more panic.

After glancing in the direction of the men who controlled their fates, she stepped close to Cassian again and let her head fall against his chest, breathing softly before asking once more. "Why would he command such a thing?"

Tightening his hold to draw her close once again it took every ounce of strength and restraint that he had in him to not act on his desire. She was so close, nestled against him and making him extremely aware of everything about her. The delicate smell he remembered flooded his nostrils while enticing curves, soft and ripe, pressed against hardened muscles that suddenly ached for her. Raw emotions that he had thought well under the rein of control were surging through him and dreams of a future they could not possibly have were ignited and fanned to life by the smoldering embers of her enchanting presence.

The kiss was no longer enough, he wanted to pull her closer, to gently press her against the wall, lift the edge of her dress just enough to… The hair on the back of his neck stood on end and he turned his eyes just enough to see that the lanista was looking at them with the most devious expression he had ever seen. It sent shivers down his spine and he wanted nothing more than to shield her from it and what it would mean.

Tiberius had leaned his chair back against the planked wall and stretched his legs straight beneath the table with a goblet of wine in his hand. Through years of practice Cassian could, just barely, read the lips of his master as he spoke to the silk merchant. "Felix," He altered his attention back to his company. "My champion is removed from the sands until wounds delivered during the test and in the arena before are healed. This means that he is of little use to me. Perhaps your house might benefit by his presence a little longer than the singular night you had mentioned in your letter?" He laughed slightly and took a deep drink. "For what use is a fighter absent the ability to fight? I would offer him as a temporary loan, a gift of sorts, to be returned when he stands ready to train again if it pleases you. I only ask that he not be seen to greater damage."

Felix turned to cast a glance towards the pair of slaves in the shadows, catching Cassian's eye briefly. If he was surprised at their intimacy, he showed no sign other than a raised brow. He turned back to his companion and extended his hand again. "You have my word, you man will be returned to you no worse, indeed I think he will be greatly inspired towards further victory." Cassian could not believe their words. It was likely that Felix' mind had already begun thinking of how to use this 'gift' for his greatest advantage. "Will the man need to remain chained or can he be trusted to obey command."

"Chains are in place as lesson to pride which has recently seen him so overcome with rage and lack of control that he made the attempt to strike his Doctore, a man who had once stood his friend." He shook his head. "Vitus also spoke of him breaking words of insult to him though such disobedience has never been witnessed by me. I would leave the choice to your discretion."

Violetta raised her eyes to his in the same moment that Felix cast a second glance to the corner. Her breath caught in a panicked gasp and she tried to pull away, causing every fiber of his being to protest the absence of her in his arms. She sank to the ground at his feet and drew her knees to her chest, wrapping her arms around them with a desolate sigh leaving him confused and concerned. Determined to do whatever was needed to ease the panic in her Cassian scooped Violetta into his arms and sat her upon his lap, with his arms around her. He would have plundered her mouth as before, trying to erase her fear with passion, but it was not the time.

He yearned to hear his name on her lips in passion fueled cries, but even more he wished to know her with the intimacy of lovers who know each other's inner thoughts, with nothing between them. He had wanted to brand her soul with his kiss, driving all thoughts of slavery and bondage from her mind and summon only thoughts of the sweetest pleasures to be shared between them. Had this circumstance been as private as their other meetings there was nothing in this world that would have stopped him from proceeding as he had before. He grew hard at the mere memory of the sweet taste of her mouth, the press of her full breasts naked against his chest and the utter bliss of her hips pressed against his rock-hard erection. He had attempted to find some solace in the memory until Tiberius had turned his eyes on him. In that second his peace had been destroyed. The look was one of malice and joy and there could be no escaping the sinister resolve that shone in them. A deep foreboding made its way through his mind, dread overtaking him in a moment of rare fear of the will of the Romans.

The tavern was now crowded with many from the market and the air was getting heated, causing them both to sweat and bringing a small hiss of pain to her lips. Looking over at their masters he wondered what words were broken to cause the embrace of arms between them. Violetta must have noted the tension in his body and turned her head to ask quietly. "You are troubled? What worries you Cassian?"

"Last time such a look was seen in Dominus' eyes two men met their fate upon the cross in the training yard as a lesson for us all to never defy his will." He had not forgotten that he had yet to answer the question she had put to him regarding the loss to Proximus that had led to her pain, if the words of Vitus could be believed. He inhaled sharply and whispered. "Apologies" through a tightly clenched jaw as he maintained his locked gaze with the lanista, barely noticing the Roman merchant's amusement at the glare between them.

"The cross?" She whispered in fear, eyes widening as she turned to look up at him. Suddenly pale she spoke of her fear. "What grievous thing could you have done to earn such from your Dominus?"

The rain and winds of the true storm beat against the walls of the tavern as the sky flashed and a clap of thunder roared so loud that it shook the foundation and drowned out the noise of its patrons. She startled at the sound and a small yelp escaped her. It was absurd; to be frightened of the boom and crash of nature, but she must have been because she bowed her head to rest upon her arms as she waited for whatever answer he could find for her question.

"There is nothing that I have done that would justify that fate and I cannot see him pursuing such a thing." Every nerve was on edge and he felt as though he were standing in the fighter's tunnel in the arena awaiting the sound of the horns to command his entry to the field of battle. He had never been this defiant and yet if felt right in the defence of his woman. He listened to the storm raging outside and smiled slightly, its fury matched his own as though Jupiter shared his emotions for once. "Let him bring what he will, I will face it as I always have though with a greater hope now than I have ever had." What had begun as a growl softened as he brought his hand gently to her shoulder, attempting to offer comfort in a touch.

When his hand rested upon her shoulder, she turned to lay her cheek upon it even as her back flinched at the contact against him. "I would never wish such upon any man nor could I bear it such a thing came to pass for you." Stealing a glance in the direction of the table she added. "I dread what accord they have agreed upon. What game would they see us used in next? Was the previous one not enough?"

"Catch your dress." He said gruffly. It had been slight but there had been a flinch at his touch, reminding him of the taunt of Vitus and how her flesh had been put to the lash. He had to see for himself if the man's words were true or just another attempt to agitate him to the point of dangerous disobedience. He reached for the knot of fabric closest to his hand and with a swiftness born of much practice he released it, using his other hand to draw the shawl away and reveal the marred perfection of her back. The bright red lines and bloodied scabs that could scar brought him to an instant outrage and had Vitus been present there was no force on earth that could have saved him from death. He slid his hand down her side. When she flinched again, he pulled the fabric further away to reveal a wound closed with delicate but undeniable stitches. "There will be a cost for this, I swear it." He growled, barely able to contain his violent loathing of the act and the man who had seen it done.

CHAPTER 7

Holding the thin material against her chest Violetta turned her head away as he peeled the fabric from her back. "The women say that the marks should fade in time, needle and thread was only needed for the one and I was told that it will scar but it may not be bad." She shook her head and whispered thanks again though he barely heard it through the blood red curtain of rage in his mind. "The pain was made easier by your gift. Without it I do not know if I could have born the lash, even with it I found it harder than I imagined." She blushed as she finished. Did he know she felt the weight of shame that he was seeing these marks on her? Did he think her less beautiful because of them?

"They tell me that I spoke to you as I lay in the cloud of the drug, but no one would tell me what it is that I said. I owe you my gratitude for the gift." She was babbling with uncertainty, to fill the silence and try to calm the murderous rage in his eyes. Taking a breath to try to calm her rush of emotions she watched as Cassian looked towards the table just as Felix rose with a sudden fury in his eyes.

Felix had obviously taken as much as he could stand of the lanista and stood to ready himself to depart now that it seemed the worst of the storm was over. He had raised his hand to beckon for her when he caught sight of the expression on Cassian's face and the material of her dress clutched tight in his fist. His mouth twisted in an angry frown and he stalked towards them as the lanista left through another exit. Had he even considered that he was simply inspecting the wounds that Vitus had so viciously informed him of? She could not ask her master these questions but there was no doubt that Felix was in a strange mood that she could not decipher, anger or an uncommon elation, either one was likely to be dangerous to her and perhaps Cassian as well.

"Gratitude is not needed. I am glad that I was able to see it to you though I would have preferred it to come from my hands instead of those that I had to send it with." Cassian's voice was soft like rich velvet and she could feel his breath against her neck like the caress of his hands as he retied the rough material of her dress and quickly lowered his hands back to his side. "The man approaches to return you to Hades itself. Know I would stay at your side if it was allowed." He said calmly, his palm quickly resting in the small of her back before he stilled completely.

Felix grinned deviously when Violetta rose to her feet, she could not help but shiver at the displeasure in his expression. Although Felix did not rage as his son did in violent outbursts his temper was a thing of reckoning, cool and calculated which made her want to run and hide, both of which were impossible in the tavern. When he stood before them, she wisely kept her eyes cast to the ground while he snapped his irritation at the gladiator behind her.

"Touch again that which is not yours, slave, and see it put from reach forever." He maintained their stare as he brought his hand slowly up the front of Violetta's body in a show of ownership, groping the softness of her breast through the thin fabric, cupping the weight of her before flicking a finger across her nipple to make her gasp. Chuckling to himself when a blush of what he likely thought to be shame flickered across her face he continued, not seeing the seething hatred flash in her eyes. "Now attend, both of you, I would see no further delays to my return home." His grin broadened as he prepared to depart. "Cassian, you will hold coverage so that I am not overly dampened by a sudden deluge."

With a quick glance over her shoulder Violetta saw Cassian glowering at Felix, his eyes trailing the path of his hand with indignation growing in them. He could not have known that both father and son took the same perverse pleasure in exercising their power in small moments of mockery like this.

"I thought she was my gift?" Cassian said with a hint of anger in his voice. He had to know better but still his expression held some hope that his reasoning at least might see Felix' anger lessened. It seemed to her that now he saw the 'gift' of her as a planned manipulation by Felix from the beginning; he was meant to feel for her so that she could be used to control him as the Roman wished. For the span of a breath she thought she saw him contemplate walking away from her and the pain that her use could bring him. As she lifted her eyes to meet his, fear growing inside her, he smiled, brief but warm, and she knew that no matter what happened, he would not leave her now. There had to be another way to survive this.

The final part of Felix's command sinking in Cassian repeated it questioningly and Violetta felt the first twinge of hope. "Attend and hold coverage for you?" He turned his head to look for Tertius only to find the space that the man had filled moments earlier was already empty and the merchant's laugh filled both their ears.

Felix laughter continued as Cassian looked for his Dominus. "Do not bother to look for the lanista, it is my words that command you now. Attend with haste for I would not be delayed." He moved towards the door as Violetta trailed behind him, glancing over her shoulder at her lover with a shocked expression. How had this come to pass?

By the door there rested a pair of poles with a tarp wrapped around them that would, when held firmly, provide similar coverage to the screens used by the noble ladies of the city when they were hiding their fair skin from the sun. This was what Felix gestured to impatiently while Violetta's mind raced in circles, trying to understand his words; he now commanded the gladiator? What could that mean but that he was to return to the villa with them? She found herself caught between the glorious rapture of seeing him daily and the fear of what atrocities he would bear witness to and perhaps even be victim to if Vitus was permitted even a little power over him. Had the lanista deemed his champion beyond redemption and sold him to the merchant or was this a furtherance of the game that they both were played with as pawns for the amusement and increased status of the Romans.

"Your words?" Cassian asked, as surprised as Violetta by Felix' statement. "By what decree was that made true? Have I been deemed worthless and sold in a tabletop bargain?" His questions received no answer but the back of the man's head as he turned to leave, pausing expectantly, waiting for his command to be obeyed. The brief smile in Violetta's direction was obviously forced but she returned it with hope. At least they would be together and might be able stand united against Vitus. It was with resignation on his face that Cassian picked up the poles and skilfully angled them above the merchant to block the fall of the rain but not his view or the public's ability to see him which, was likely Felix's first attempt to humble her champion.

Following the men from the tavern, Violetta put her head down to brace against the wind and tried to angle herself behind Cassian and Felix so that the tarp might give her some relief as well. Winding through the streets of Velletri towards the villa grounds the trio passed several clusters of townsfolk hiding from the deluge whose eyes widened at the well-known face of their arena champion. Even in what would appear to be a lowered state the women of the elite had unabashed lust in their eyes as he passed. Violetta, behind him and unnoticed as anything but a drenched slave, reeled with the unfamiliar pangs of jealousy. How many of these women had known him intimately? How many had watched the rumored demonstrations of his skills beyond the sands? Her mind spun, and spirits plunged at the thought.

As they reached the wall surrounding the villa Felix quickened the pace to reach the dry warmth of his home. Violetta tried to increase her own pace to catch up but nearly slipped in the mud. "Leave those out of doors." He commanded, brushing past Cassian to enter his house, leaving the two slaves to enter after him he did not see the gladiator usher the woman in ahead of him as though those few seconds of warmth would make a difference to the chill that gripped them all.

Violetta wrapped her arms around herself to stop her teeth from chattering but looked up with a small smile when Meridius stepped into the hallway, nodding his head in answer to the command summoning him to follow Felix and attend the man's bath and drying. His bright blue eyes lingered on Violetta until Cassian stepped into the hall beside her and then his face flashed with confusion. It seemed that he did not understand why the man had been brought home with them either. Snapping fingers pulled him away before she could speak to him as the Roman called over his shoulder. "See yourselves dried and dressed in something that does not fucking drip upon my floor and then attend with haste."

After he dropped the poles against the wall she watched as Cassian raked a hand through his hair, to clear the wet tangles away from his face. He briefly nodded at Meridius who he had seen with Felix on more than one occasion now. That he was friend to her was obvious with the way his eyes kept finding their way back to her. The words of the man he was to call 'Dominus' for the time being made him smirk but that turned to a sigh of frustration when he found himself still without explanation as to why he was in this house with her.

He shook his head then looked up, finding her eyes and then nothing else mattered to her as he said with a tender smile. "You look frozen, Violetta. Let us fall to command if only to keep you from falling ill."

"Yes Dominus." Violetta nodded her head carefully to Felix, sharing a brief glance with Meridius before meeting the eyes of the man at her side, her living heart. "Come." She beckoned with her hand. "It will not be hard to find a change of clothing for you in this house for linens abound." She stopped herself from reaching for his hand, if Vitus appeared and saw her touching him it would bode disaster and the heavens knew how he would react to the presence of his irritator within the walls of the villa, but she could not find energy to care. Walking down a smaller corridor, dark and warm behind the kitchens, she took him to the top of a steep stair, cut into the stone.

It was as if Cassian sensed her desire. Catching her hand, he took it into his own for the briefest of moments, pressing a quick kiss to her palm before releasing it to follow her lead.

He had never looked so out of place and tense, even in her master's decorative pool with eyes upon them, but she had to have faith in their connection. If she believed the gods were behind this, she might have thought they were answering her prayers by sending him to this house but what would a man like Census need a gladiator for? There was no one to fight here, no one that would dare to face him, and Cassian was not a house slave and never would be. For the briefest moment she feared that Felix would pit Cassian against Meridius and that she would see the two men she loved most fighting against each other for their lives. "There are quarters below. They lock it at night, when the house is asleep. We must hurry, we have little time, for patience is not a virtue in this house."

Smiling at her somber expression he added. "I would dare to make a wager that no form of virtue has ever graced this house, except for that which I hold in my hand."

She smiled at his comment. "Precious little virtue, only honor in trade and business."

Coming to the bottom of the stair they set foot in the dampness of the slave's quarters; on both sides of the stairs lay a darkened passage lit only by sparse torchlight where curtained doorways on either side marked the rooms. Turning to the left, walking quietly, she led him past rooms that were empty of their occupants, who were upstairs at work. Ducking through the curtain of her own cell she reached for a pair of cloths used for bathing. Placing one in his hand she made for the doorway again. "I will return shortly with a dry tunic and linens. Await me here?" She asked, looking into his face with a nervous smile on her lips. She presumed many things in bringing him to her cell, she did not know if he preferred the solitude of his own cell, as he surely had in the ludus as its champion. Felix had not said where he was to be housed and until she was told otherwise, by either man, she would attempt to keep him as close as she was able.

Rushing to find dry garments that would fit him, she found that most of the discarded tunics in the washing room would not likely fit his shoulders. The women working the piles of cloth amid the steam and vats of water watched her wordlessly as she dug through trying to find something, anything, that would fit. He could not stay in the wet clothing and begin his time, however long it might be, by disobeying Felix's command. At last a few tunics and stretches of linen were found and she made her way back towards the room only to be stopped by guards descending the stairs.

"Where is he?" The leader asked. "Dominus would see chains removed." Nodding silently, she led them down the hall and parted the curtain, bowing her head after she glanced silently towards her shackled lover. She prayed that he remained calm, he did not know what they were permitted to do if he offered resistance.

"Your new Dominus bids chains removed to allow tasks fulfilled but shackles will remain as reminder of new position, do you understand?" The guard asked, holding the key where Cassian could see it while he waited for his answer.

The only evidence that he was displeased at their condescension was the slightest twitch of his jaw before he extended his hands. He nodded a brief affirmation then smiled at the sound of the key turning in the locks as if it was the sweetest sound he had heard all day. "Gratitude." Was all he said instead, the sentiment genuine despite the circumstances. "The man will see us now? Census? I do not even know if I should address the man as 'Dominus' or something else since Tertius was too great a coward to break words himself."

The guards scoffed and looked at Violetta. "She will see you to where is needed when it is needed. We do not have time to educate fallen fools." They said before leaving with laughter echoing behind them.

Closing the curtain behind the guards, Violetta sighed with relief that he had been unshackled and turned back towards him. "He will be some time. Dominus will require a hot bath before we must stand in attendance." Lifting her eyes at last she gasped, her breath coming in sharp, shallow pulls as she drank him in with her eyes rising slowly from the floor.

As he spoke, he had peeled the rain-soaked garments from his body and tossed them to the floor one by one until he faced her in naked splendor. Retrieving the cloth that he had earlier discarded so that he could wipe the last remnants of the rain from his body while he returned her dazed stare with a wink that sent a blush to her cheeks. "You have seen me in this state before, did you forget my appearance?"

She shook her head slowly. It took only the sight of him to pull her mind back to the memory of him pressed against her, the rapture she had felt with his arms wrapped around her. Her eyes never leaving him she stepped across the room to pull a clean, light blue, linen dress from the box against the wall. Her hands were shaking, and she shivered while fumbling to untie the knot fastening the dripping fabric in place. "How could I forget the image of a god?" As the dress fell slightly away, almost completely to the floor, she pointed to the clothing on her pallet that she had brought for him. "I was not sure if they would be suitable for you, if not we have enough time that I could go and get you something more appropriate."

She could feel Cassian watching her through half-lidded eyes, the reaction of his entire being was physical and immediate. Crashing through both of them was a wave of desire, hot as liquid steel. The incredible pleasure of their nearness and near nudity, flooded her senses and glazed his eyes. She wanted him as much as he wanted her, but it was never supposed to be like this. He should not be shackled and serving a master he did not know for the furtherance of a game he did not know the rules of, and she should not be fearful of every sound, worried for the appearance of Vitus at the door.

With a sharp intake of breath, he was the first to attempt to regain in his control. "There is only one thing here I find to my taste." He said with a wicked grin on his lips and a low growl in his voice.

"Only one?" She looked up at him with distress in her voice, she had been almost certain that what she had brought would fit him. It was not a subligaria for the arena, but he would not want to be so exposed in this house. When her eyes met his she began to understand his meaning with a soft smile raising her lips. Walking towards him carefully, the dry garments forgotten on the pallet as she dared to reach a single hand to touch him. It was as though she were caught between her worst nightmare and most sacred dream.

CHAPTER 8

He was in her cell, his heart beating beneath her palm with nothing but a few inches of air between them and yet, he knew that his being here would mean he would bear witness to the debasement she was put to daily. The barbs of Vitus would surely find their mark, and he would be helpless to stop them. Tears sprung to her eyes and he opened his arms in silent invitation. Violetta closed what distance there had been between them, wrapping her arms around the strong core of his chest with a ragged cry before silencing her lips by pressing them to his skin.

He lowered his head and embraced her warmly, his hands running up and down the exposed skin of her lower back, careful not to come close to the lash marks upon her shoulders. His hand carefully cupped her bottom while he brought their lips together but the moment they met; a storm of passion whipped to life inside him. A growl sounded deep in his throat, like a savage animal in need. His hands fisted into her hair, the dark damp silk caressing his fingertips, his tongue thrusting to penetrate her lips then searching the heat of her mouth for something not to be named in the need for carnal fulfilment.

There would be no mistaking the dominance in his kiss this time. Like the man he would be if not a slave. It was meant to mark the woman's soul and steal the breath from her lungs while calling for her total surrender to his will. Suddenly mindful of the possibility of their discovery he slowly released her and stepped back. The dew of sweat on her chest and the rigid organ below his waist both stood as evidence of their shared desire to complete what had been started but there was not time, yet night might bring it for them both if the gods could see them together in the dark.

As his mouth claimed hers, his priestess gave into his mouth's demands and pressed her body against him. She would have moved in swift passion with him had he dared to join their bodies in the brief time they had, but he could not risk her safety. The whimper that ripped from her throat when he broke the contact between them made him crave her like the breath she stole from him. He loved knowing that he left her burning with desire, possessing her in a way she could not yet understand. She could not know yet that he would give her anything she ever asked of him, even if it meant his life.

Blinking he focused his attention, smiled into her eyes and released his hold so she could turn back to the mat. When she picked up her dress to tie it in place, he could not help but allow himself the opportunity to watch her unabashedly. His body protested the separation though his mind knew it was necessary, but it was her next words that touched his heart with her faith in him.

"I do not know what awaits at the command of Dominus, but I would have you know that no matter what happens, I can bear anything with you by my side."

A brooding expression came to Cassian's face as he stopped his hands from reaching for her hair and stared somberly into her eyes. "The mind overflows with the thought of what possibilities could be created by malevolent minds within these walls. Vitus is cruel and his hatred for me is like a living thing. I do not know how I have earned it. That he uses you as a weapon against me is something that I cannot begin to explain the agony of or understand. Now I am here, not to simply hear of what has been done, but to stand witness to it while being unable to protect you."

He reached for the tunic she had brought for him and continued as she started to untangle her hair. "Though the concern of what he might do troubles more than the rest of this strange predicament." He would be helpless to protect her against the hands of her masters. If he was allowed, he would offer comfort after the fact, but would it be enough? He could not understand the game that was played by the Romans and if he did not understand it how was he to win?

Wrapping the linen of the dress around herself he noticed that Violetta made certain to leave the marks exposed to ensure that Vitus did not have to search her to find and expose them. "The cruelty of Vitus goes beyond what you know." She said, over her shoulder. "I wish that I could give voice to reason or even guess why Felix brought you here when he knows the way that his son feels, but there is no cause that I can think of." When she paused a stillness came over him, wondering at her thoughts, then she added with a faint smile. "Perhaps the whim of the wealthy is to seek to lower the pride of the man whose skill they envy as much as they revere?"

She placed her hand softly on his arm before adding. "It is a mercy that those of the house are rare to visit the cells so at least here we are afforded some small moments of peace from them."

He looked down at her small hand with a smile and asked as he took it in his own. "Do you think it is a game that he plays? To bring me to my knees?" He shook his head firmly. "If that is so then I promise to see their venture to failure. I will break for no man." His resolve strengthened as he let his gaze wander the room again, taking in further details with the closer scrutiny. It was as small, but clean, space. Simply furnished with only a small cot and wooden chest at the wall. A window was cut high, well beyond reach but he was surprised that there were no bars. "The Romans do not visit the cells and there seems to be little concern of escape. Violetta? Why is that? Do they have guards?"

"The guards have permission to kill any who would attempt escape. They are held unchecked in punishments administered before the prisoner is brought before Dominus." She shuddered softly. "It is not only the family that is full of perversion here." She followed his gaze to the window with a shake of her head. "There have been attempts at escape of course but after the offenders had been punished by the guards Felix had seen fit to flog and crucify the men and command the rest of the household to watch. He also installed the barred gate at the top of the stairs to the cells that is locked and guarded each night after the slaves are accounted for. They have guards check and count us, as if we were sheep and they the shepherds."

Stepping towards the doorway Violetta paused. "We should attend soon. I would not wish for words of my bringing you to my cell to be broken with Dominus if he is angered."

"They are permitted to kill absent awareness of your Dominus?" It was unheard of to him and yet in this house it could not surprise given the standards that Census ruled by. Forced to endure the lechery of his offspring as well as himself it seemed that those under his mastery lived, not tethered by collar and lock, but by chains that were built day by day out of fear.

She stood, sweet in her insecurity, by the door and suddenly he found himself overcome with desire. Pulling her tight to his chest, his mouth descended to hers once again with a heated demand for acceptance and sweet submission. He would have lifted her body to press against the wall then and there had it not been for the sudden and unwelcome press of steel to his back and a hand gripping his shoulder reminding him of the first night they met.

"Dominus awaits." The guard growled with unwarranted anger as he forced them apart.

Violetta stepped back as a guard gripped her arm tightly. She brought her free hand to her lips, tingling from the bruising pressure of his urgency. Locking her eyes to his face after darting a panicked look to the steel pressed against his spine, she answered the guard. "We attend with urgent speed; steel is not required."

The guard who had her arm twisted it savagely and growled in her ear. "Slave bitches should know when to shut their mouths before I find another way to silence you." Cassian glared as the guard pushed Violetta roughly from the room, releasing the hold on her arm and nodded for his companion to follow with him. Rage went through him like a wave of heat, but this was not the time to act with violence, not yet. The fool, with no idea of his danger, positioned himself between Cassian and his woman, rushing them towards the stairs.

How long had it been since he had been threatened with steel? Had it happened since the night she had been gifted to him? He did not recall, but that did not stop him from wanting to explode with anger fueled violence. He could feel his hatred of this place building and he had not been there an hour. This place was filled with the worst of those that reveled in the power they held over those forced to servitude and he did not know how long he would be able to stand it. The simple act of the guard's aggression had made his fists clench. Even if it was not Violetta, he was not the manner of man that stood idly by when any innocent was brought to pain. He was following, playing the part of the obedient dog but he was on edge, frustrated in the knowledge that anything he might do would put them both at a greater risk.

The guard turned to catch Cassian's eye and chuckled at the defiance blazing there. "You have yet to be broken of such defiant spirit? It may have been of value to your past Dominus but here in this house it has no use." He looked Cassian up and down. "It will be a pleasure to see that fire doused by the hand of Census." He nodded to his companion, who drew his sword as he followed them to the kitchen. They would make no mistakes with his handling. He was too dangerous a man to disregard, even simply walking to the study of the master of the house.

Talking as they walked the romans discussed the slaves as though they were not present; wondering aloud at the arrival of the city's champion and what it could mean. "What this new toy is for I do not know, certainly not for fucking. He still has his Spaniard for that." The other guard shook his head and replied. "Maybe he wants to finally push Vitus to snap and have him take the girl as amusement." He reached out to trace a finger down one of the lash marks on Violetta's back as she walked ahead of him, forcing Cassian to stop himself from breaking that finger. "She chose these over his bed, which is understandable but still, his wrath now could be deadly." He sneered simply to add to the anger he saw in the man's eyes. "It would be a shame to lose such a fine piece to that animal." The men shared a laugh as they neared the door to the study where Felix was waiting but it was the sound of Vitus' angry voice that cut the air as they arrived.

Cassian felt as though he could not breathe, the very walls of the villa had closed in around him and every step seemed to take him towards some uncertain doom. The guards were right to mock him, even the flickering light of the torches that danced across his body, accenting the strength hidden beneath the tunic, seemed to mock his inability to protect that which was truly his. He had to find a way to close his mind to the voice of inadequacy or he would never survive, neither would the woman who held his heart. If it took all his strength, he would not fail her, not here in this house where she needed him more than ever.

Closing his eyes, he pressed a hand to the wall when the guards shoved him to hurry, if they wanted the champion then that was what they would see. Resilient and controlled, he would treat each day as though he was upon the sands and he would stand victorious each night and find a way to bring his prize to his arms. He could not carry a sword here and likely would not even hold a rudus, but he could use the same cunning and subtly to achieve his goals while force could not be exercised.

The sound of Vitus stayed not only himself, but he saw Violetta freeze as well and so he squared his shoulders. He gave no indication of his displeasure when they were both pushed into the room to confront her abuser and their shared tormentors.

CHAPTER 9

Felix looked up slowly and a smile slid across his lips, his brows arching in amusement when Vitus spun on his heel to glare at them raising Cassian's hackles when their eyes met.

"It is true then you have brought the great champion of the city to reside in our villa. This is indeed a pleasure I never dared to hope for father." He hissed while he slowly began to circle both Cassian and Violetta like a cat as his father began to speak.

"I am not used to being kept waiting by my own slaves, commanded to attend me with haste. Violetta, you are aware of this and know better than to do so." The older man looked back and forth between the two of them. "I would have an explanation as to cause such delay that guards had to be sent to fetch you to answer my call. Which of you would offer such words?"

Felix tapped his fingers together in a slow cadence awaiting an answer while Vitus paused behind Cassian to whisper. "Perhaps, father, he was putting the girl's body under inspection." His voice was full of mockery as he added. "Tell me champion, does she not look lovely marked as I told you? Perhaps you will be next to take the lash beneath my hand? I promise, the same choice will not be offered to you." Cassian looked at Felix waiting for him to deny the request of his son, but his face was the same mask of disinterest that it always was when faced with the exposure of his son's perversion.

"The fault was mine." Cassian stated when it looked as though Violetta was about to attempt to take the blame. He forced himself to ignore Vitus treating him as nothing more than a harmless fly, buzzing for attention. "The chains between wrists made it impossible for me to change from wet clothing, as you had commanded, and so the guards with their key were required to see it completed." He glanced at the woman beside him. "The desire to obey was present, but the ability was removed until that task was completed by the men of your house. Violetta carries no blame in this as she retrieved the garments in good haste so that we could attend you as soon as it was possible to do so."

His heart was thundering in his chest so loudly that he could swear that they should have been able to hear it. He found it hard to catch his breath while he waited, hoping that he had saved Violetta from the harm that would surely come if Felix thought her deliberately disobedient. He then turned his head slightly to address Vitus without looking directly at him or letting the indignation in his eyes show. "I made no inspection, but simply dressed as I was commanded, then made my way here." When their eyes did lock, he squared his shoulders and continued. "As for marks, they prove the truth of your words but nothing more." Directing his attention back to Felix he made an offer in the attempt to appease. "If it is desired, by my Dominus, that I see the same marks upon my flesh then I stand his to command."

Vitus grinned wildly and gestured for Violetta to retrieve the whip from the side table. Cassian wondered if it was the same one the monster had used on her only days before. He sighed with relief when Felix called for her to halt.

"Violetta, fetch wine for Vitus and myself." He glared at his son. "You would do well to remember the man is mine and not your own. He is a weapon not a plaything." He stood to emphasize his point. "I will not have him whipped, not while I have use for him in my house." Coming out from behind his desk he paced, tapping the tip of a finger against his chin. "What other skills do you possess outside the sands and bedchamber? Are you trained to serve at a Roman table?"

He could not recall a time when he had ever been put to the lash for the pure amusement of another, his skills were too valued by the lanista to be risked on a whim. He had seen many others suffer it and it was not something he wished to ever live with. Words could not describe his relief when Felix put a stop to his son's sadistic game of wills. He refused to give in to the pressure of anxiety weighing on him but drew a deep breath and forced his voice to be calm as he answered. "I have never been put to use outside that which you have named though I am more than willing to follow the will of my Dominus."

Felix took the cup of wine Violetta served him and nodded. "All skills shall be used soon enough though some are best saved for a more glorious occasion." Taking a deep drink, he continued. "For the time being you shall serve this house in same the capacity as any other slave. The kitchens, the table, any task that I set you to you will do without pause or question." He gave Vitus a hard look. "My command and mine alone is the one to which you will answer, and it will not be superseded by any other." Then his eyes met Cassian's, his hand gripping Violetta by the shoulder to stop her beside him. "I trust that you understand this, that you are capable of understanding what it means. If this simple girl from the North can see it done, then a man of your experience should find no trouble in learning what is required of you here."

He flinched, what could Felix possibly mean by the words 'all skills shall be used soon enough'? Did he mean to have him fight? Was he to stand executioner for some fool who had dared to displease him simply to provide entertainment? Was he to fuck Violetta or gods forbid, some other woman, to spark their lust?

He stood before the Roman's in a tunic and yet he had never felt so exposed. He did not have the familiar fabric of a subligaria or even sandals. He felt as though he had been returned to the nightmares of his youth, valued for nothing but his raw sexuality and natural ability to pleasure a woman. It was only the iron cuffs on his wrists that kept him from believing that he had somehow gone back in time to those horrors of his past. He was not so foolish as to believe in this house of horrors and deprivation that he would not be used poorly.

Felix had to know, even if Vitus did not, the parts of his past that he wished hidden from thought and revelation. To think that these things would not be used against him would be like stepping into the arena and expecting freedom without the glory of combat. There seemed nothing to lose by bringing his questions to voice now and so he took a small step forward to ask. "Am I your possession now? Am I to stay beneath this roof for the rest of my days? Never to stand upon the sands of the arena again?"

Felix released the hold on Violetta's shoulder and met Cassian's angry glare. With a smirk he shook his head. "You do not need to concern yourself with that for now. There is the chance that you may yet find yourself upon the sands once more. Do not concern yourself with those thoughts now, you have new skills to learn."

Felix sipped his wine and continued. "For now, you shall share tasks with Violetta and my man Meridius in my apartments and personal care." He turned away dismissively and made his way back to his desk and the papers on it. "I will expect you both in attendance at table tonight." Meridius entered the room, with his hands full of parchment rolls. From the way the Spaniard scanned the room he assumed he was there to attend the merchant with the business dealings of a silk merchant. He would not be able to repeat anything Felix said to anyone, it was well known that his tongue had been removed some years before. Suddenly Cassian wondered how it was that he communicated with Violetta for years.

"Go and she will show you what is to be done. Immediately." Was the sharp command from the older Roman behind the desk.

The champion lowered his gaze, not out of respect as it appeared to the Romans but to avert his eyes from the depravity he saw reflected in Felix's expression. "I stand a gladiator," He said, to himself or to Felix he did not know, perhaps the words held little meaning now. "The sands are my life, not the floors of a villa no matter how grand. Dominus, I have skill in the care of weapons and of armor. Perhaps I would be better suited to aiding your guards instead?" It was not a total lie, but he hoped it was convincing enough to earn him a reprieve from the personal tasks that were obviously planned to break the spirit that the Romans found so displeasing.

Felix had begun to sort through his papers, barely looking up to respond, which was a disrespect that Cassian felt like a physical strike. "I will remember that. I was not aware that Tertius set his gladiators to such thing." The smirk on his face betrayed his intent before the words came from his lips. "You are indeed still a gladiator. That fact is undeniable, but here you stand absent sands or gladius and thus are no more or less than any other slave." His smile broadened. "Perhaps you may find yourself of use in the kitchens to sharpen knives there. Now remove yourselves to task while I attend matters of worth."

"Sharpen knives?" His voice was almost a whisper, the man might as well have put the blades mentioned to his gut. "Yes Dominus." He hated to submit to the man on any level and this task made it worse. The knives stood as a reminder of the blades he was no longer entitled to. He could see in Felix' eyes the glee, bordering on deviance, brought with each blow to his pride. It would not have surprised him if, beneath his fine robes, the older man was practically pulsing with pleasure. He took a step back and turned to exit only to find Vitus in the doorway. Would he allow him to pass without a word or was he to begin suffering humiliation at his hands already?

"Hurry to attend tasks, do not allow my presence to hinder the great champion of Velletri, the god of sands, from his urgency to arrive in the kitchens where many knives are waiting for your…skills." He swept his hand towards the door as though to usher him from the room to the hallway beyond and the woman waiting in it.

Cassian saw that Violetta looked ready to run to his arms, but the fact that Vitus stood in the doorway, watching every step either slave took, must have stopped her. "It is my pleasure to obey when it leaves you far behind me." He retorted, stepping past the man and raising his eyes to meet Violetta's.

A soft smile lit his lips, drinking in everything about her from the curve of the hips that seemed to fit perfectly in his hands to the swell of her soft breasts making his mouth water but it was the brilliant blue of her eyes, filled with trust and affection that stole his breath until he managed to say, calmly under the circumstances. "Show me the way to the kitchen so that I may see to this task, however unsavory?"

Nodding Violetta turned and started walking towards the kitchens. "You'll find it in this direction." The back of her hand brushed against his as they walked, with a soft blush upon her cheeks that made him want to pull her into his arms, seeking comfort for them both. The innocent contact sent a thrill through him, but when she finally turned her head to speak to him her eyes widened in a fear that caused Cassian to turn his head to see what she saw.

Vitus had followed behind them like a wild scavenger stalking prey it was sure would soon fall to its wounds. Knowing what the man was capable of, Cassian hoped it was only words he was looking to break, though he was likely to use those to cut as deeply as a sword. "Dominus." His head was bowed as they both turned to address him waiting for him to make his move or to move past them, as he hoped.

"Violetta, my little flower, in your rush to see Cassian to the kitchen you neglected to take a task for yourself." His lips parted as his tongue flicked out to wet them before he drew his breath in a hiss that chilled the champion's blood. "It would not do for you to stand idle until evening meal while the champion works so very hard in the kitchens, slaving away in the heat. When you have seen the present task completed you will come to me."

He put a brotherly arm across Cassian's shoulder and whispered in his ear. "I am sure that you will find the tasks of the kitchen to your liking. I am certain they will suit your intelligence. Since my father does not allow for me to set you to tasks that would make use of everything you are capable of, we will both have to do our best to make the most of this situation." He grinned wickedly. "I am sure though that I will find more…pleasure in this than you shall."

Cassian reached for Violetta's hand, entwining their fingers in open defiance of the Roman's presence. The few minutes they shared together since leaving the company of Felix had been more calming than hours spent alone in the ludus. Her presence eased his rage while setting fire to his blood in a way that was primal and savage in its need, already his body fought to claim its fill of her, to come together in a thundering rhythm of hips, breathy gasps and moans of the pleasure that built between them. He had been ready to lean close and tell her the thoughts on his mind when the voice of Vitus had stopped them.

Once again on edge, Cassian was ready to relinquish control in a second should a threat be made against Violetta. The way the Roman spoke it was as if he was baiting him to snap and strike simply to have a reason to punish him, as if using his woman to bring him anguish was not enough. He pulled away from Vitus' embrace and met his devious expression with one of unbridled hatred. "Then you should see me to what use you would dare, in defiance of your father's words."

Vitus laughed and stepped between the would-be lovers. "You would like things my way gladiator." He gestured a hand towards Violetta. "It sees you once again between her thighs, with me between your cheeks. All the tales of your skill in the beds of the city's elite cannot be wrong. You must be worth fucking."

Cassian could not believe that Vitus thought he would willingly take cock in ass even bated with the temptation of being with Violetta. He was outside his mind if he believed that such would ever happen in this life.

"It is your choice." Vitus said with a dangerous arrogance as he maintained eye contact with Cassian, daring him to react.

The groan that passed Cassian's lips was one of disgusted dismay, his hands clenched as he fought the urge to use them to end this vile excuse for a man. He choked back the bile rising in the back of his throat as wave after wave of nausea hit him at the thought of sharing Violetta with Vitus. The choice was his? Really?

"Many in this city boast of me in their beds and the pleasures brought by my skill, you do not stand among them." Determined to call the Roman's bluff Cassian reached for the hand that had been across his shoulder and pressed it to his chest. "I would see it change so that you too may boast the bedding of another slave that held no choice in the matter." Releasing the grip, he altered his gaze to catch Violetta's hoping that she might take hope in his meeting the bastard at his own challenge.

The Roman seemed taken back at his words and even more surprised at the firmness of his grasp. When Vitus' brow arched in surprise, his lips pulled back in a grin. "You would submit your body to me? You are wiser than your companion then for, to her pain, she rejected that choice."

A quick smile passed between Cassian and Violetta, he thought it had been too quick to see, but Vitus' nostrils flared suddenly in agitation. Cassian was surprised when he pulled his hand free from his grip but when he brought the back of it across his face the surprise turned to anger.

"Do not think to mock me you shit. My father may command exclusivity to you, but I will see you brought to your knees before long. By one means or another you will break." His eyes flashed angrily before he spun on his heel to stalk down the hall with a flush on his cheeks. He paused before turning in a doorway to give Violetta a glare as if to remind her where she was due in a brief time unless she wanted him to come and find her.

CHAPTER 10

His instinct had been to block the blow, but he had allowed it to land so as not start a physical fight. He would have easily won but it would have allowed Vitus to become the true victor. The feminine manner of his attacks was becoming amusing to Cassian, the slap in the house of Tertius and now here. Maybe there was more to his desire than just the cruelty of dominance.

"You stand a mockery of men Vitus Census." He said to himself as he laughed at the man's swift departure. The hatred between them was becoming stronger with each encounter and would soon reach a level of deadly venom forcing one of them to fall.

"If only there were some way that you could avoid him." He said soothingly to Violetta. Her arms were wrapped around her chest and the joyful, nearly defiant look that had shone in her eyes was dimmed once again. His entire being screamed to hold her, to comfort her and wipe away the fear he saw in her eyes. It was his actions that had brought it to life, and he was at a loss for how to make things right for her.

Violetta stayed utterly still until Vitus was out of sight then she turned, at last, to embrace him in a silent cry of fear and need. Her arms wrapping tightly around his torso begging for the comfort that his embrace could offer.

"I am the property of the father not the son, but at times, I am tasked to serve him as well. I might be able to avoid him today, but it cannot last forever. If all else fails, he will seek me out. His perversions know no limits and for some reason I am his favored target when he is in such a mood." She was shaking in fear for what the Roman might demand. Every fiber of his being screamed the need to pursue Vitus to fight for her safety, but his touch seemed to calm her slightly and so he gave what comfort he could in that moment.

As a slave, Cassian knew that she should see him to the kitchens and then attend Vitus, but as her lover he could not bear to think of what that would mean. He could shut his mind from it while she was still beside him. His mind filled with how he could help her avoid being used as a pawn in a contest whose winner had already been decided.

"Since I draw his interest away from the other girls, they are quick to lend aid when they may, perhaps it can be arranged for present avoidance at least?" She whispered fearfully.

He drew her into his arms, wrapping them tight around her small frame, smiling when she closed her eyes and breathed deeply. He offered a prayer for the first time in years, for the hours to pass with speed. He longed for the quiet hours of the night when they would be locked below the floor in the space of cells so that they could find solace in each other. He doubted they would listen, his gods, to the prayers of a man who had doubted them for years.

He hated himself for the words that were about to come out of his mouth, but it was unavoidable, for now. "No. You must go. There stands no choice, if you do not then he will come to find you." He wanted to hold her tight for the rest of the night, his need to protect her was stronger than anything he had ever felt before. Indecision gripped him when she clung to him, seeking comfort from his embrace, then in a flash it was gone when she whispered his name against the material of the tunic.

"Cassian...I cannot do this. Not when you are here now."

Gently touching the side of her face so that her eyes were locked to his he lowered his mouth to take hers swiftly but instead of the fierce heat that his body demanded his mouth softened, gently moving over hers, persuading her to open for him so that he could taste her with a hungry moan. She tasted like honey; pure and so sweet that he could not get enough of her and yet the longer he held her, the longer they stayed locked together, the greater the price to be paid by them both at the hands of the Romans.

They were both lost in his kiss, the gentle pressure of her mouth against his intoxicated him like summer wines. "Stay safe." He whispered, "I will be waiting for you." He could not say what he meant, the words 'I love you' seemed stuck in his throat and best not said as she was to face the sadist he had angered. Carefully letting go, his hands lingering on her skin, he turned towards the kitchens, there were knives to be sharpened, torment to be endured and vengeance to be planned.

The kiss had kept them in a state of bliss until he broke the words that brought reality crashing back. Though he wished she could stay forever in his arms Vitus would not become more forgiving with her delay. He only hoped that she knew that he would be there for her at the night's end, no matter what happened.

Violetta pointed him in the direction of the kitchen, they both knew that if she joined him there, she would not be able to leave. Instead she whispered softly in his ear. "My heart is yours, even if the Roman claims my body for now."

He sighed, watching her turn to run the distance to the room where the monster was surely waiting eagerly for her.

Cassian watched her go before finding the kitchen, following the smells of spice and meat that had begun to invade the air. He ignored the voices around him that whispered his name as more and more of the slaves began to appear, staring after him as he walked past. He could hear the whispers of:

"Is that Cassian?"

"How is it that Cassian stands among us?"

"Is he no longer the champion?"

He knew that it would be merely moments before everyone, slave and Roman alike, knew that he was within the walls of the villa. It would be only a few precious moments after that when they would know that he was to serve as they did, bowing and scraping to the filth that commanded them.

He stepped into the heated confines of the kitchen and looked around at those inside. Their whispers and stares gave him precious little concern when compared with the knowledge that his woman was now at the mercy, or lack thereof, of a sadistic monster in the guise of the son of her master. The man had to be stopped before Violetta was injured or worse at the whim of his savagery.

"Cassian?" A pot clattered to the floor, released from the grasp of the cook with its contents spilling out across the tile. She did not move to recover it or to clean the contents but instead she stood with a bewildered look in her eyes as she stared. She was older than Lycithia, stout, with hair that would have once been called black and teeth that reminded him more of a horse than a woman. Everything about her repulsed him but her lust was obvious, with a flush of arousal blooming on her cheeks as she asked. "What...? Why are you here? Now?"

He knew that he had found the weak spot in the staff that would help him to achieve his desire. Laughing softly, he came to her side and crouched to retrieve the pot. "If you would hand me a cloth, I would see this cleaned, before asking for a favor."

"A favor of me?" She asked breathlessly. "Here in the kitchen? Before the others?" She smiled and placed a hand to his chest. "It is not my usual but for you, I would make an exception."

It took him a moment to grasp the meaning of her words, but the truth of the advantage became clear in the space of a few seconds. Annoyance coupled with his amusement at her lustful assumption crossed his mind, but still he traced the tip of a finger along her jaw and gave her a seductive smile. "Not here, not today, but do not discount what the days ahead may bring."

His voice turned to soft velvet, a gentle tease as he set aside the pot and continued. "I would just ask that you show me to the knives and put a whetstone in my palm. Dominus has set me to a task which I would obey as swiftly as possible."

It was not usually his way, but he knew how to use a woman's affections for his personal gain. He had no intention of letting the aged cook anywhere near his cock but allowing her to think that he might could serve him well in the future. As the woman moved to do as he asked, he considered how it would be beneficial to teach Violetta to do something similar. He hoped, perhaps foolishly, that she was not in too much agony now, that Vitus would not take his wrath out on her but instead save it for the proper target. "Be strong." He whispered to himself though it was for her ears.

Hours later his task had swiftly become tedious, filled with mindless repetition. Knife after knife passed across his palm and the stone that he used to bring them to a razor's edge felt as though it was becoming a part of his flesh. He heard rather than saw the bustle of the slaves around him coming and going as they did their tasks to prepare for the evening meal, yet not once was Violetta mentioned.

Concern was starting to grow for her as the time passed. More than once he had looked up to see anticipation and longing in the eyes of the cook. He had found some slight amusement in flashing a smile at the older woman and watching her blush as though he had groped her before she returned to her tasks with the dreams of hours in the arms of the god playing in her eyes. Even that mild amusement did not last long though when his focus kept slipping to Violetta with Vitus for more time than he cared to count. Surely, he would release her soon so that she would be able to fulfill the command of his father to serve at the dinner table that night?

The blades at his fingertips offered such temptation. It would have been so simple to take one in his palm and hide it had he been wearing a subligaria as he was used to but with only the tunic there was nowhere to hide such a thing. Even the smallest of the blades could be easily seen. He needed that piece of clothing. That night or in the morning. It was not only to hide the weapon he desired but to give himself a feeling of coverage instead of the constant concern of exposure to the eyes of others.

After what felt like hours the word of the man who ran the kitchens for Felix summoned all who were to serve the table to prepare themselves. The gladiator stood, preparing to change from scullery dog into a server of meat and other foods. "Bastard." He cursed beneath his breath, one day he would have vengeance upon Census for this.

A hesitant shadow in the doorway caught Cassian's attention. He raised his eyes to the arched entryway and saw Violetta standing there, briefly, before moving away. She was the picture of agony; her hand at her mouth and tears glistening in her eyes, the stains of those already fallen on her cheeks spoke of brutality suffered absent the ability to stop it or the madman that took pleasure in it.

His nerves were frayed almost beyond his control and now he had to tolerate this as well? Stepping in the direction that she had disappeared he found his path suddenly blocked by the blade of a guard's sword, the tip rested at his throat while the man holding it barked the command. "Stay yourself, slave, or see blood shed for your refusal."

The words of the guard paused her steps. She turned, perhaps thinking that they were directed at her, but when she saw the steel at his throat she cried out, horror in her expression. Their eyes locked for a breath before she turned and stumbled her way down the stairs. Did she race to find water and a cloth to cleanse the scent of Vitus from her body? The tears from her face? How badly had he hurt her? How much of the Roman's rage was his fault? Cassian closed his eyes at the thought that his pride and temper had brought greater harm to her delicate body and haunted soul.

The steel at his throat stopped his advance and his hands raised in the total submission that they demanded of him as he stepped back with a lowered head. All of this was new to him, new and despised. The mind games and brutality without justification were not the worst of it. None of them could even breathe, take a step, without someone watching them. The guards were all but unseen until they appeared from thin air with allowance to kill if their whim was justified. Soon enough he would ensure that there was steel in his hand, ready to defend himself and Violetta from their hands.

He was pondering how he would achieve it when suddenly the solution came to him. Felix had commanded them both to serve the evening meal. She would be in there with him. Perhaps there would be the chance to speak with her, to comfort her with his arms if not his entire body.

"Dominus has commanded that I am to serve at his table tonight along with Cassian. I pray that you do not cause him to be angered by the delay of his meal without cause?" His head turned at the sound of her voice. The truth of her words caused the guards to step back and give her access to the kitchen, and Cassian access to her.

Stepping into the warmth of the room she approached him with a forced smile. "This task is not as difficult as others this day. If you do as I do there should be no incident or cause for words broken with Dominus or his son." Her voice was calm, but her eyes told him of the sorrow and pain of the past hours. "There is nothing about this that you cannot do." She nodded for him to pick up his tray as well while she stood, warming herself against the chill of her trauma, before the cooking fire.

The flames of the oven glowed behind her and exposed her body in perfect silhouette through her dress so clearly that she might as well have been standing naked before him. The high firmness of her breasts stood out amongst the luminescence of her creamy soft skin. His mouth ached for the taste of her more than the food being prepared around him. The narrowness of her waist coupled with the soft curve of her hips made him think of nothing more than spanning her with his hands and pulling her close to…with a slight shake of his head he forced his mind and eyes elsewhere. This was not the place for such things and the heavens alone knew what Vitus had done. That sobering thought snapped his mind back to the present and the near past, his muscles tensed in anticipation of his anger. "You were crying." He stated his voice a low growl. "What harm did he bring to you? What happened in these hours?"

Violetta pressed her eyes closed against his query. "You ask questions you cannot want answered with truth." She opened her eyes to meet his, tears threatening to spill down her cheeks once again. "Let it be sufficient to know that his anger is sated. Though I fear I raised it further when I disagreed as to whose cock was greater, yours or his. The truth was not a thing he appreciated." Her brave smile faltered as she lowered her head, waiting for the tray of food to be handed to her by the cooks.

"The man holds concern for the size of my cock? He would compare us at every turn?" His eyes were filled with disgusted horror at the thought, shaking his head he looked at Violetta. "He broke word of this while harming my woman? Has he taken leave of what sense he has?" He hissed angrily to himself as a young slave brought him a tray of sliced fruits arrayed to look like a flower on a silver tray. He gripped it tight, his indignation forming a smirk as he became not a gladiator, but a server though it was justice in the form of steel and not fruit that he wished to serve the cold-hearted Romans that night.

"Why is it that he hates me? I have barely broken words with the man, what cause does he have for such atrocities against me or you?"

Violetta took the jug of wine that was assigned to her hands instead of the tray she had expected and joined the line of slaves that prepared to attend the dining room. Looking over her shoulder at him she answered in a hushed voice. "He bears concern for all things he fears superior to himself and hates that which proves him less than a man." She straightened, bravely hiding her fear despite the pain that must be wracking her body. "What have you done?" A smile flashed briefly across her lips. "You have been given and accepted as a gift the thing that he desired for six years and with that acceptance you came to possess that 'thing' as he can never hope to."

"He wishes to possess you in more ways than that which his father already does." It all made sense to him with that explanation; Vitus wanted Violetta to love him. Pulling himself together with the composure he used when he entered the arena to fight in the games, he squared his shoulders and lifted his head. A smile that bordered on arrogance played across his lips as he joined the line of slaves moving to serve the meal right behind Violetta.

He stepped closer to her, his body brushing agonizingly near to hers, so that he could continue to whisper to her. "That is why he now seeks vengeance in the means of sadistic perversion and forced sexual conquest. I swear to you that I will find a way to make him pay for what he had done to you, in this life or the next." His jaw tightened, clenching to choke back more words as they entered the dining room and the subject of his vow came into view, lounging as he spoke with his father.

CHAPTER 11

"You are not hearing the words that I am saying. I have no care if you take the girl when I have no use for her. I do not care if she finds it pleasurable or not, it is one of her uses now, but it is the screams." Felix took a long drink and glared over the edge of the cup at his son. "I would not have them echo across the yard and disturb my work." He gestured to Meridius standing at the wall. "Even he was disturbed and spilled the ink across the desk. I will not have it Vitus. Silence her or be denied the sweetness of her thighs."

Cassian watched shame burn brightly on Violetta's cheeks. Everyone in the room could see it and they knew that the Romans were talking about her. She poured wine into the cups at their sides with a grace that denied her feelings. No one would comment or defend her honor except Cassian and even that would not be for hours later, if they found time alone, for he would not bring her shame on top of the hurts she already bore because of him.

Vitus reached for fruit from the tray Cassian held at his side while replying to his father. "I offer apologies father; I fear I was lost in the moment and did not notice the volume of the sound she made. I assure you that in the future I will find a way to silence her." He turned his head to smirk in a boastful crowing of his victory in the battle between them.

The tension between the two men could have been cut with the knives upon the table, the animosity so thick it was choking to any that heeded it. 'Who will see your own screams to silence when the times comes that you meet my blade?' The dangerous question hovered on the tip of his tongue, but he could never utter it. If he did, he would be gone from this house and put to the cross which would leave Violetta alone and undefended.

Though perhaps not, he caught the eye of Felix's man upon her with a concern deep enough to match his own. Did something lay between them? Or was it something else entirely that caused such anger in the blue eyes of Meridius that turned to briefly meet his own?

Turning his gaze away from the Spaniard he met that of Vitus for a moment before realizing that a change of tactics was what was needed. Forcing himself to a model of perfect submission he lowered his eyes from the contact that the Roman was reveling in. Staring at the ground he mused to himself that it was a shame he had never been trained in the arts of service, how would it be possible to hold him to blame should an accident occur. He kept his face the picture of innocence as he took the jug of wine from Violetta. Slowly tipping it towards Vitus so that he could refill the nearly empty cup. He hid his smile when the drink reached the edge of the chalice and spilled over, soaking Vitus' hand and pouring onto the fresh robes he wore, instantly creating a pool as red as blood on the silk.

"You fucking cunt!" Vitus bellowed, leaping to his feet to jab a finger in Cassian's face. "If you paid more attention to your work instead of dreaming of her this would not have happened." He pointed the other finger towards Violetta then looked at his father instead of the man now holding the offending dish straight and steady. "He did it on purpose, that shit did it on purpose and I demand that he…"

Felix cut his son off with a wave of his hand. "You demand what Vitus? That the man be whipped for an accident?" The amusement faded from his face. "I made a promise that he would not be destroyed and to whip a champion for such a minor mistake is hardly worth the effort it would take to restrain him." The accounts he had dealt with that afternoon, combined with wine seemed to have put Felix in a somewhat indulgent mood. He took some cheese from the tray he had pointed for her to offer him with a smile. "Violetta perhaps you had better take back the wine, after you find a cloth and water to clean the accident. I feel that your hands might be the steadier. Perhaps the fruit might be a better task for you Cassian." He turned his attention to the gladiator. "Unless of course you have some skill at carving meats?"

Cassian doubted greatly that Felix believed that it was an accident, but since it had barely disturbed the meal and could be easily dealt with, he seemed to have decided instead to test the gladiator's control and his intelligence. By placing a knife in his hands and commanding him to serve the man who had only just finished laying his hands and body upon the woman he desired he thought Cassian would snap, but he had better control than the old man guessed. He watched as Violetta quickly darted from the room to get the cloth that Felix had commanded, but as soon as she reached the confines of the kitchen she let loose a round of laughter that rang with disbelief and could be faintly heard from the dining room.

She rushed back to the dining room and began to try cleaning the mess of juice from the stained robe until Vitus shoved her roughly aside. "Still your hands, it is ruined." He glowered at Cassian and his father. "Are you going to just let him stand there grinning like a fool?" The rage boiled in Vitus's eyes and made Violetta bow her head to avoid the look as she stepped to take the tray from Cassian. Letting her hands rest on his for the briefest of moments as they shared a smile, and he fought the urge to wink. "Allow me this burden so that you may see to the meat." She said to him quietly, her tone not matching the spark in her eyes. He had done such a simple thing but the look she gave him was like that of a hero standing victorious. He would have words with her as soon as possible to discover the meaning in her look and why slaves had begun to watch from the doorway.

The twinkle in her eyes gave him hope but when the knife was placed in his hand for a moment he paused. The weight was a reminder of what he was capable of. What he wanted more than almost anything was to use it as he had been trained to and end the lives of both Romans before they drew another breath. He knew that there were guards outside the door, but it would be impossible for them to reach him before he took both their lives. He noted how Felix watched him, perhaps a weapon was even now pointed at his back should he make the move. He knew it would be worth his life, but if this was to be how he was to live, for now, he was going to have to maintain control.

He looked at Violetta and knew that once again the gods had put him on a path that offered the choice to pursue his own desires or seeing to her safety. She had been given to him as a gift, her heart and soul in his safekeeping, and so he would put aside his own wants for now to look after her and her alone. He lowered his head and set his hand to the task he had been commanded to do. He had to trust that whoever guided his fate would give him another chance, another day, since he gave the Romans this unknowing reprieve.

As he watched, Violetta shifted her stance carefully. The pain in her body must be starting to register as the adrenaline slowly faded from the trauma of the day. Her face was bruised from what he assumed was the hand of Vitus. It was a pain she had likely grown used to from years of abuse, but he wondered if the man had harmed her more intimately and if that was what caused her to clench her jaw and blink away the tears that sprung to her eyes.

The smug look on Vitus's face told him everything he needed to know about his thoughts. He sought to boast that he could have her at any time he desired with the snap of his fingers. While it was not completely false, Cassian was sure the Roman intended to make it painful to be in the arms of the man who loved her. Vitus wanted to break and bruise her body until passion from any man held no desire for her. There was no way that he could understand that love eased all pains and the tender touch of a lover could heal the ache of bruises and no amount of cruelty could change that.

All other things in their lives were a passing pain, fleetingly brief. Though each minute they had ever had alone could likely be counted on Felix's abacus, it did not matter to him. The story of their love was being written with fire on his very soul and time shared with her stretched to eternity in his mind.

The minutes stretched into hours and hours felt like days while they waited for the Romans to conclude their meal. He saw in the shadows of the doorway the quickly passing silhouettes of other slaves, curious to see if the rumor was true and that the gladiator had stained the robes of Vitus and yet remained unpunished. When he saw the faces of those that did not serve in the kitchen he wondered if the story was circulating. The Romans were blissfully unaware of the sensation and buzzing whispers as they finished their meal.

He was grateful at least that Selenia had not been present as she had been invited to a meal elsewhere that night.

Finally, having finished their meal, Felix and Vitus rose to depart the room with Meridius stepping away from the wall to follow Felix and one of the other women falling into step resignedly behind Vitus. Other slaves entered the room to begin clearing the remnants of the meal while Cassian and Violetta stood still, waiting as though carved from stone until they were alone in the room. Cassian had forced himself not to allow his indignation and rage to show in his eyes while serving the Romans so when his woman returned from the kitchen his body had clenched once again with the yearning to hold her and give up the control that had almost been lost when he watched her attempt to clean Vitus' robes.

When he had looked into Violetta's eyes and saw them dancing with some secret joy, he had stayed his words of concern. What the cause of her happiness was he could not tell but he was grateful for it, nonetheless. The eventual departure of the Romans left him staring across the table at her, hoping for the day when he could make those that hurt her pay for her pain.

"Cassian?" Violetta called to him softly, as though she thought him caught in a dream. "We can leave the room and retire to quarters below. I do not think there will be call for either of us again tonight. Come with me?" She beckoned with a motion of her head and a smile lighting her features, hiding the pain and discomfort of her body that he knew she must be feeling.

His name from her lips was the simplest of enchantments and yet the most potent. A smile lit his eyes for the first time in hours, but it was brief all the same for the knife in his hand demanded attention. They stood alone without guards as far as he could tell. The fates were with him if he chose to make the bold move, did he truly dare? If he wore a garment that would have provided a place to conceal a stolen blade there would have been no doubt or pause, it would have been done; but the damned tunic provided him with nothing. He stared at the steel, the flickering lights of the candles taunting him and painting the blade a tempting gold but he released a sigh of resignation, stabbed the tip of the blade into the tabletop and turned from one temptation to another: Violetta and her beckoning eyes.

Stepping towards her he was aware that his thick hair was tousled, his eyes tired and his face strained with the force it had taken to not allow his instincts to take over when dealing with the Romans. They were the same instincts he fought when he wrapped his arms around her waist and pulled her close to feel her warm and welcoming curves. Primal instincts, ones that were taught in a world where a man killed or was killed and claimed what was his with the force and passion of a man that might not live to see the next sunset, screamed for release.

He allowed his mind the few moments of dreaming that he could hold her forever, simply walk to the cells below and not return until morning, sating every urgent desire between them after calming her fears and soothing any pains she might hide. His line of thought was broken by the growl of his stomach and he released his hold with a smile when she turned her head to look at him. He had not realized his hunger went beyond that for her until he considered that he had taken no food and barely a sip of water since leaving the ludus that morning with Tertius. No wonder his control was so difficult to maintain. "Lead and I shall follow." He whispered in her ear.

CHAPTER 12

Violetta leaned into him, letting them both enjoy the moment of calming embrace before leading the way back to the kitchen that was still full of activity; many hands cleaning, taking care of the left-over food or preparing for the next day's meal.

A young male approached them with a plate in hand, boldly addressing Cassian while she smiled, holding on to his hand. "You must be hungry, I took the liberty of preparing a plate for you, before the best pieces were claimed by others." He looked at Violetta and then back at the gladiator. "Is it true? You spilled wine upon Vitus and were not struck down?" he asked, his words stumbling together in awe of the man before him and curiosity about the deed that had set the tongues of the villa wagging.

Violetta set her tray down upon the table, and Cassian watched as its contents were quickly attended to by the youngest of the kitchen staff to whom the fruits were likely a luxury. If this house was like that of Tertius then the children only received fruit when someone understanding, such as Violetta, held the tray. He had noticed that she chose their location specifically to ensure it was beside them.

"Tiber has dreams of the sands and often forgets that introduction is the better way to begin the breaking of words." She chuckled softly and then watched as the action of the kitchen slowed to crawl as all ears strained to hear the answer given by the new man among them.

"Did you tell him to take himself to Hades?" Called another young man near the fire. A chorus of similar questions began to rain down upon him, showing the extent that the tale had grown.

She was beaming with pride in him as she watched the shock of their attention overcome his normally stoic features until a guard yelled from the hall beyond the heated confines. "Still tongues before it is done for you!" The louder voices ceased but the whispered buzzing continued as many gathered close to their new hero.

The words of the guards caused his expression to darken slightly.

"You are welcome to die at the attempt." He whispered fiercely.

When the young man stepped forward again with a plate of food Cassian reached out with earnest gratitude. "The act itself is true though no words passed between us."

He grinned and took a large bite of the meat, offering the plate to Violetta to eat from as well. He had seen the small scraps that the black-haired cook, Irissa, had handed to her and hoped by his actions that he was confirming to all present that she was his woman and he would not allow any of them to harass her without consequences.

"Is there wine to be had?"

His laughter danced around the food in his mouth and he nodded encouragingly to Violetta who seemed to hesitate to eat with him as he took more from the plate. The attention surprised him even if the thought behind it did not. "It was nothing but wine. A simple 'mistake' made by one without training with such things. As for being struck down, you may see that I yet stand among you without mark."

Violetta smiled and took the offered food at last, the anger on the face of the cook was something he noted with some concern. He wondered if she ate only so she would not shame him or offend with a refusal. Reaching for a cup of water she sat next to him on the bench, leaning close to join the conversation's hushed tones.

"No one, ever, has done such a thing without retribution being immediate. You stand as a hero to all within this house." She leaned closer still and laid her hand upon his arm to draw his attention down to her. "And as such deserve the worship due to a champion." She smiled, her eyes shining with affection though he thought he saw lust sparking in the blue depths. It seemed to make her happy to see him elevated among those she knew for who he was could not be hidden by the simple redirection of his work.

As they finished the food and drank the water in her own cup, she leaned back against him gently. He did not want to take her from the friendly fellowship in the kitchen, but he was eager to have her alone. To press his lips to hers and share the taste of the wine that had been secretively slipped into his cup. He wanted to know if his hand on her body could wipe away the memory of Vitus and the pain of what he had done.

Cassian pressed his cup into her hand, his fingers lingering over hers as he guided it to her lips. "Drink, it will ease discomfort and relax tensed muscles." He murmured in her ear before pressing his lips to her cheek. "There are none here who should stand up to him as I did. The price for them is higher than for me and it is not worth their pain." He stretched out the hand that did not hold the cup and captured a strand of Violetta's hair between his fingers, sliding it until he had wound it about in a spiral and her head leaned against his knuckles.

Their eyes met with mirrored but unspoken desire, the soft growl of lust in his throat changed quickly to one of angered frustration when he saw the reddened mark upon her cheek from the strike of Vitus' hand. "Change hero to fool and find me better described." He said darkly, Census had stripped him of everything, rendering him powerless, or so he thought, with the agreement with Tertius. The knowledge of what Violetta lived with under this roof had made up his mind, he would fight for the right to protect his woman and find a way to see her removed from this Hades on earth. "Retribution will come, my priestess. I give you my oath. Tonight's celebration comes prematurely but the true cause will come soon enough."

He leaned closer, his body towering over hers, with his golden-brown hair tumbling over his shoulders as he brought his forehead to meet hers. The arousal he felt being so close to her was agonizing, tantalizing. Setting the cup down he used both hands, calloused as they were, to run over the divine softness of her skin. He wanted to pull her up against him right there, take her mouth passionately, hungrily, and slowly work them both into a fever of passion that would only reduce to a smouldering simmer after they had stoked it to an inferno. He knew this was not the time, or the place for such passionate exhibition, so he merely smiled and kissed her forehead while continuing to play his fingers through her hair. He loved watching the reaction that such a simple affectionate touch had on her.

He could see her pulse was racing and there was a familiar flush to her cheeks. While their foreheads had touched, and they breathed in the same air, the feeling of intimacy with her, even though they were surrounded by the others, was incredible. She stroked his own hair away from his face and smiled, wetting her lips then whispering. "I do not think there is any here who would call you a fool, my love." She smiled and glanced briefly towards the door, and he knew he would follow like a pup if she left the room now.

Lowering his hand from her hair Cassian knew that his lust for her was making itself physically evident in ways he would rather not share with the crowded kitchen, so he closed his fingers over Violetta's and drew her to her feet. What he was about to do was a risk, perhaps the guards would not allow it or those around them would draw too much attention to them, he did not care. He pulled her lithe body flush with his and lowered his head until, with a wicked grin upon his lips, he took possession of her mouth. A deep feral groan and a rapid dart of his tongue were all that was needed to ignite his carnal need for her. His body responded when she pressed back against him, leaving no doubt as to what they both wanted. Now.

Violetta smiled up at him, nestled into his chest; warm, safe and cherished. "I would lead you to a cell if you are of a mind." She said softly before adding louder. "I am sure you must be weary. I would see you to a place where you may take your rest." Making certain that the guards heard her words she stepped back from his hold. Her eyes danced, daring him to follow as she walked away slowly, beckoning him to follow amid the knowing chuckles of her friends around them. He would not deny her, and her eyes said that she was certain that it was his touch alone that could wipe away what Vitus had done.

He nodded his farewells to those in the kitchen who had surprised him with the heartfelt praise which had returned some of his dignity. A smile rose on his lips and he winked, acknowledging the ruse she intended. "Rest is a thing much longed for at this moment. I would see my bed for immediate use." Laughter lit his eyes when the words left his lips, a play in tandem with hers that saw a jump in her pulse.

Her hips swayed seductively as she walked away, driving him to rush and catch her by the waist, turning her to face him. He tightened his hold, the feeling of her pressed against him burned his blood, each of her soft curves meeting the tautness of his muscles was irresistible. He kissed her swiftly, hot and full of passion, the taste of her sending him careening over the edge of reason and control. His need for her was stronger than even his common sense. Primal and dangerous he nodded towards the door as he released her only so that she could move in the direction of the cell where they could come together at last.

She returned his kiss then stepped back, nodding to the rest of the company as she left the room and stepped into the cooler air of the hallway. Passing a guard that had been outside the kitchen door she said over her shoulder to him. "I will see you to your cell and pray you rest well." He hoped that either the ruse would work or that the guards would not give exceptional care to their actions because of the late hour. At the top of the stairs she paused and turned her head to look back at him once again, her hair gliding across her back as their eyes locked and she beckoned him to follow before descending to the bottom where she waited, eagerly, for him.

He had just reached the doorway, watching her move down the hall, when he noticed a jug of wine filled nearly to the brim. Closing his fingers around its handle he took it into his possession without a care in the world and followed Violetta as though this was the most natural thing instead of something so new it set his heart racing like an untried boy with his first girl.

He followed Violetta like a man in a dream and a bemused smile flitted across his face when the guards he passed made no move to stop him or to take the jug from his grasp. He almost wished one of them would try to stop him and he slowed his pace to bait their action but still they made no move. He could not decide if it was a trap or if they thought to allow him at least this one comfort of the ludus but still he nodded his appreciation and made his way down the steps in a rush to be alone at last with the woman he craved.

CHAPTER 13

She watched each step bring him closer and her heart rose to her throat as her lips parted in a smile of genuine delight. Her eyes falling to the jug in his hand she shook her head, marveling at the daring of such a thing and curious that the guards allowed it. If they had ever shown something similar to human kindness, she had never witnessed it. With a teasing smile, she pointed down the hall away from her cell. "There are empty rooms this way if the champion prefers solitude instead of companionship." She lifted a brow, daring him to accept that as she stepped in the opposite direction towards her own cell. She waited with eager breath to see what he would say, what he would choose now that they had the night before them without the interference of Romans to come between them. "What would you choose? The arms of a woman or the company of wine in solitude through the night?" Her voice was teasing while the anticipation between them grew and crackled like lightning in a storm.

"Does Dominus not care where it is that we sleep?" Cassian asked her with a grin. "If not, then what should a man choose?"

She knew that he wanted to be with her, but his mind seemed to be filled with laughter and jest. It felt good to let loose the tension of the day and play. She wanted to see him laugh, not a chuckle but a real laugh.

Walking towards the empty cells Violetta watched as he leaned his back in one of the doorways, stumbling backwards when his shoulders met with curtain instead of the planked door he must have been expecting. He laughed at himself and drank deeply from the jug while keeping his eyes on her.

She was shocked, filled with questions at his strange request. "Dominus cares not where we sleep as long as we attend when commanded." She smiled slyly. "But the man in the cell next to that snores loud enough to wake the dead." She laughed and took another step backwards towards her own cell. "I do know of a cell that would find you warmed nightly with a much sweeter sound to send you to sleep."

Cassian grinned and stepped towards her, the wine swashing over the edge of the jug. "Is that so? Snoring...I never could abide the sound of it. What sound would you see greeting my ears to lull a champion to rest?"

She continued her backwards steps, now all but certain of the game he played. "Your name on the lips of a woman who bears great affection for you." She flashed a smile at him and winked as she paused at last in the doorway of her cell "The choice is yours champion." She said with a laugh, stepping through the door and allowing the curtain to fall behind her.

He followed quickly behind her, inhaling deeply when he stepped into the shadowed confines and the curtain closed softly behind him. "Choice is removed for I stand before you a shackled slave." He laughed, the sound as deep and rich as she had wished. His features were suddenly mischievous and devilish in the flickering torch light and he drank deeply from the jug once more before setting it aside and sweeping her into his arms.

Violetta gasped as his mouth was instantly upon hers with a moan of satisfaction. His kiss was hot and demanding with a hunger that could never be satisfied. His hands caressed her back with the tenderness she needed, coming to rest on the rounded curve of her backside before he nipped her bottom lip with his teeth. "Does choice meet with the woman's approval?" He teased, bringing one hand to brush away a strand of hair from her eyes.

Laughter turned to deep gasping breaths when he pulled her into his arms, but she was quickly silenced by his mouth on hers. Nodding she entwined her arms around his neck to pull him closer to deepen their kiss as desire flooded her senses. All she could think of was her need for him. With a nod at his question she replied breathily. "Oh yes, much approval."

His actions were feverish as he pushed aside her dress. His eagerness to see her bared before him as he laid her down atop the straw mattress was almost boyish but the look in his eyes was every bit the man of passion she knew. Cupping her breasts, kneading and squeezing the soft flesh before lowering his mouth to devour her mouth again. He tasted like wine and the fruit from their shared meal. It was agonizing pleasure when he took his time descending her throat, his tongue flickering against the rapidly beating pulse in the hollow at its base. Every time his lips touched her skin, she felt the fire growing between them. His tongue traced a path to the tightened tips of her breasts before taking them into his mouth, suckling her with a moan of hunger and delight at the way her body responded to him.

Her breath exited in a gasp as she rolled her body into his hands while her own moved down his back to reach the hem of the tunic and pull it higher so that her fingers could dance across the skin of his lower back. Her breath was coming rapidly but still she wanted more. This was heaven and she did not know when they would have the chance again for the Romans might part them in the morning or they might have days or even weeks together. Violetta pulled the tunic over his head with a teasing giggle as it covered his face "I would see your full glory once again champion."

He drew a breath at the gentle teasing of her touch, a smile in his eyes shone at her words while she raised the tunic high enough to reveal the size and strength of his physical desire for her. The demand for satisfaction had him slowly inch down her body, his mouth and hands blazing a trail until he rested between her thighs. Cassian gently kissed a line across her stomach while his finger swept against her core, testing the dampness evidencing her mutual desire and her readiness for him. With the look in his eyes growing even more predatory he slid the palms of his hands under the curve of her buttocks to lift her hips, raising her to meet his mouth.

She was shivering in anticipation of his touch and the feeling when he teased her with the brush of his fingers that made her shudder in his hands. Raising her head slightly Violetta looked down to see him naked between her knees and all thoughts except pleasure were forgotten the moment his mouth met her flesh. She gasped his name like a prayer, her hands splayed on the bed, searching for something to hold on to.

His name on her lips drove him to even greater efforts. The quivering of her delight turned into shattering spasms of pure pleasure as she came apart in his arms. His mouth was devouring her, sucking, licking and even nipping with the gentlest drag of his teeth down the length of the sensitive nub in the center of her sex. Her hips thrust against him and her back arched as she felt the first wave of her climax take her. One hand that had grasped at the bed found his hair and her fingers threaded through his hair while the other covered her mouth to stifle the sounds she made. He slipped his hands from beneath her using one to grab the wrist of the hand that stopped her cry. "Let me hear you Violetta." He growled, replacing his tongue with first one then two fingers which he slowly began to pump in and out of her body.

Her breathy gasp made him grin, and it was impossible for her to deny the primal response she saw taking over him. His face grew tight and his eyes dark with lust and newfound passion. For a moment, he looked so fierce, so dangerous, that it scared her, but she knew, without doubt, that it was all for her. His countenance, the physical proof of the frantic desire, could not be chained by the will of Rome and neither could their passion. His heart thundered as her hand slid across his chest, and his muscles flexed to the rock-hard tension that he was conditioned for, but when he lifted his chin to look through the mane of hair falling over his face, he smiled as though the view would have made the gods themselves weep at the sight of what was for his eyes alone.

In that moment Violetta saw all that he was: the deadly gladiator who killed without pause. He was he champion and protector of her soul, but more than that she saw the man beyond the confines of slavery whose love shone for her in the heavenly glow of his amber eyes. Though he may not be a man to use words to say how he felt she understood what his eyes said, along with the reaction of his body pressed against her and the power of it all took her breath away. "Kiss me again Cassian." She managed to whisper, pulling him down to her lips.

He lifted a brow in playful reply to her demand, a proposition on his lips as well as the smile brought by the relaxing effect of the quality wine. He was bold and comfortable when he teased her with his response. "And what do you offer in exchange for this kiss Violetta?" He traced his tongue around the outline of her lips and beckoned for her to part them by playing the pressure between them until he gained the entry he desired.

She returned his kiss with a whimper, defenseless against his advances. She broke the contact to whisper breathlessly "I offer anything you desire in exchange for more kisses." Though she tasted the wine on his lips the intoxication of his kiss was all she needed. There was not a wine in Rome that could compete with the feeling of his body pressed to hers, so close to joining and yet too far.

He took a breath and blinked, pausing before speaking of his desire. He wanted something. She could see it in his eyes but there was a hesitation in his words that had never been there before.

"Show me…show me again how you are not a Roman noble?" His voice was not as powerful and commanding as it usually was. The tender, boyish tone was even more endearing than the gladiatory tones she was accustomed to.

Smiling up at him as she rose to her knees on the mattress, a hand reaching first to his hip then sliding to take him into her grasp while the other moved up his chest to push him gently to his back. "Lay back and see exchange fulfilled." She feathered kisses from the base of his throat down the chiseled plains of his chest before flicking her tongue into the hollow of his navel. Looking up she saw the grin spread across his face as he followed her command, his hands behind his head while he watched her kiss her way down his body, surrendering to her erotic offering. His grin brought a smile to her own lips before she nipped and licked her way down to his hardened shaft where she dragged the width of her tongue from the base to the tip then took him deep into her throat with a hungry moan.

He kept his eyes down, watching as her lips closed around him like an act of love. Her tongue flicking across the width of his shaft as her lips moved the length of him, each stroke taking him deeper as though she were starved for him. A sound of raw pleasure slid from his lips as he arched, unable to stop himself from thrusting carefully, despite his body's obvious need for release. She could tell that he needed more but still she did not stop, not yet. It was an aching rapture and the most exquisite torture that drew a lusty haze over his eyes as he wrapped a hand into the long soft tresses of her hair.

Violetta coughed slightly as she misjudged the length of him, and he tapped the back of her throat as he thrust. Calming her breath, she began instead to lick the raw evidence of his masculinity, his hand in her hair bringing a smile to her lips with the knowledge that she brought him to the brink of his control and that he, like her, had needed something to keep tethered to the moment before cascading into orgasmic bliss.

"Apologies." He whispered with a soft sincerity. He used his hand to carefully guide her up so that their eyes met, and their lips could touch in a soft brush that grew to a bruising crush in seconds. His free hand skimmed the sensitive skin of her back until he cupped her bottom. Sliding out from beneath her, he gently rolled her to where he had just lay. Cassian stared down into her eyes as he positioned himself between her thighs.

She shook her head at his words, there was no need for apology between them. His kiss brought a moan to her lips and she let her eyes close in anticipation of what was to come. Even as he lay her down on the mat Violetta kept the fingers of one hand in contact with the flesh of his hip, unable to stand not touching him. Even with her eyes closed she could feel him watching her. A blush crept across her skin and she almost reached to cover herself, but a slight growl stayed her hands and she peaked through her lashes at him.

His eyes were sparking with passion and his jaw was tightly clenched as if he was working hard to hold himself back. The vein in his neck twitched for a second before he cursed to the heavens and groaned, letting her hair run through his fingers like water as she watched his face change from tender to that of a man savage with need but even though her heart pounded with excitement she was not afraid of him, not now.

He raked his hand down her chest from her throat to the apex of her thighs where he was settled between the lean muscles and stared down at her, easing her open with his last bit of gentility before plunging into her with one smooth, hard motion. He closed his eyes as she watched him. He then gripped her hips and thrust again after withdrawing slowly, his body urging hers to match the rough rhythm he set as he released the reins of his control and gave over to the raw sexual pleasure of their joining.

Her back arched and a gasp tore from her throat. Her body was on fire for him and he was feverish with a passion he had never shown before. She watched his face for a moment before her own ardor took hold and her body responded to his in a primal way. She returned his thrusts as forcefully as she was able, gasps and moans flying past her lips that were still swollen and bruised from the crushing power of his kiss. Reaching to entangle her fingers in his hair she drew him down to further their kiss for a moment before every stroke of his body inside her made her break apart in his arms.

There was nothing left but his primal need for her, the urge to claim her, take her as his, forever, was becoming branded upon his soul every time her body moved in response to him. The savage fire inside him had only been tempered by the lovers of his past but this woman had the power to extinguish it, to bring him peace if they could find relief from cruelty. He wanted to give her the world and the freedom to explore it at his side, but in its place he gave her this; his heart, soul and body delivered in hard thrusts and deep grinding pleasure that was building pressure at the base of his spine and throughout her entire body as she clenched around him.

He could not give her the promise of a long future but by the Jupiter he would make what life they had together worth the living. His body tightened at the thought of her waiting for his return from the sands and he knew he would not last much longer. Opening his eyes, he caught reflected in hers a love so pure that nothing, even death itself, would be able to touch it and for the first time he truly understood the depth of love. A wave of purely physical rapture crashed over him then and he came with a roar, the force crashing through him and sending his seed deep within her as his body clenched again and again.

He felt her tighten around him, his name on her lips like the sweetest prayer. Watching her come apart from the pleasure he gave was a boost to the ego damaged by the confusing actions of the Romans that owned the house. He smiled as she closed her eyes and pressed her ear to his chest to hear the beat of his heart. A smile crossed her lips, and he wished he could enjoy that sight each night until the afterlife took him.

She nestled in his arms and fit against him more perfectly than he could have imagined. This feeling, her falling asleep in his arms, felt so unfamiliar and strange but it was the most natural thing he had ever felt. Her breathing slowed as she drifted off to sleep. He knew that he would join her soon, but first he lay still, staring at her face while the moonlight poured into the room, giving her an angelic glow, and kissed her cheek. Laying his head next to hers he allowed sleep its hold trusting their dreams would be filled with this moment alone.

The crispness of dawn came sooner than he had hoped but as the first rays of light penetrated the darkness of the night before and bathed the woman in his arms with the warmth of its glow, he found that he felt no weariness, only inspiration.

He woke her with a kiss, slumber disappearing from her eyes at the insistent persuasions of his mouth and tongue. The intense, fierce hunger of the night before had transformed into the slow and easy exploration of lovers. Naked and touching, their limbs entwining, he put his hands low on her soft skin, stroking her until she heated beneath his fingers and her body arched against him hungrily. He bent his head to circle his tongue around her nipple. Sucking her rosy peak into his mouth he nipped her with his teeth, playing her body with his hands and mouth until she was writhing beneath him, open and ready with a yearning that matched his own.

When he entered her it was slowly, his eyes locked to her face as he memorized the way that her cheeks flushed as she took him into her body. He fought the urge to dissolve into the pleasure of the sensation of her tightening around him. Buried full hilt into her Cassian stilled, the pleasure was like a wine to his senses that he wanted to let linger, to embed in his mind forever how she looked, smelled and felt joined to him in total bliss. Holding her eyes with his, he thrust slowly, trembling with a tenderness he had never felt before as he withdrew and returned. His stroke lengthened, building a rhythm between them that had no sense of rush or urgency but was simply the physical expression of their love.

When her eyes closed and she began to cum Cassian let himself go, he surged hard and furiously against her until he crossed over into the chasm of bliss and exploded inside her with a violence that shocked him. He had never felt like that when reaching climax, even with Nala he had never felt as though his release was something pulled from the core of his being, his very essence combined with the force of his love for the woman beneath him. His breath ragged he pulled her into his arms with all the tenderness of a man who had just realized his heart's desire and found it laying in his arms. The realization that he could lose it, lose her, in the mere seconds that it took a blade to slice through his flesh came crashing down and reluctantly he let her go with a gentle kiss. Even his considerable strength and determination could not hold back the rising of the sun and the tasks they must do while it blazed its path across the sky.

CHAPTER 14

Violetta had muffled the cries of her passion against his chest but when his arms encircled her, treating her as gently as though she might shatter in the breeze she pressed her lips to his chest, then rising to his neck and then at last the firmness of his lips in an ember of passion.

She knew that if Vitus had his way the man she loved would be brought to his knees, broken spirited and shamed, perhaps even taken from this world but she could not bear the thought of living without him. As sudden as their connection had been, she knew that there was something real between them that the Romans would not understand or if they did it would be used against them. Never had anything in her life, even her own safety, meant as much to her as he did. If it meant she had to give her body to the sadist to keep him from turning the full force of his hatred to Cassian she would do so if it saved him.

When he released her, the heat of his arms withdrawing leaving her with a chill she sighed and looked up into his eyes. "Another day in Hades awaits us up those stairs but here, in this moment, in this cell, I stand in Elysium with you."

What he might have said in reply was lost when their conversation was stopped by the sound of a guard's footsteps in the hall. The curtained door was pulled open and a command was barked by two men stepping inside causing Violetta to cry out in alarm, thinking they had come to harm them.

"Cassian, attend." One of the barked, his sword drawn as he advanced towards where they lay on the mat "You are ordered to return to tasks in the kitchen. Immediately."

"Lower blade there is no need for it here. I stand unarmed as you would well know." He lifted his hand and stood, naked, to face them, standing between the sword and herself. She had suffered at the hands of these men before and cringed at the thought of a reprisal. She was awestruck as Cassian brushed the steel aside and stepped past its carrier to draw their attention to him and him alone. "I would have a subligaria before beginning my day and the tasks your master would put me to."

"And who are you, slave, to make such a demand?" The guard asked with a sneer as he turned to look down at her, now clutching the thin blanket to her chest. "The man who fucks the bedwarmer of Felix is either brave, a fool or both."

"I stand the Champion of this city and the man who causes its name to be upon the tongues of all the Republic." Cassian replied, his arms crossed defiantly. "So, bring requested cover or use your sword. Choice is yours, but I will not wait long."

Violetta wisely made use of the men staring at each other, facing off in the battle of wills, to scramble from the bed and find her dress. Wrapping it quickly around herself she marveled at his boldness. Her eyes flickered to the guard and she waited, with bated breath, to see if he would strike or comply.

"Arrogant shit." The guard sheathed his sword at his waist with a scowl that quickly turned to a jovial grin. "And the best fighter I have seen in the arena in over ten years. If it is simply fabric that delays you, then I would not have it so." He left, returning moments later with the material in his hands. "Now dress and prepare before I am put to lash beside you both for the delay."

Finishing the fastening of her dress when the guards departed to wake the rest of the slaves Violetta whispered to him. "Cassian you risk much for simple linens. Does the dress of a gladiator matter so much to you here?" She pressed a kiss to his lips then stepped away to run a comb through her hair that had been tangled in the night. Aware that he was watching every move she made to see if she was still hurting or if their passionate night had caused her new pains, she did her best to be graceful. She wanted him to wrap herself in his arms again, but there was no time though there was some solace to be found in the trivial act of preparing to meet the day in each other's company as if it was a common thing instead of a newfound joy.

"It but keeps from the sight and hands of the cook who would have for herself that which I prefer for you alone." With that statement of intent, he hoped to ease her nerves regarding the need for coverage and put to rest any thoughts that he might also seek his pleasures elsewhere while inside the villa and their company parted. He kissed her firmly, his tongue thrusting between her lips as his hand slid beneath her dress to cup the soft cheek of her backside. "Give it no other thought, little priestess." He said with a wink and stepped out to meet the returning guard.

A surprised burst of laughter came from her throat and she lingered in the cell a moment making his head turn at the sound. Had she doubted his ability to get what he wanted? He was a type of man the likes of which she had never encountered before, even though Meridius was bolder than most in this house even he paled in comparison to Cassian and what he would dare. It was as if no one could refuse his charm or deny that he was a man beyond the understanding of those around him. The gods had touched him, and it was obvious to all that he stood in their favor.

Nights and days passed, turning into weeks beneath the roof of Census. The bright hours of the day were spent mostly apart from each other and avoiding Vitus as much as was possible. Cassian hated the dulling of his mind caused by the monotony of sharpening every blade beneath the merchant's roof but lived for the hours of the night. When darkness fell upon the house and the Romans were at last sleeping soundly, then came the hours he treasured most of all. This was when Violetta came to his arms, in the bed they had shared since his arrival. No matter what the day had brought; mindless conversation within the kitchen or the heavy hand of a Roman, in those hours it did not matter. They had each other for solace and the fire of their passion washed away the stains of everything else.

Cassian was surprised to find how easy it was to share himself with Violetta. He found himself spilling tales of his childhood before becoming a slave, telling her of his first fights in the arena and some of the tales of his time serving the house of Tertius before taking the sands. He told her things that he had not even told Arturo and he marveled at how it did not feel strange but comforting. She recounted some with him as well, her life before slavery though not her life in the villa. They both left that subject alone so that they did not have to face the reality of its brutality when they lay naked in each others' arms.

Each night he watched her as she slept and wondered how long they would be granted these nights of bliss before someone would try to ruin what they were sharing together. His wager was on the Spaniard, Meridius, the jealousy in his eyes grew daily and soon it would overflow to the destruction of all. Kissing her temple, he lay himself down to let sleep take him and bring dreams of a future with Violetta to his mind and rest to his body.

The thought of the hours spent in Cassian's arms the night before continued to bring a flush to Violetta's cheeks as she entered the bustle of the villa kitchen while the morning meal was prepared and the other meals of the day were being planned and in some cases the preparation had already begun. She scanned the room for him but with the press of the crowd it was difficult to spot him. With a soft sigh, she quickly found some bread and water, watching the preparation of Felix's breakfast with the scrutiny of one who would bear the punishment if it was not done to his liking.

Her focus was so intent that she almost did not notice the jealous eye of the cook who had spent the days staring at the man with whom she had spent her nights not sleeping beside. "What is it? You are staring Irissa."

The woman stayed quiet, glancing over her shoulder at the guards near the door obviously watching Cassian as he sat to eat before starting the monotonous task of sharpening blades. Her voice a harsh whisper Irissa hissed. "We all heard you last night. You are becoming the whore of the villa. Dominus, Vitus, Meridius and now this one. Do you think your supposed beauty will earn you favor or are you simply a slut who does not know when to close legs and mouth?"

The room had gone silent as she had vented her small tirade and left Violetta staring at her in confusion and anger. "I have never shared Meridius' bed in that manner. The man stands as a father to me." She hoped Cassian would feel relief at her words, but the cook was becoming dangerously aggressive.

Irissa stood and paced towards her, carrying the food that she was to deliver to their Dominus so that she could not run away or seek the protection of anyone else. "Oh, is that why you seek each other when either is troubled? Why everyone here has seen you leaving his room at strange hours and why more than once you have spent nights in the bed with he AND Dominus?" She looked her up and down with an obvious sneer or disgust. "You behave as though a whore and then when a champion comes you decide that he is to share your bed as well?" She looked around at the other women and few men who were still in the room. "I have had enough of this little bitch thinking herself better than others and I will see her brought as low as she deserves."

"How do you think you would achieve such a thing?" Cassian's voice rang out as he stood, anger blazing in his eyes with fists clenched against violence at his side as he stepped towards the two women. "With more bold lies against my woman?"

Violetta sighed with relief when he arrived at her side and met the eyes of the cook who fumed and sputtered at his intervention.

Standing next to her Cassian radiated anger and an edge of violence that she had not felt from him since the first nights in the villa. "You name her a whore and yet it was you who was willing to part thighs before all those here if I had but given you the word?"

He shook his head, revulsion in his expression, as though the woman was more disgusting to him now than before. When he turned to look at her Violetta was shaking, though with rage or fear that he might believe the words of the cook she could not tell.

"The things we do upon the command of Dominus say nothing to character but only the intelligence to pick survival over fates worse than death, especially in this house." He concluded, letting it hang in the air that the cook was now as hated by him as the Romans she cooked for.

The appearance of Meridius in the doorway, obviously waiting for her, forced him to save any other words until a later hour when they might have more privacy. "I'll be here, for you, when you can." He whispered to her with a nod and a brush of his hand down her back before she took up the tray and joined the silent man to go and serve their master his breakfast. With a final dismissive glance at the cook the gladiator took his seat and returned to his task. He had a look of concern on his face that made Violetta think he carried more worry over Irissa's words than he had implied he felt.

Violetta would not have been able to express out loud the relief she felt leaving the kitchen behind Meridius. She wished it had been anyone else who had come to the kitchens to find her, especially after the accusation of Irissa which she would now have to answer for to Cassian, but at least it removed her from the situation.

Her eyes met the man beside her, and she was annoyed to find his filled with amusement at her predicament. "It is not a matter for laughter. She tried to say that we are lovers, even without the command of Dominus."

She shook her head; such a thing was impossible for many reasons, but the greatest was the truth she had defended herself with; he stood as a father in her eyes. The look on his face told her that the protest had fallen on ears as deaf as his tongue was mute. "Please do not make this worse." She asked quietly, following him into the room where Felix lounged upon his bed waiting for them both.

Watching her set the tray down beside Felix, Violetta read the laughter in Meridius' eyes and it made her angry. She was worried that the man would become a danger to her relationship. It was clear he did not agree with their pairing, but he could not wish her any more pain than she already endured on a far too regular basis. Helping her serve the meal and prepare the merchants robes for the next day he tried to catch her eye, but she was determined to avoid him and kept her eyes cast to the ground even when Felix voiced his own observation to her behavior.

"Do my eyes deceive me Violetta or does the morning sun find you in better spirits than most days?"

He had to know the presence of the gladiator in the house would have the effect upon her that he was noticing. Felix was not a fool. He had to know that if free either Cassian or Meridius would be more revered than he was. Even muted by a blade Meridius had a presence that commanded attention and the gladiator was a natural born leader of men.

"Come my girl, break words of answer and see me amused this fine morning." He coaxed as she refocused her attention to him.

It was impossible to hide the smile in her eyes and in the rare moment that Felix was not commanding or terrifying she could not help but answer with a sliver of truth. "I found peace in my slumber Dominus. The gods blessed me with good dreams. Your concern is a kindness, gratitude." She could see that Meridius was frowning slightly at her reaction to the question, but she could not help the joy she felt and to lie to Felix would lead to a greater pain than the displeasure of the man that stood as her father.

Pouring his wine and preparing his robes to distract herself from the moment that the man rose naked from his bed and grinned lecherously at Meridius before stating. "I too found myself in a pleasant slumber thanks to the effort and skills of Meridius." She shuddered when he laughed and ran a hand intimately down his back, if there was anything in this life of slavery that she knew her father hated, it was when Felix chose to be demonstrative in his physical desires in front of others.

"I am glad that you find yourself rested Dominus." Violetta replied softly. "What business shall you attend today? A trip to the city market again or the docks?" She was flipping through the robes hanging in his cabinet, trying to select the appropriate attire. "Or will you be at home with Vitus and Selenia today?"

The shared relief in the change of topic was palpable between Violetta and Meridius while the Roman ate and ceased his narrative of the dreams brought on by the night's activities in his bed. "Today I am bound for the docks but will return before noon to bid Selenia farewell as she returns to Rome in continued pursuit of a husband, which she seems to think impossible inside this city. How she still thinks to find one without the guidance of her father is a mystery to me."

He shook his head and stood, pointing to a burgundy robe with plain but fine linen undergarments. "I will take Meridius with me to the docks. I would not have you among such coarseness or in a place where you might be easily spirited away and never seen again."

"Gratitude again Dominus for sparing me such company and risk." She said with a bow of her head. She had hoped he would say that she was not to be included in that outing for it meant that there was a chance that she might find moments alone with Cassian to explain her relationship with Meridius. There was nothing for him to be concerned about, but with the meddling and manipulation of others it would be easy to see it for something it was not. She had to stop that from happening, stop him from misunderstanding and turning from her.

"I am sure that you are going to be successful in your ventures today Dominus." She said with a smile, adjusting his robes, pausing when he leaned forward to sniff her hair.

"I would have you bathe before I return Violetta. I would not have you smell of the kitchen when you attend me later." He stated simply, ignoring when she took a deep breath to stop herself from protesting what was inevitable.

What would she tell her lover? What would he think? Was it possible that he would understand?

"Of course, Dominus. As you command. I will bathe and find clean dress right away." She turned away to do as he wished but stopped when he snapped his fingers for her to stay and see the task of dressing him finished before bathing and cleaning herself.

Her mind was in turmoil as she and Meridius finished the task and cleaned the remnants of the food. The thought of going to Cassian, hours after they made love with an earth shifting finish and telling him that she had to attend the bed of the man who seemed to delight in antagonizing and humiliating him, seemed impossible. What would he do if she returned to their bed used by the other man?

Following the Roman and Meridius out into the hall her face was filled with questions that she knew would be impossible to have answered if she did not find the nerve to speak to the man she loved. With a nod to Meridius she left the men to take the clothing to be cleaned. Lingering a little she tried to sort her thoughts so that she could explain to Cassian, try to make him understand that she did not do this because she wanted it, but simply because she was commanded to it.

With a fresher confidence, even though she did not have an answer yet to what he would say, she made her way towards the kitchen. She was determined to find a way to say what was needed, though she would need to have a few moments alone with Cassian to hopefully make him understand. With a forced smile on her lips she stepped into the room, eyes widening in horror at what she saw.

CHAPTER 15

The cook, Irissa, had clearly taken offence at the brush off she had received from Cassian. As a Gladiator she saw him as fair game among the women of the house. His reputation as a lover was well known to slave and Roman alike within the city and the thought of him settling down with a single woman seemed as ridiculous as it appeared to be disappointing.

Stalking towards him she glared as she placed her hands on her hips. "What does she have that I do not possess?" She snapped. "Are my breasts not as soft? As able to fill mouth and hand as her meager offerings." A seductive smile lit her face as she took his hand and cupped it to her flesh, pulling it from the confines of her dress. "Tell me it is not more to your liking?" Snatching the other hand and forcing it beneath the material and between her legs, moaning as his fingertips brushed her damp sex. "Is it not as hot and tight as hers? Why her and not me, or any of us? What is so special about that little whore?"

Cassian pulled his hands back with a look of disgust, wiping them on the rag at his feet. "I have neither time nor desire for such pursuits at the moment." He looked up at her with a shake of his head. "And I prefer to take them with one that does not offer so boldly to any man that catches her eye." He returned his focus to the knives and sharpened each to a razor's edge. His face showed that he had rarely felt such a sense of revulsion more than this woman and her crudeness. "Call my woman a whore again and find the strength of my temper turned against you."

The cook stepped back as though his words had burned her, eyes blazing with lust turned to hatred. "You will live to regret this champion, or should I say former champion for now you stand nothing but a shadow of the man who once held that title." Leaving him with her words hanging in the air she turned to find Violetta in the doorway glaring. "He is not worth the effort. Maybe a little waste like you does deserve him. The stallion has been gelded." She laughed and went back to the fire to attend the meat cooking there, leaving the lovers to stare at each other, each deep in the anguish of their own thoughts.

When he registered that his woman was so close, he stood and stepped towards her. "Violetta? Are you hurt? What happened?" The moment his hand touched her skin, he could do nothing except pull her to his chest and wrap his arms around her, savoring the sweetness of her scent as it gave him the peace he was beginning to crave. "I am here for you, tell me, please, if he hurt you again." He cupped her cheeks in his hand and stared down into her eyes, searching for the truth in the captivating blue.

She shook her head slowly. "Nothing. I am fine Cassian, I promise. He did nothing to me…this morning." She let the words hang in the air between them and leaned forward to capture his lips in a kiss, soft and gentle but almost timid as though she had a fear of his rejection. "Dominus has taken Vitus and Meridius to the docks and I pray that Selenia is soon to depart to her own amusement. I would beg a few moments with you. Alone?" She looked at the others, especially Irissa who still glared from the fireside.

"My time is yours to command." He said with a teasing smile, angling his body against hers as he dropped his hands to rest on the gentle curve of her hips. Pulling her as close as he was able and while still allowing them both enough space to walk, he directed their shared steps towards the door of the kitchen, eager for any time free of the stare and repulsive behavior of the cook.

Cassian looked at the guard lingering near the entry and shared a nod of understanding. He suspected that the man was an admirer of his skill upon the sands of the arena since he had said nothing when the eager youth from the kitchen brought him wine instead of water to drink as he worked upon the blades as Felix seemed to delight in commanding him to.

"Do not be long, champion." The guard uttered as they passed him. "Though there is no need to rush either." He said with a conspirator's wink and a look of his own towards the cook. Cassian knew they had shared a few lurid moments in recent weeks, and he was obviously eager for another chance, especially when she was angry and worked up over his rejection. It would likely make her even more willing and enjoyable. Even before they had left the room, he was stepping towards her, his intent shining in his eyes.

"I will be mindful of the time." Cassian said with a smirk, heading down the hall with his fingers entwined to Violetta's. Looking at the stairs and knowing the answer already he asked. "Do we dare descend or would the temptation be too great?" His voice whispered hotly in her ear so that she knew that for him the answer would be yes.

Simply being near her sent him into a state of arousal so intense it was painful but if the memory of the groping of the other woman left him burning with anger, what could it be doing to his woman? When her smile faltered his grin slipped, he was right: she was upset about the cook. Following her towards a room still darkened by drawn drapes he asked, his voice fighting a panic she had never heard before. "What is wrong? Violetta tell me, please. If it is the actions of that foul woman do not let it hold a thought. She is vile and jealous of everything that you are, and she is not."

Violetta suddenly looked as though she wanted to wrap her arms around him and hide from the world. "I may not be with you tonight, or I may not come to you until late." She looked up at his eyes with tears in hers. "You may not want me to come to you after I have finished my tasks this night." There was a deep fear in her voice and the shame that washed over her body was palpable bringing questions to his mind at what the Roman had devised now. "Dominus informed me that I am to attend him tonight after the evening meal, with Meridius in attendance as well. I cannot refuse him though I wish to the heavens that I could. I pray that you believe me."

"Census commands you to his bed? Tonight?" Cassian stared at her as though she had just told him that it was himself and not her that was to bed the man that night. "With me in his house and knowing that we hold meaning to each other he would still command this? Or will it be Meridius that takes you?" His voice was choked with emotion ranging from disgust to near blinding rage.

The idea of his woman lying in the bed of the old man, beneath him while he took his pleasure in the sweetness of her body was making him physically ill. He had known it was possible but had thought, had hoped, that while he was beneath this roof, she might be spared the act. Maybe he could have dealt with the thought from afar while in the ludus, leaving the blame of it being the lack of his presence but it seemed that this would not be the case and a fresh new kind of torture had suddenly become a very real and visceral thing in their lives.

"Tell me of the Spaniard." He said with a growl in his voice. He hated that she flinched at the anger in his voice and he hoped that she knew it was not directed at her for what she could not control.

"Meridius stands in the place of the father who saw me to slavery's chains. He would never hurt me or see me with lust filled eyes." She flushed deeply, remembering the single occasion he had proven that was not the complete truth. "I can trust him with my life, I know that. When…when it is the three of us in Dominus' bed it is not me that Padre is commanded to pleasure." She held back a sob "Cassian, apologies but there is nothing that I can do to fight this. He will have his way or else there will be pain to pay for it and I cannot bear the lash again. Please try to understand."

He took a deep breath, trying to calm his temper so that he did not lash out at her. She was innocent in this, but he could not believe that Meridius had never lusted for her.

"I would not ask you to bear that, but how can I stand by waiting for him to finish with you and send you back to me in tears. As a man and one that loves you, I cannot see you used in such a way." He looked up to the heavens, searching for answers or perhaps an inspired solution to the problem. He would shed the blood of every Roman in this house before he could be at peace with this. Suddenly the solution came to him. "Tell him you bleed. He will not command you to his bed then." He offered her a small smile of hope "And you will be free to join me in ours instead."

"It may work." Violetta said with a cautious hope in her voice. "If he believes me then I would have some days before he would call me to any task in his presence." Taking a deep breath, she sought his eyes, but there was hesitation in her voice. "I knew you would not want me to come to you after, that is why I had to tell you. I did not want you to think that what Irissa said was truth. I have not, willingly, been with anyone but you." She paused, her eyes telling him that she was still afraid of his anger. "Cassian, I do not know what I must say or do to show you that what I say is true but name it and see it done. Please?"

The soft plea in her voice brought him out of his internal darkness, he realized she thought he was angry at her. The idea might seem laughable to him, but it was a very real fear for her. Had she never known love or even real friendship?

"Violetta? Did you think that the command of Felix would turn my desire from you? My heart?" He gently cupped her face in his hand and brushed the pad of his thumb against the smoothness of her cheek. "I do not think there is a force in this word strong enough to do that." He pulled her close, wrapping the safety of his arms around her slender shoulders and holding on tight, pushing aside any doubt about his sincerity. "You are my woman, gifted by more than Felix, I would not let him destroy what we have or can have."

He kissed her lips with a sweet gentility and continued "If you came to our bed after such a thing you are right that I would not have taken your body, I would have held you with the intent to comfort, to heal the hurts done by the other. As you would do for me if I came to you in pain."

Violetta let him hold her and sank against him while he spoke. "I would do anything to ease your pains, champion of my heart." She stepped back and tried to smile "I know there is not much within my power, but I would do what I was able."

"For that you would have my eternal gratitude." He whispered, kissing her once again.

"There is little worry now, but I would still take leave of you for the luxury of the bath that he has commanded me to." She smiled when he did, unable to stop herself from mirroring him. "I will discover the 'inconvenience' shortly after and see myself to our bed this night." Her fingers lingered in a loving stroke down his arm with a twinkle in her eyes "Unless you would rather join me in the bath?" Though they knew it was impossible it was a pleasant idea in his head before he went back to the hungry eyed cook.

"If only I stood able to do so I would be a happier man." Cassian said with a light laugh and a wink. "You will be safe alone?" His question was teasing, but he was hiding the deeper concern that the guards might make an attempt on her while their master was away. "I would not want to leave you feeling unsafe as well as longing for my company."

With a gentle nod Violetta stepped from the room "I bathe in the slave's quarters. There is little to fear from the Romans while I am in there."

She left him behind as she descended the stairs and quickly made her way to the room set aside for the slaves to bathe in the warm water of the shallow bath. He imagined her alone and in the dark except for the single torch lighting the small room she stripped and stepped into the welcoming water. He could almost hear the moan of delight slipping past her lips as the heat began to ease the ache in her body from all that the previous days had brought.

He left the thought of her there and returned his focus on dealing with the jealousy of those like Irissa who could not be alone in her feelings though she was the only one bold enough to give them voice. What more would the woman do to see her own desires fulfilled? Perhaps she would be persuaded by his firm refusal of her advances to leave things as they were and return her attention to the guards where they had been before.

CHAPTER 16

When Cassian returned to the kitchen, he was relieved to find the cook had been somewhat satisfied by the guard that had allowed him the privacy with Violetta. She still glared at him with a dangerous rage in her eyes when he sat down to continue to sharpen the knives.

There was a small knife, dropped by one of the workers in the kitchen, that no one seemed to have noticed. It was just beyond the reach of his hand but if he moved slowly, he just might be able to reach it with his foot. Grateful that this time he had the subligaria he desired to hide it in he slid his foot across the tile and eased over the tool. Slowly he moved back to his normal position, just waiting for the chance to pick it up and hide it without the others noticing. The house had begun to buzz with activity that he assumed meant that one or more of the Romans was making their return.

Violetta rushed into the kitchen, her hair still damp but braided across her shoulder, and flashed a worried smile at him as she stepped close. "I do not know if I can do this Cassian. Lie to him? I have never done so in all my years here." She whispered, gripping his hand, her own shaking with fear. "How do I do this? What if he asks for proof?" Her eyes searched his and they did not note Irissa watching the lovers like a hawk hunting a mouse. "I do not know if I can do this, take the risk."

Cassian took a deep breath, as champion of the house of Tertius he had calmed the nerves of more than one recruit about to enter the arena for the first time and he looked at this as being a similar situation. "You will do it because you need to. Your capabilities will let you do it and the reward is worth it, I promise." He gave her a soft, tender, smile and cupped her cheek in his hand before laying an encouraging kiss on her lips, a simple thrust of his tongue to remind her of what he would be doing later.

"As for proof," He added with a smirk, breaking the kiss reluctantly and picking up a knife. "I can help with that." He sliced the sharp blade across the tips of his fingers and squeezed until the blood pooled. Locking eyes with her, he lowered his fingers beneath the edge of her dress and smeared the blood at the top of her thighs and swiftly wiped her crease, hating that he could not linger there and see her come apart. "Now the tale appears as truth. Go and see to your tasks if that is what is needed. I will see you in our bed soon, I hope."

Breathless at his touch Violetta nodded carefully and retreated a step. "I will do what I can to be with you shortly."

Turning, she fled to the office and the returning masters whom they both knew she must convince of her state. If they discovered her lie it would be worse for her than if she had not even made the attempt for Felix was the type of man who hated lies above all else.

Meridius was just helping Felix to remove his outer robes when she stepped timidly into the Roman's presence. It was with relief she noticed that Vitus had either not returned with them or had already removed himself to his own chambers.

"Dominus?" She called softly, pausing with a trembling lip when he met her eyes "I...I cannot attend you this night as you requested." When he lifted his eyebrow and opened his mouth to demand an answer, she lifted the edge of her dress to reveal the blood on her skin. "I would not wish to come to you, unclean." She bowed her head in submission to the anger she was sure would come but also to hide her relief in the fact that she would not be sharing his bed.

Felix had been in the process of stepping towards the girl when she revealed the reason behind her abstaining from his bed. "You bleed and yet you stand before me? Dirtying my house with your offing? You know where you are commanded to be. Get to the cells and do not stand before me until you are cleansed of this."

He waved his hand in dismissal and Violetta had turned to depart to comply with his command when a guard stepped into the room "Dominus? The cook begs immediate audience with you."

"The cook?" He asked, his face a deep frown of confusion "What could she want?" Felix nodded for her to be admitted, barely noticing that Violetta lingered near the door.

When the older dark-haired woman entered the room, she bowed her head until Felix commanded her to speak. Raising her eyes, she glanced at the Roman and then Meridius beside him. "The girl lies to you Dominus." Irissa said, pointing to Violetta. "She does not bleed but lies so that she can lay tonight with the gladiator. They were together all through the night and again this morning. I heard them as did many others." She frowned when Meridius shook his head but grinned happily when Felix strode across the room to pin Violetta to the wall by her throat.

"What is this treachery?" He growled in her ear, his hand squeezing tight and flooding her with panic. "Speak quickly before I find means of drawing the words from you." His hand was raised to strike her then looked from the cook to the guard. "Wait, let us hear from the man who offers me such offence. Bring the gladiator, and my son so that he can see how such betrayal is dealt with properly." He turned his attention back to Violetta and released her throat, stepping back as she coughed, trying to breathe again.

She could feel the bruising on her throat, but she turned blazing eyes to the cook. "You bitch. You could not let me have this one joy, but you must see it taken from me? For what? He will never want you."

"He will, especially when you are exposed for the whore you have become and sent to the cross for betraying our Dominus." Irissa sneered with a look of vengeful glee.

The woman seemed to think that Violetta had been favored for so long that, now, she wanted to see her brought down to the lowly position of the whore of the villa. Stepping closer while Felix waited for the arrival of the others and Meridius glared silently at her Irissa whispered "When I bed him, in the depths of his grief, I'll think of you and how you thought yourself special when you were just another filler for his bed, for a brief time."

Cassian did not even know the cook had left the room. He was focused solely on getting the knife beneath his foot into his possession. He had leaned down with the intent to take hold of it while he scratched his ankle, he had just covered the blade with his palm when a booted foot crushed his hand to the tile. Before he could look up to see who it was, he felt a hand in his hair that jerked his head back until the only thing he could see was the eyes of this new tormentor.

"The champion of Velletri is summoned by Dominus, now." The man's tone of voice left no doubt that he held no respect for the gladiator or his title. If there had been any it was quickly dismissed by the fact that he wrenched him from his seat, still holding tight to his long hair as he finally removed his foot from the hand it covered.

Cassian had no choice but to move wordlessly while the Roman pulled and twisted his hair then gripped his wrist as though he had attempted something violent instead of simply scratching his ankle. When the man at last released him, he stumbled into Meridius who nearly knocked Felix himself to the ground. Steadying himself he stepped away from the Spaniard and looked around the room. He had thought perhaps the guard had seen him attempt to retrieve the knife but when he saw the black-haired cook with a look of gloating satisfaction in her eyes and Violetta looking as though she were about to cry, with red marks about her neck he realized that this was much more serious than picking up a knife. "Dominus? You sent for me?"

Felix's face twisted in a dark grin as Vitus stepped into the room, preening like a peacock and asked, standing beside his father. "What brings such urgency and vexation that you would all for me so soon after our return father?"

Cassian's frown deepened when he saw that Meridius glared at him with murderous rage. What could be happening that would bring so stoic a man in such a dangerous mood he wondered then looked to Felix for explanation.

"If I am to believe our cook," Felix started. "This gladiator has been taking liberties with a piece of my property that you desire for your own possession. My thoughts were to include you in the discovery of the truth so that you may bear witness to the proper way of dealing with such...betrayals." His eyes glared at Violetta who stood trembling in fear before turning to Cassian, newly arrived and still confused. "What do you say to such accusations Cassian? I want the truth from your lips, slave, and not some falseness created to protect the girl." He nodded to the cook to speak her charge again so that he could see the honest reaction from the man before him.

"I heard them in the throws last night for hours uncounted, again this morning at dawn." Irissa was near to laughing as she gave her report "Her moans filled the hallway, Meridius himself would be able to tell you if he yet had his tongue." She smirked and stepped towards the gladiator. "He kissed her in the kitchen as well, before my eyes and those of many others. He cannot deny the truth, there are far too many witnesses." She crossed her arms, turning back to laugh quietly at the distressed horror on the Violetta's face and Cassia felt his blood boil with rage.

The daughter of a whore had betrayed them. Her jealousy was what had brought this down upon them? He glared daggers at her, if looks could kill or if he only had the free use of his hands, she would not be long for this world. Flinching inwardly at what he must do now, he stood silent, his face a mask of calm he did not feel. His heart was racing and full of fear for his woman as they stood together in the den of the lions that were their enemies. "She speaks truth, in a manner of bold fact." He said solemnly "Yet her simple mind did not see the fact that I stole what I wished with forced seduction." He stopped himself from looking at Violetta and hoped that the lie might protect her from the worst of their punishment.

Violetta' head turned like the snap of a whip at his words of forced seduction. Her eyes locked to his in question and she opened her mouth to speak, but Felix stepped between them, earning the unknowing gratitude of the gladiator. He was trying to protect her but was this the way to see that done?

Felix looked deep into Cassian's eyes and smirked. "You mean to tell me that you used seduction and force to take my body slave? That she was not willing to lay with you? Last night and this morning? What of this kiss mentioned in the kitchen, was that forced as well?" Felix growled, Meridius brooding over his shoulder with eyes blazing at the man's suggestion.

For a heartbeat Cassian considered what a match it would make between he and the mute man, the father and lover fighting for the rights to protect her. It seemed to him that Felix might have had the same idea for suddenly he was more amused than angry. Had Cassian given him inspiration to invite the elite of the city and a few from Rome to his house for a celebration of contest? Or had he simply sighed his own order of execution?

"Break words gladiator, are you a man of any honor or simply a ravager and seducer of women?" Felix asked, making Cassian cringe visibly at the trap he put himself in with his defence of Violetta.

While Cassian stood as mute as Meridius, Vitus gleefully walked over to Violetta. Gripping her chin hard and forcing her eyes up to meet his, he asked with a devious smile "Did he force you my little flower? Did he pry you open and plunder your body as a bee to a delicate blossom?" He pursed his lips in mock sympathy before slapping her across the face. "I hope he did not do too much damage though it is less of a personal concern than a legal one. What do you say eh?"

Having stolen a quick look at Violetta he had intended to inspire her with the need to join his conspiracy, but the second Vitus' hand raised to strike her all his control and thoughts of deception were gone. Cassian moved as though in the arena, throwing the offending Roman against the wall before he drove his fist against his jaw with a roar. It had been bad enough to know that the man was violent towards her but to stand and watch was not a thing he could do. There was no force on earth that would let him stand, unfettered, and watch anyone bring her harm. He let his fists fly against her chief tormentor and felt the satisfaction of vengeance even though he knew it would be short lived.

Felix nodded for the guards, who stood staring in surprise, to seize the man as he continued to pummel his son. "Cease! Cassian cease!" He yelled over the sound of the men, not noticing when Irissa ran from the room when faced with the violence of the man she accused.

Cassian paid no heed to him, for he was too engrossed in his chance at vengeance. He did not notice when the merchant stalked to Violetta and despite the shaking of Meridius' head not to do it the Roman gripped her hair tight, wrenching her to her feet from where she had fallen because of Vitus' strike. Her fearful cry echoed through the room and down the hall making him pause long enough for Vitus to deliver a blow to his ribs while two guards finally gripped his arms to stop the champion's attack.

He felt as though he had lost his mind for those few minutes, except the knowledge that the man beneath his fists had hurt her and hurt in more ways than the slap that had sent her to the floor. He knew that no Roman would see what had happened as an excuse but if the ever-present weight of the shackles on his wrists without explanation were not enough, then perhaps the indignity of being placed as a houseslave doing nothing but sharpen blades instead of wielding them had to carry some weight as reason.

"Cassian!" Violetta screamed from the far side of the room. The fearful panic in her voice cut through the thoughts of every man in the range to hear it.

The sound of his name being screamed from her lips in agony brought Cassian to a halt and all thoughts of further blows stopped. The realization of what had happened dawned on him and he took a large step back from the wall. What had he done? What purpose could it serve besides pain? He shook his head to clear it and bring back sensibility and clarity, but he caught Violetta's panicked eyes filled with fear and pain that was caused by his actions. Searching her face for hope he murmured. "Apologies...gods I..." There were no more words he could find to speak. Nothing would come to his tongue for there was simply nothing to be said that could excuse what he had done.

Vitus drove his fists into the stomach of the man who had caused the blood to drip from his lip and nose onto his pristine robes. "Apologies?" He sneered as his fist struck again "You think your apologies will save you or the bitch?" He reached for the dagger at his waist when his father's voice raised to its full strength stayed his hand. "Father? You would not deny me the right of his blood for this assault and surely you want hers for the betrayal?"

The question hung in the air as the older Roman released his grip on the girl, shoving her into the arms of Meridius. He cradled her carefully, tilting her head to check the bruising while his eyes asked her how bad the pain was. Cassian cursed himself for causing another hurt he could not mend.

"Vitus! Desist. I would not have my word sullied by your rash actions." His eyes flickering back and forth between the bloodied face of his son and Cassian who was trying to calm his breathing. "Break words on your actions here or the sands will not be the only thing you never live to see again for I will see you upon a cross and dead before the dawn." He pointed his finger back at Violetta sending a stab of dread and resignation through Cassian. "And her to join you after she sees your lifeblood spilled upon my yard as you spilled her maiden blood across your cock." He glared darkly. "Speak quickly and with truth."

Violetta's eyes were filled with terror as they locked with his even though she was held in the safety of Meridius' arms. If the truth of their feelings was to be revealed to Felix and Vitus, even if they were somehow spared death, they would be parted from each other forever. He watched as her spirit broke and tears slipped down her cheek. Her lips trembled in fear of what punishment was to come in moments and she shook her head to beg him silently not to tell.

He clenched his jaw, holding back the cry of despair that was crawling up the back of his throat while his body recoiled as Vitus continued to strike. They would send him to death on the cross instead of even an execution on the sands? The shame of that fate drained his will to fight any further but when she nodded her head the meaning was not lost on him, even in the height of his misery. She did not deserve this, none of it and his share of it more than anything else was causing her pain.

If Vitus were not so envious of him Cassian had no doubt that the cruelty delivered to her would have been less for Felix himself was not the sadist that his son was. When the blows stopped he pulled himself to his full height and tried to steady his breathing so that the lie he knew he had to utter would sound like the truth though he prayed Violetta would trust him enough to see through it to the truth of his feelings.

"She was given to me as a gift, was she not Dominus?" He looked from her to the Roman glaring daggers at him. "Mine to make use of as I see fit? Does the location of my rest change a champion's right to his prize? She is mine and I take her when cock beckons need, thus she obeys your command when she falls to my will." He scoffs. "She is not…we are not lovers she is my whore and your son mocks us, all of us, with his constant abuse and I have had more than enough of it." He looked at Felix and Meridius. "Surely a man of honor understands that I could not let unjust abuse of one so small be allowed?"

"I cannot deny that she was given as a gift." Felix mused but then looked at him. "And you do stand as undefeated champion. Still words should have been broken prior to use as I prefer not to share, nor have my heir share, with a slave's cock." He curled his finger to summon Violetta from Meridius' arms to stand between them. "What answer do you give girl?"

"Forget the girl and whose bed she has been in or not. The slave attacked me father." Vitus pointed at the gladiator then at his face. "My blood is spilled because of him, what do you say to that?"

Cassian could see that he wanted Violetta as his own, but more than that Vitus wanted him dead. Perhaps what the

Roman wanted most was for Violetta to see and understand the power he would wield in her world as soon as his father was dead if Cassian didn't find a way to save her. "Father, whatever your vow to that stupid lanista I do not care. I demand vengeance for what has been done today."

His face was weary as he turned to face his offspring. "I have spoken to you often of the violence you apply to the slaves, this one in particular. Do you not wonder that some men, even though they are slaves, find it distasteful?" He laughed and shook his head. "What demand would you make that a magistrate would hear?"

Looking from one man to the other as though he was deep in thought. Cassian knew it was impossible to let him go unpunished, but would he break his word to appease a son he obviously did not love?

"I ask again Violetta," Felix said firmly "What answer do you give to Cassian's words of force and seduction?"

Her breath was shallow, and her eyes were lowered not meeting those of Cassian so he could not tell what she felt, what she thought, of what he had said. "Your will, my body Dominus. I thought only to fulfill the accord made." Her eyes flickered briefly toward Cassian before turning her back to him and facing Felix completely, her face a mask of submissive repentance that broke his heart. "I say truly that I found little pleasure in his brutality except that I might be fulfilling your desires by my actions." She moved back to the wall with her head bowed as Vitus crossed the room towards his father with his fists clenched angrily at his side. Cassian wished he could go to her and offer comfort but who knew if they would ever have the chance again?

CHAPTER 17

"See the man to a barred cell and the girl to her own. Have them both cleaned and prepared for display at the feast this night. I will see this settled before sunrise." With a turn and wave of his hand the slaves and guards were issued their commands.

Guards took Cassian by either arm before dragging him from the room while Violetta's eyes followed him, mournful and afraid of what was going to happen next and even more so of what would happen that night. His eyes held the silent apology of his heart, the tears in her eyes like daggers to his heart as he was roughly gripped on each arm and dragged from the room and her sight.

Whatever future awaited them was not now in the hands of the fates, but in the mood of a Roman who had no reason to spare his life besides his prowess in the arena. He found himself overwhelmed with the feeling of dread and the unfamiliar sensation of fear. How many times over the long count of years had he raised hand or voice against those that sought to dominate him? Precious few, so why did he do this now? All his training, his strength and endurance had given him nothing, nothing to prepare him for the sight of the woman he loved being struck and accosted by the man who took pleasure in assaulting her for no other reason than that she did not want him.

He glanced over his shoulder to see the third guard approach Violetta. He was relieved when she started to walk so that he had no excuse to touch her. The misery seeping through her every pore was palpable and he watched her begin to spiral into misery that would soon consume every thought.

Cassian wondered how many times she and all the others had ignored the arduous cries from Irissa's cell as she had lain with any man who would have her, including more than one guard. There had even been times in the kitchen while she was preparing Dominus' meal that she had set the task aside to see to her own desires. All these things had been hidden in good faith and yet one public kiss between himself and Violetta had her breaking words of it to Dominus as though a crime had been committed. If only there was a chance for revenge upon the vile woman but even words with her were to be denied as the day was now to be spent in solitude, dreading what plans Felix would devise for their punishment.

Slowly descending the steps to the cells, Violetta considered how her heart had leapt for the briefest of moments when he sprung to her defense, but it crashed back to the ground suddenly when the reality of his actions truly sank in. Vitus would be within his rights to demand Cassian's death and perhaps her own as well. At the bottom of the stairs she saw Cassian being led in the opposite direction and sighed, they would be nowhere near each other until they were presented to Felix for whatever humiliating 'entertainment' he devised to use them for. Would there be guests? Perhaps the lanista would be summoned and would take him back to the ludus. If that happened, they would never see each other again but at least he would live and that could be enough for her, to know that he lived.

She cringed as she stepped back into the cell, barely willing to lift her head to face the room where only hours before she had lain blissfully in the arms of her lover. He had held her, kissed her and made her feel as though all the world was within their grasp. Now it had been stolen away, dashed to ruin and lowered by the jealous lips and lies. Passing through the curtain she could feel the eyes of the guard on her back and shivered as she kept her eyes downcast, trying to make herself as invisible as possible even though he was staring at her like a wolf stares at a sheep on the hill.

"Remove dress." He said curtly, anger in his eyes as he stepped towards her "I would see the body that tempts a champion to lose control."

"Dominus gave no order to undress." Violetta cried in a panic, crossing her arms across her chest and stepping back. She would not simply stand by and let this happen, not again.

"I said to remove the damned dress." He growled, ripping the fabric from her shoulder as he pushed her back towards the wall. "I would see the body of the whore that will cost the city its champion and I will see it now." His eyes roamed her exposed skin as she uncrossed her arms and the fabric fell to the ground revealing her completely. "Lay on the mat, on your stomach." He instructed, licking his lips hungrily.

She closed her eyes and shuddered as he began to circle her slowly, his eyes taking in every exposed inch of flesh with unmasked lust. When he told her to lay on the mat, she began to prepare herself for what she was certain was coming. Her face pressed against the straw mat Violetta steeled herself against the violence and the stink of wine on his breath. It seemed like an eternity had passed when she dared to open her eyes and find that she was left alone in the cell, her dress gone from the floor, he had left her there. Naked and burning with shame, she had rarely felt so alone in all her life.

"Cassian…what have you done to us?" She whispered, crawling beneath the thin blanket to hide and to rest.

Cassian followed the guard with weary footsteps, his pride had made him a fool once again. Was she hurting even now? Had the guards been given freedom to do as they wished with her? The thought of it brought him such a feeling of dread that he found he could hardly breathe, and it was only the cold of the stone wall that pulled him, briefly, from his cloud of self damnation. He watched, wordlessly, as the guard pulled heavy chains attached to rings in the wall and fastened them to the cuffs already on his wrists.

"Cassian, the great champion of Velletri, now a mongrel champion only of piss and shit. Soon all the city shall see you dead upon a cross for what you've done." Had he spoken or the guard? He did not know and could not care.

He sank to the floor, heedless of the stone scratching his back. His head bowed, he let his hair fall lifelessly over his shoulders and sank into an oblivion of dark thoughts and pleading for the safety of Violetta as she stood innocent of his crimes. His nightmares seemed to be brought to reality when suddenly he felt a warmth at his feet and opened his eyes to see the dress that she had been wearing tossed in a careless pile by the man that had led her in the opposite direction from his own cell.

"Slave." He called with a devious grin on his lips. "Your bitch has good form. I pray Census sells her to the whoremongers so that I may join all of Velletri in taking my pleasures between the thighs of the woman who caused the fall of the greatest champion this city has ever seen." He gripped the steel bars and leaned closer to hiss even more distressing words. "That is if Vitus does not fuck her to death himself first."

Cassian had never felt so confined in all his life, the chains were only part of the feeling, but they were the newest. He could not remember being in chains before, in the ludus such punishment was reserved for those destined for the pits, the mines or the cross with no hope of return. Whatever debauchery Felix had planned for him and Violetta that night would no doubt be an attempt to see him dead or at least lowered so much in the eyes of the city that he would have to regain his title once again and thus see he and his heart parted from each other permanently.

He raised his eyes to meet the mocking gaze of the guard with his own filled with hatred while he reached to take hold of her dress. A cold sweat came over him, the urge to retaliate if only with words was so strong but it would not help her, not now. Perhaps if Tertius attended tonight he might find some way to have her brought to the ludus and out of harm's way but so long as he stayed beneath this roof he would do whatever it took to see her as safe as he could make her. He would teach her to hide the pain and to show no fear to the monsters around them but until that opportunity came, he would take the chance that the gods were real and entreat them to give her strength and endurance to survive this. Staring up to the heavens he sighed, would they hear him? In a sign of surrender no one would ever see in the arena Cassian bowed his head and let the reality of his helplessness wash over him completely.

The final preparations were being made to the villa as the hour of feasting drew closer. The silk banners and candles danced in the evening breeze while slaves moved speedily to lay out food and drink. Maya was with Selenia within her chamber, applying those final decorations and oils to perfect her appearance. Her mistress was thrilled for, if her father was not lying, the Imperator Claudius would be in the villa tonight. Though he was wed he had two sons that were not. If she caught his eye and made the right impression, then when she returned to Rome it would not be hard to arrange a meeting with them and perhaps finally land herself the husband of great social standing she had hoped for.

"Make sure you look your best tonight Maya. I would not have Claudius think I hold with ragged slaves." If only the woman knew that Maya knew the man, his family and the ways to impress him from her years serving him before her relationship with a gladiator was discovered and she was sold in anger to the elegant Roman woman. Every day she missed Proximus more, yet there was no word if he lived or who he had been sold to.

Walking the halls of the villa in search of the baths and a more elegant dress Maya found the office where the master of the house and his son sat talking. Deciding to wait for another slave to attend their masters who could also direct her to what she needed she stood outside the door, unable to help but hear the words within.

Felix sat across from his son shaking his head and near to laughter. He had sent word for Violetta and her champion to be bathed and oiled for the evening. She was to be decorated in subtle jewels with a fine chain looped around her wrists and strung between them, threaded through a loop in the collar at her neck in case she needed to be controlled by force and to expose his displeasure with her to every eye. Her dress was to be layered translucent silks arranged to expose her enticing charms to the eye but not the flesh.

Setting aside his wine, he returned to his son. "Vitus are you sure you want to match him with blades? Even if Tertius agrees to this course of action are you prepared to risk your life for the slight?" He shook his head at what even Maya could see was arrogant foolishness on part of his offspring. Maya thought it should have been enough to have the man lashed or sent to the pits to fight for his survival for a night. It seemed though that this hot-headed fool would not be appeased by either.

"I am sure of my skills father." Vitus said smugly. "I will see his blood upon my blade for daring to strike me." He stood and placed his hands upon the desk, leaning across it aggressively. "I want her father. Exclusively. The thought of sharing the woman with a slave shrivels the cock and it lowers me in the eyes of others. You must see this for what it is: folly. End the bargain with the lanista and his gladiators. Turn your mind back to silks and away from the sands of the arena. Upon my victory give possession of her to me and let her be marked as such." He sounded certain that his father was still considering the agreement with the lanista. Maya wondered what he would do to end it.

Felix took another drink, his face a mask of complete calm as his son sputtered in his rage. Maya had to hide her desire to laugh behind her hand in case they saw her. "You would do well, Vitus, to remember under whose roof you still reside and who stands the Dominus here. Violetta is my property to do with as I would, and I have a mind to her fate. If," He paused with a shrewd smile on his lips. "If you are victorious against the champion, I will consider your desire unless I receive a better offer from Tiberius Tertius himself."

Vitus's face flushed red with an anger that scared the girl watching from across the hall as he spat his reply. "If? You doubt me? My own father? What if I do not stand the victor? Will that see you give him wine and the woman for his use until he has finished with her?" He paced to the window and then back again. "What of my honor father? The slave struck me, that cannot go unpunished and should not be rewarded. It sets precedent for the others."

Felix' smile changed to one of languid indulgence. "If you do not stand the victor then I doubt it will be of concern to you, but the accord will be maintained until Tiberius has no further wish for it and then Violetta will be sold in the market or in private exchange for there has already been whispers of offers to possess her. Either way it shall soon be decided." Adjusting his robes to his satisfaction he left Vitus stewing in his own rage to make his way to a smaller office where both slaves would be delivered prior to his guest's arrival. He gave Maya, lingering in the hall, only a cursory glance, perhaps thinking that she was meant to gather information on his son to be used later by his favorite child. Hoping to avoid the dangerous son, Maya followed Felix, sharing a smile with Meridius as he joined his master with the gladiator close behind.

Cassian looked grateful to be shaved, even if it was to look presentable for the torment that Felix had no doubt devised in the past hours. Now he stepped into the small office with his hair tied in a knot at the back of his head while his skin glistened like gold, coated with oils scented with a sandalwood spice that wafted to the hall. His shoulders were squared with the dignity befitting his title and his though body submitted to command his eyes brazenly met those of Felix with a look close to defiance as the candles danced silently between them.

She watched as Felix grinned broadly when the gladiator entered the room looking every inch the idol of death that he was. "Shackled and chained yet still so proud. The trappings of slavery have little hold on you, do they?" He asked, circling slowly, looking over his shoulder as Violetta entered the room.

Her hair hung free from ties in a dark cloak across her shoulders, accenting the paleness of her skin and the translucence of the golden dress. The delicate collar and attached chains to her wrists were unfamiliar to her and her uncertainty showed in her eyes as she raised them briefly to meet his.

"Dominus." She whispered, her breath caught in her throat at the sight of the man beside him, glowing as though touched by the gods themselves, but she quickly looked down, suddenly remembering that she stood all but naked before them. Maya could see that the weight of the collar and chains paired with the knowledge that the entire party would soon see her so displayed was more than the younger girl had strength to face.

"Ah yes, Violetta. You do truly look the part of a temptress tonight." Felix stepped closer to take the ring around her neck into his grasp, pulling it slightly so that she fell off balance and had to lean against him to steady herself. The Roman turned his head to watch Cassian while his hands slid beneath the sheer fabric covering Violetta. Maya cringed for the girl that had been nothing except friendly to her on the few occasions they had spoken. "Truthfully I cannot blame you for taking her when cock beckons and had you not raised your hand against my son, I would have given no care if it continued." He shook his head and removed his hand. "But now I fear it will come to worse for both of you."

Before he had the chance to explain what that might mean a slave appeared in the doorway. Maya was filled with relief when he gestured that she should follow him after her message was delivered. The merchant and his son would never need to know what she had heard while waiting.

"Apologies Dominus but the lanista has arrived and requests private words with you." His eyes quickly moving between the suspected lovers he nodded and followed to meet his guest, Meridius joining him, obviously trusting that they would behave themselves with the fear of punishment hanging over their heads.

Cassian hung his head, the word "Dominus" barely a whisper to acknowledge the man who held the power to break him though he did not know it. It seemed his lie had been believed which was the only peace that he could summon in that moment. He refused to give in to the feelings of tension and become a slave to the utter despair that threatened to overwhelm him. Raising his eyes briefly to look at Violetta he cursed his own foolishness and closed them with a sharp intake of breath. Her beauty was like that of a goddess come to earth, standing only feet from him and yet he was forbidden to touch her.

He was stuck, feet bound to the ground by the unspoken threat of Felix. He took a deep breath and released it to try and steady his voice, he could speak to her, they had not been denied that at least. He raised his eyes once again to meet hers, his body rigid in reaction to her, he had never wanted anything in his life, even freedom, as much as he wanted her. "I love you." He whispered, his voice choking on emotions held in deep check. "Never forget that you will hold my heart, always."

Violetta's eyes lifted at his words. "You have my love, all of it. No matter what comes this night you own my soul." Pausing, perhaps at the thought of who now spoke to Felix, when she spoke again it was a whisper. "Tertius is here? Do you think it is possible that he comes to see you returned to the ludus? Buy you back from Census?" Her eyes shone with hope and his heart surged at the sight, perhaps she was right to hope?

"Tertius?" He scowled deeply and shook his head to remind himself of his vow to submit to the will of the Romans until she was either safely within his grasp or forever removed for it. "I have no thoughts towards what his intent may be. I do not even know that I have in fact been sold. No words have been brought to my ears of any plan or explanation of why I am here." He sighed, wishing he could reach out and touch her, just to feel the touch of her hair on the tips of his fingers. He had to keep her safe, if he was able, for she was his top concern now. "It is possible that this is all he had in mind the entire time, but I have no way to tell. Violetta, promise me that no matter what happens you will stay as safe as I can make you, do not worry about me but look after yourself and stay alive."

She nodded and smiled at him sadly "I do not think he would want you dead, your value to him is too high. There is little that I can do to aid you in this fight except to play the part they expect, fearful and obedient."

Her eyes searched his pleading for something he could not give. "Cassian? Please, I beg you not to sacrifice anything, especially yourself, in this game of madness that they play." She took a single soft step towards him but checked herself before getting any closer. The sound of sandaled feet in the hall seemed to have paused her. "Hades comes for one or both of us." She whispered to him before bowing her head in the expected position of submission.

CHAPTER 18

Tertius had his most charming smile upon his face as he entered the house and hall of Felix Census, extending his hand as the man himself approached. "Good Felix, once again you grace me with your lavish hospitality. I came as soon as I received word that there was something of importance that you required words regarding. My wife will join us presently, you know women, taking twice as long as a man but looking three times as splendid."

He reached out to take the glass of wine that Jovian had already acquired for him from the merchant's house staff. "I hope the matter is one that is more pleasant and not an offence caused by the property I loaned you." He sipped the wine, doing his best to hide his unease.

Felix extended a hand to greet Tertius with a smile that unnerved the lanista, but he could not identify why. "If only it were indeed a matter of pleasant chat and gratitude my friend, but it seems that I have misjudged my son's hatred of your man or of your gladiator's ability to hold restraint. There has been an incident and now my cock for a brain son demands the chance to cross blades with your gladiator. As if he can defeat a champion." The merchant scoffed loudly, shaking his head at the foolishness of his son but the lanista could tell he was waiting for his reaction to the information.

Tertius could not hide surprise he did not feel. Sipping the sweet honeyed wine, then swirling it within the fine goblet to spread the sugary essence through the liquid he tried to find some words to break. It was not a surprise that Cassian was yet unbroken. He was no longer sure that change for the man was possible at all. He had been through more, exposed to more, in his life as a slave than most and until the appearance of Violetta in his life he had been completely unchanged. "Your son would die Felix, surely he knows that is the only possible outcome when facing Cassian? What would he risk his life in such trivial contest?"

Felix shook his head. "You know as well as I do what the outcome will be, it does not matter what skill level Vitus thinks he has, he is not a swordsman." He handed Meridius back the cup and nodded for more. "Cassian laid fists against Vitus' jaw when he saw him strike the girl. His fists flew fast enough that Vitus could not block them let alone strike back until two guards disabled your man by taking hold of his arms. All of this comes from the accusation of my cook that your man spent the night and early hours bedding Violetta. I had not forbidden it, but it had not entered my mind that he would be so bold as to do so without permission."

His eyes met Tiberius' filled with questions. They both knew if this was a lesser slave this would have meant certain death, but a champion gladiator was worth more than his weight in gold. Untold amounts had been offered for his purchase five years ago and yet the lanista did not think it worth parting with the man.

"The sentiment behind such insult is easily understood, but I would not see the man dead or injured." Tiberius said, handing the empty cup back to Jovian and shaking his head refusing more drink while he was talking to the merchant who currently had his prized gladiator in his possession. "This is no ordinary slave we are discussing Felix. This is Cassian. He is unrivaled for skill in all the republic, standing undefeated by all. I am certain that you can find some other way to pacify your son. Regarding the girl, if you did not command him to leave her untouched, I see no reason why he would not assume that she was his to use as he desired since she was given to him as a prize more than once. No other action would be expected, it is Cassian, the only thing that drives his passion more than a beautiful woman is the glory of the arena."

Felix nodded and held up a hand. "Tiberius, I do not want the man dead. I have already talked Vitus down from demanding the cross."

Feeling a flood of relief Tiberius held his cup out for more wine at last, smiling when Meridius filled it promptly and handed it to Jovian. The amusement of watching the boy blush and fluster under the stare of the Adonis-like man that served them almost offset the disappointment and inconvenient stress from having to deal with the foolishness created by Felix's son.

"Would it be possible, could the man be convinced to stay hand from a death blow? Fitting reward would be offered of course." Always with a head for business Felix sought to find the gain in the situation but the lanista was ready.

Tertius gave the idea a little thought and then looked up at Felix. "Where is he? I would break word with him towards this." He wasn't sure that Cassian could be convinced to not kill the man if the opportunity was presented to him, but he would do his best to convince him that it would serve him and his woman better if they did as he requested. He could try and bring the girl to the ludus, away from this place that seemed to crawl with a depravity that made even his skin crawl. That might satisfy the Celt.

"He awaits command in the small chamber down the hall. My man will lead you there as I must see to the blades to be used in this folly." He gestured towards the door, "If you have no use for the girl's presence then send her to the hall and she will be dealt with."

Felix turned and made his way to his office where the weapons were kept and were currently laid out, ready for his inspection. Stepping into the room he was surprised to see his son already in attendance. "Vitus? I was not expecting you to be here." He said dryly with a shake of his head that communicated the disdain he had for the foolishness of what his son wanted to do.

"Why is the lanista here father?" Vitus demanded. Word must have reached him of the man's arrival and seen his curiosity piqued as to why he had been invited the same night he intended to send the gladiator to Hades. "Is it your intent to sell the man back and deny me my rightful vengeance for what he has done?" He demanded, picking up one of the swords laying across his father's desk, weighing it in his hands.

Felix picked up the second blade and swung it smoothly, with an ease and skill that defied his years. "I cannot sell what is not my property unless it is in brokerage for another. This is not the case, of course." He set the weapon down and smirked at his son. "The man is not mine and has never been mine. I had meant to make a display of him and his skill, perhaps drawing the magistrate and others of note to witness his prowess beneath our very roof. The fit of temper displayed in reaction to your move against the girl has brought that plan to swift end." His wrath at the disruption of his plans was evident as he swiped up the weapon once again and swung it in a swift arch that stopped merely inches from his son's shocked face.

"But you did not speak to me of this loan father?" Vitus let the blade in his hand fall slack as he stared at the weapon that was close enough to kill him if Felix was not more skilled than most remembered. His son's mind had to be reeling from the reality that his assumption that Cassian had been sold due to an injury that would not permit him to return to the sands was mistaken and the man was in fact in top form, ready to battle to the death.

"There was no need to break word to you in its regard and even now I would not be doing so if you had not been so foolish as to challenge the man to combat." Felix set the blade down upon the desk and turned to face his son. "I had no idea that your jealousy of him would drive you to such foolishness. Since you do not have the sense of mind that I thought you were born with I had to strike yet another bargain with the lanista to ensure that should the gods favor Cassian with victory your life is to be spared." He spat the words, unable to hide his anger that his promise that the champion would be returned uninjured was in jeopardy. If there was a mark on the man, he knew that he would have to offer some sort of compensation to the lanista to make up for his broken oath. He worried that if things continued in this direction the balance of power in the relationship between them would soon be tipped and it would not be in his favor.

"Father I...apologies." Vitus said in a voice that related his embarrassment. "I will not dishonor you tonight when I meet the man in combat. I am sure that your word will remain intact for I too vow to show missio if the situation allows for it." He stated, standing tall and proudly before leaving the room to ensure that his armor was prepared, he would not risk anything but perfection now or it would not be Felix who saw to his fate.

Tertius walked into the small chamber he had been guided to, leaving Jovian outside its doors so as not to crowd the space during his confrontation with Cassian. He looked around the room, his lips curling in jealousy at the opulence displayed in a room that obviously held little purpose and yet it was decorated with more finery than any room in his own villa. One day he would live with the means for such luxury he swore to himself. His eyes drifted to the young woman that had somehow won the heart of his champion.

He watched her tremble beneath his gaze, the slender body shaking like a leaf under the force of a gale wind. The mockery of a dress she wore hid nothing from his eyes and seemed, in fact, to enhance her appeal with the curtain of grace it gave her. Her breasts were high and firm with a luscious curve that made his hands ache to cup them and run down her side to the captivating curve of her hips that pulled his eyes to the shadowed darkness of her femininity. Who could blame a man like Cassian, or any man for that matter, for having fallen in love with a beauty of such enchanting delicateness?

For a moment the lanista thought he should command the woman to wait with Jovian in the hall, but he was suddenly reminded of the last woman who commanded the man's heart and how she had been able to aid in bringing him to heel. Cassian never knew that Nala had been sent to his bed and though unwilling she had accepted the compensation and done as commanded to mold the young gladiator to near perfect obedience. Even her death had been useful against any lingering rebellious nature, until now. Since he was seemingly so enamored with this Violetta if he allowed her to stay, she might prove useful in influencing Cassian to agreeing to the desired outcome.

Sitting himself on the edge of the desk he finally altered his attention from the girl to the true object of his interest. He would be better off asking instead of demanding that he do as this. If he was honest with himself, he would have been able to admit that he had likely done the man a greater injustice than intended by the punishment of this visit disguised as a loan or sale. If he added insult to the already injured pride it would do nothing but make things more strained and difficult on all involved. "Cassian, I have favor that I would ask of you this night." His voice was calm but unwavering.

Cassian eyed him warily. "You make a request of a mere slave Dominus?" Which was understandable as he had never made a request before. In the ludus it had been commands that were to be obeyed without question. "Do I not now belong to another? Has permission been given to agree and it is truly my choice?"

"The property of another?" The question caught him off guard for a moment before the reason dawned on him and brought him to laughter. "Why would I sell my greatest asset? Especially to a merchant and when you have just regained title." He shook his head and chuckled again to relieve the tension that he could not have if this meeting was to go as he needed it to. "No Cassian you stand, as ever, my gladiator. Felix has brought words to my ear that his son desires to cross blades with you tonight as a means of settling some dispute between you. I want to offer you an alternative."

Violetta looked up at the words as Tertius had expected her to do. "Apologies Dominus, Vitus seeks to set contest with blades? Not practice weapons?" Her eyes flashed with intense fear. "He wants your life." She said to Cassian in a panic, forgetting the presence of the Roman for a few seconds. "Vitus means to kill you."

"This means instead of demanding that I lose you come to offer what? Supplication?" Cassian shook his head and stared past the man on the desk and watched the world out the window for a few moments. "Would you see me fall again? Is there a purpose for this beyond my destruction?" His voice was full of frustration. "Is it the mines you wish me for? The pits? What good am I, a 'greatest asset', if I am constantly ordered to loss at the hands of men I can easily defeat?" He squared his shoulders and looked Tertius in the eyes. "My answer, Dominus, is no. With deepest apologies."

Tertius hid his anger behind a smile of deep sincerity and removed himself from his seat on the desk. Walking towards Violetta he placed a seemingly tender hand upon her shoulder, giving her the answer he knew she was looking for. "Vitus thinks he is the better swordsman. The thing is as laughable as it is foolish. No one can best Cassian." His hand closed over her a little tighter. "You are, of course, aware of the words between your Dominus and myself. The agreement is profitable to all involved but that would all be lost if your... lover...was to end the life of Vitus."

The man's meaning was not lost on her and she bowed her head under the weight of his stare, pleasing Tertius with her demure grace. "Vitus is a fool to think such is possible." She said softly. "I think that if Cassian were to end his life Felix would not be able to keep the accord, for pride's sake if nothing else."

She raised her eyes to glance at the man in question. "Cassian? Is there any way you could defeat Vitus without taking his life? Do you think you could hold back a death blow?"

It would be impossible for Vitus to do the same, but Tertius prayed that the man would be convinced by the pleading in her eyes and voice to see the reason in what he was being asked to do.

In a strange way Violetta had become the most dangerous thing in the champion's life. This tiny woman had the power to break his will and his control. Not by any action of her own but by her innocence and vulnerability. The depth of Cassian's emotion for her made her deadly in ways she would never know. There was nothing left for him to lose, except for the hope for a future, the hope for love.

Cassian straightened and looked him in the eyes. "Do not use affection to bend my will Dominus. I will not be so foolishly used as that." It was daring to speak in that tone to him but there could be no chance of misunderstanding between them, not this time. "Unless you would offer a greater gift in return for what you are asking of me."

Tertius' eyes narrowed into a glare at his refusal. Though it showed that despite what had happened his fighting spirit was still unbroken. He would fight again provided he could get out of this house alive; it was still dangerous.

"Do you mean to bring a bargain before me then, Cassian?" He let his hand slide off Violetta's shoulder as he stepped up to the champion, his smile swiftly changing from charming to a challenging smirk that dared him to be bold. "Make offer and see if your worth is still enough to see it met."

"In exchange for mercy upon Vitus at the end of the match I would see chains and shackles struck from myself and from Violetta. She should be able to move about the house without the fear of abuse. If she is to indeed be my prize, then I would see her unmolested as long as that title stands."

The lanista took a deep breath. "Cassian, I have no say in what a man does with his own property. The slaves beneath his roof are his own. If you had wanted a different woman each night to warm your bed with wine for days on end, I could see these things done but what you ask..." He shook his head and stepped back. "Apologies Champion, you ask the impossible."

Tertius watched Violetta hang her head and as the shadow of defeat wash over Cassian's face. She had to know that what he had asked for was truly impossible to ensure, even if Felix granted it Vitus would never comply.

"The impossible." He muttered in resignation to the reality of their fate. "See us both freed of shackles and it will be easier to spare his life as that is what you truly desire."

Tertius looked from Violetta to the chains between Cassian's wrists as resignation to the fact that he might never hold her again settled over the Celt. There was little left to debate, and he did not have the time for any more of it.

"If our hands can be freed, I will spare Vitus."

CHAPTER 19

Felix entered the room just as Cassian uttered his agreement, setting the gladiator back on edge. "It sounds as though you were successful Tertius. What terms are there that I should know of?" The Roman grinned his victory over him but remained cautiously away from the man that had just agreed not to kill his son.

Cassian shook his head, not meeting the eager gaze of Felix as he voiced his answer. "Agreement stands in favor of your son. The act is foolish, but it is not I who will learn lessons this night." He would make sure that even though Vitus should live never again would he think himself able to cross blades with the gladiator.

Felix nodded. "It is good to see that wisdom was not lost in a fit of temper, even if control was lost. This shall not be forgotten in future endeavors if your Dominus still wishes for them to continue." He extended his hand to Tertius with a friendly grin and a look in his eyes that seemed to invite the lanista to further conspiracies that Cassian was sure would haunt him and Violetta soon enough.

"Come, let us dine and break words before the spectacle is presented. The company for that shall arrive at a later hour." He beckoned Violetta forward to join them with a wave of his hand. Every man in the room paused to admire her as the light played itself through the sheer fabric and cast golden shadows upon her skin.

"Cassian, I have thought towards appreciation for your sparing the life of my son, if you would wish it?" Felix said, pausing in the doorway, much to Cassian's annoyance.

A flash of anger was quickly concealed in his eyes before he lifted them to meet those of the man who had just addressed him with a tone of trivial indulgence, as though lives did not hang in the balance of his pleasure. He took a step forward in approach, letting the back of his hand brush against that of his woman when she lingered, waiting for Felix before departing. The contact was barely anything and yet it was all that he could offer in comfort, in apology and so much more than he might never get the chance to voice again. The Roman was going to offer appreciation for his sparing a life that was not worth his effort to take up blades against, but the choice was as far removed from his hands as his freedom was. "Such is yours to give if you think it warranted, Dominus." He answered as calmly as he could manage to utter the words.

Violetta had dared to lift her head a little at the touch of Cassian's hand, and he forced himself to deny the reflex to grab hold of her and not let go but instead he savored the contact, brief and sweet though it was. He wished their eyes had met so he could take the memory of their brilliant colour with him that day and all to come.

Felix nodded with a smirk playing on his lips at the words expertly spoken by a slave who was better schooled in these games of will than the man who commanded him. "Well spoken Cassian." Clapping a hand to his shoulder he leaned close to speak softly, pulling Violetta to his side as he did. "In appreciation for my son's life I can ensure that lash never again bites the tender flesh of your prize. What do you have to say to this?"

He refused to respond instinctively by pulling away, but met the Roman's stare for a few moments, sharing the scrutiny and weighing the truth of his words. His self-discipline kept his body tense and unmoving, except for the thundering pulse at his jaw there was no indication that he had even heard the words Felix had said. If he could give his life for her freedom, he would have walked into the flames of Hades without blinking but instead he found himself forced to accept terms that should have been her right and not a granted privilege. "Gratitude Dominus, there is little more I could ask for."

Releasing a deep breath, he looked at his own Dominus and away from the temptation of his lover's eyes he asked. "Am I to fight in cloth as I now stand, or will my usual garb be provided along with steel?"

Grinning indulgently at the acceptance of his offer Felix paused at the question as though it was asked to him and not the lanista whom Cassian was relieved to know was still his true Dominus.

"I do believe that you are to be dressed in full glory." He turned from the gladiator to face his master. "Come my friend, let us dine together in celebration of continued good fortune for us both." He then beckoned not only Violetta but Cassian as well to follow them to the main hall where a select few of Velletri's elite were gathered to join in the meal that would precede the main celebration.

Cassian was positioned behind his Dominus and Violetta commanded behind Felix, at Meridius' side. She did not dare to look at him and he did not blame her. It took a moment for him to realise Jovian had joined them with the merchant and was staring at Violetta boldly. The boy had a teasing glint in his eye that made Cassian happy that they were across the table from each other instead of next to each other. He would certainly be whispering things to her that would have his blood boiling. He watched the boy undressing her with his eyes and Violetta gave her head the slightest of shakes. Jovian responded with a broad grin that told the Celt that he had been right about guessing the boy's thoughts.

The sound of Meridius clearing his throat beside her brought Cassian's mind back to the present and away from the rage building inside. As Violetta poured Felix's wine the champion had to wonder what was going on in the youth's mind. To be so bold with his woman in the company of Romans who were treating the night like a game or some jest was something he did not understand. He knew that Jovian had almost laughed out loud to watch Violetta in such discomfort. The fact that simply looking at him made her squirm was delighting the boy to no end. He wondered what kind of reaction he would get from her himself, if she was a part of Tertius' household and he had free rein to tease her into the pretty blush that was on her cheeks. Cassian would never forgive Jovian if he acted on the pranks that he was clearly planning but it would be wonderful to see her smile like that more often.

Cassian thoughts were interrupted by his guard Julius whispering in Jovian's ear before taking the champion from the room. Glancing over his shoulder he saw the young Syrian give Violetta a sly smile before leaning down to whisper in the ear of Tertius. He then leaned to Felix who responded with a nod. The merchant's reaction sent Jovian walking slowly around the table until he edged himself between Violetta and Meridius. With a seductive grin on his lips, he leaned over to whisper then he held out his arm to her, waiting to escort her from the room.

Violetta had barely found the nerve to look at Felix, who nodded as if annoyed that she would doubt the word of the messenger, but she took the young man's arm and left Meridius, hiding his agitation, behind her. Once they were clear of the noise of the dinner, she turned to whisper to the young man beside her. "It is going to be another spectacle is it not? The night is ripe for it, as are those gathered to bear witness to the violence." She pressed her lips together for a moment to gather her nerve. "Do you like it? The bloodshed and violence of the men?" She found that she was curious to know if there was more beneath the flirting and seduction, perhaps a friend was to be found?

"It will be a sight to be seen." He said cryptically, looking at her with teasing eyes again. "You do not look at me with lust like the other women. Do you not think me desirable?" He asked, mock offence in his voice as they slowly made their way down the hall. "Cassian has told me himself that I am one of the most striking men in all the city. It is only right that you should agree with him."

"You are striking to the eyes and well looked after, but that does not mean that I should lust for you. I have Cassian and that is all I desire and all I could." She shook her head at his vanity. He seemed so good natured that it was hard not to enjoy his playful teasing. If she had thought that he meant anything by it then she would have left his side right away, but there was something comforting in his presence that she was genuinely enjoying. "How does it feel to be a man jealous of him?" She teased back. "Since he has what you do not."

Jovian laughed softly and gave a single strand of her hair a gentle tug. "You have more spirit than one would guess. I like that and can see why he cares for you." They stood at the doorway. "There is little he has that I could not, if I asked for it." He stated matter-of-factly. "Except the sands." Standing outside the door to the room where Cassian had been delivered to his armor the boy's eyes grew serious. "I envy him the granting of his desire even if what he wants is not what I would wish." He gestured for her to enter the room with a strange look of solemnity in his eyes that made her pause.

"Beware of Vitus, my friend. He is in a vicious state that I doubt even you would be able to sooth." Violetta whispered, glancing back towards the noise of the feast. Meridius had just paused in the doorway, his eyes narrowed as he watched them. "Also, Meridius. He does not take kindly to most other men, not if they show interest in me. A protective father really." She offered a gentle smile. "Be safe and I shall see you soon. When a gladiator becomes a god for the entertainment of those gathered."

"I do not fear him, and you should not fear for me." Jovian whispered in return. "My mouth upon his neck and hand upon his cock would turn angry words to moans of the sweetest pleasure." He smirked at her. "Now go and do the same for your champion before he enters into combat, however brief it may be."

Laughter danced over his lips and he winked at her before sauntering back to the noise of the celebration that was beginning to grow in volume and members who were becoming excited at the news that they would see their champion cross blades with one of their own, however unpopular he might be.

Violetta watched him go with a bemused look on her face, the youth was more than he appeared but guarded himself behind flirtation and humor. For some reason he did not want to let others in, even in friendship. With a shake of her head she turned her attention to the room to which she had been brought. When she saw the man within shining in the light of the candles, his silhouette like that of an Olympian god, she knew why men feared him.

"Cassian?" She called in a whisper, feeling unsure in his presence for the first time since the night he had been invited to the feast hosted by Felix. "I have been sent to help you into your armor, though you will have to instruct me for I have never done such a thing before."

Standing before the armor that had been laid out for him; the quilted fasciae, bronzed leather greaves and manica resting beside the leggings that he wore in each fight in the arena, he looked intent upon something deeper than the fight ahead. He had been reaching for them when her voice sounded, timid and unsure, from the doorway causing him to pause as though he had forgotten the purpose for what he was about to do.

"Help me to my armor?" Cassian could not hide the confusion from his voice. "It is a task that I have never before required aid to complete. Why does he send you now?"

Violetta's confusion matched his and she lingered in the door uncertainly. "That is what I was instructed to do. Why would your Dominus have wished me to aid you in a task that requires no assistance? Jovian bid me to come quickly, he seemed to think it urgent that I come to you." She took a few tentative steps towards him and he wondered if his master had sent her to offer him solace or if it was a trap set to expose the truth of their feelings.

Cassian took her hand and brought them to his lips, his eyes meeting hers with a gentle acknowledgment of what they shared, trying to soothe her nerves.

"Perhaps it is that Tertius would have my mind filled with distractions. Perhaps he fears that I will not stick to my agreement regarding sparing Vitus' life since my request to keep you safe was denied." His lips spread into a teasing grin as he lowered his hands to her waist. "I would have you stay, regardless of what purpose your arrival was meant for." His eyes twinkled, and he winked before taking her mouth in a kiss that reminded her of his claim upon her soul.

Violetta inhaled as though to breathe in his very essence while her fingers teased at the top of his subligaria sending bolts of desire to his loins. Slowly she broke the kiss and whispered hotly in his ear. "I do not seek to distract, but I wish to be nowhere but in your arms." Her worry at the thought of his death at the hands of Vitus was impossible to hide from her eyes and although he was the superior warrior her concerns were valid.

The Roman would not rest until he received what he believed himself owed. It did not matter how much force he needed to make it happen or what malicious deeds he had to perform to see himself satisfied; he would have it.

It was dangerous to tempt himself, very dangerous but even though he knew he should stop, he could not. Her nearness and willingness to be his set the flames of his desire scorching through his body. She was stunning and seductive with the power of her innocence, more beautiful than any woman should look. Like a mythic nymph with long chestnut locks that tumbled down her back and over her shoulders a cascading waterfall of darkness that he wanted to wrap around his hands. If the intent with her dress had been to drive him mad with lust, then it had succeeded for all he could think about was claiming her body once again.

Need surged through his body as the memory of her lushness pressed against him teased with the knowledge that it would take only seconds to be buried deep within her again. Somehow, he had to have her again, this night had to give him that. He wanted his hands upon her hips, plunging harder and deeper into her from behind as her hair flew wildly and the soft orbs of her breasts bounced in time with the sound of their bodies thundering together. He would take her any and every way she would allow him, he wanted to explore her carnally and expose her deepest desires, the urges that she would not even recognize yet. He would show her that she stood a goddess his equal in passion and that thought stilled him, pulsing with shortened breath, as he stared down at the woman who was now his single most important thought.

"Extend arms." The command was given by the guard that neither of them had noticed enter the room and brought Cassian down to earth from the rapture of his fantasy. He took a quick step past her to answer the demand of the man who had been all too happy to secure the shackles hours before. Words that lay on his tongue in temptation to speak were swallowed with the relief he felt at being free of the shackles at last. His pleased smile faltered when the same relief was not brought to Violetta before the man departed. He would have to be satisfied with what gift he had, the ability to truly fight as he was trained to do without trying to compensate for the restrictions to his movement made by the shackles.

Violetta was hardly breathing while locked in the heated gaze with him. The light chains from her neck ringing as her breasts rose and fell beneath the sheer mockery of her dress. After the guard's departure before she spoke again. "My champion stands a god once more."

Her eyes met his, filled with so many unspoken words of fear. Fear for his safety, love and desire all whirled within her expression, but the strongest he saw was the love she had for him. He shivered when her hand reached to his forearm and glided up his arm until her palm cupped his face.

"See me to the armor." Cassian said, his voice tight and rough with the restraint required to hold back his desire to hold her. He was a man built for combat, death and destruction. Every inch of his body was strong, hard and cut as though from stone and yet she softened something in him and made him care, worry, love. Before she could move to aid him, he captured her mouth once more for what could be the last time if the gods were as cruel to him now as they had been in the past. His tongue pried her lips apart and he drank her in like the wine the Romans poured freely to toast the action they had come to see. She tasted sweet with a hint of salt as though she had sipped her own tears only moments before stepping in to see him.

"Violetta," He whispered roughly. "Swear to me, no tears, not for me."

She started to nod in agreement to his command when he took her mouth, her protest was quickly stopped as she gave in to his kiss. Her heart was racing, and he could feel it through the mockery of a dress. Nothing existed but their shared breath until the guard barked from the doorway for her to do as was commanded.

"I should fall to command before I fall to my knees in prayer." She reached for the first piece of his armor. "I do not know how to do this, but I will not fail. You will stand the victor in this, I have faith. Of nothing else am I sure unless it is what my heart speaks."

"You had both set selves to purpose. Dominus is impatient for the display of contest." The guard snarled, impatient for them to finish their farewells and return to their positions so that he could return to his post.

Cassian removed himself from the kiss a man transformed into a machine of death. No longer a lover or slave but a man who embraced death as though a brother in arms instead of the enemy that his Roman superiors saw it as. He stood fearless, ready to greet Hades, though it was unlikely that they would meet this night for he knew his skill was greater than the man he was to face.

The memory of Violetta's sweet kiss and the tender touch of her hand at the buckles and laces were luxuries that he had never dreamed of. Even Nala had not attended the Doctore, then her husband, Cirandon, before a fight so the thought that his own lover might be there with him had never entered his thoughts as possible.

He had thought it might stand a distraction but instead it was a steadying act, grounding him and turning his focus to that which was most important: victory. The rewards that came with it, wine and the knowledge that even if he was parted from her his lover would not know the sting of the lash again. To see her saved was a thing he was more than willing to give mercy for, no matter how undeserved it was.

Her task finished, Cassian gifted Violetta with a soft smile before entering the place in his mind that was reserved for the moments before entering the arena, all thoughts and actions set towards a single purpose: standing a god among the Romans again.

CHAPTER 20

Every Roman in the room looked up as they entered the room. Cassian felt like death carved from flesh and blood walking among them. He watched as Violetta resumed her place at Felix's side, Meridius moving to brush against her protectively as Cassian had known he would do.

Even the older body slave could not help but to stare in awe at the champion of the city. It was a stark contrast to Vitus who also entered the room dressed for similar combat. Though his armor was finer, as would be his blade, it was evident to all which man would be the victor.

"I hope you stand ready to meet Hades at last for tonight I send you to his embrace."

Cassian shook his head with a scoff under his breath at Vitus' attempt to goad him to anger, even though he knew it meant nothing. He savored the warmth of the anger and turned to face him, his face a blend of a dazzling smile and deadly calm. "Every dawn I wake sees me prepared for that meeting." His words and tone were as smooth as the satin of the man's robes and dripped with self confidence that had been earned in over a hundred arena matches.

Reaching out his hands to take up the blades offered to him by Jovian, whose playfully flirtatious wink he ignored, his eyes met those of a Roman man across the room. He had never seen him before but there was no doubt that this was a man of importance and influence. The ice blue stare was filled with a chill that would have sent shivers down the spine of lesser men and for a moment it felt as though a snake had tightened around his neck with the intent to choke the very life from him. He abruptly pushed the image aside and returned his focus to Vitus and the contest about to begin.

Glancing towards Violetta he wished that she could be excused from the room or hide behind Meridius. It looked like she was barely breathing when Vitus picked up the blades offered to him and swung them in a simple arch before pointing them at the gladiator. He looked at his father for permission to begin the match after smirking at Tertius. "Apologies for the loss of your man. I am certain you have many more brutes of his like within your ludus stables." He laughed aloud and moved into the proper position to begin the contest.

Cassian eyed his opponent, felt the rage rolling off him in waves and set aside his own. He had seen firsthand how the allowance of such emotions could see a man to his death. It would not be his death today, for he had a greater cause to live than ever before and he would not fail. He assumed his position in the space that had been cleared and bowed respectfully to Felix and to Tertius before he nodded his head to the new Roman whose eyes he had felt upon him since he entered. "With permission, Dominus, we shall begin." With the nod from the men he prepared his stance for the attack of Vitus.

"Begin!" Felix called to the men ready to fight. After a brief look to the lanista he smiled indulgently and looked at Violetta who had a face filled with fear. "More wine Violetta." He ordered curtly then raised a cup in acknowledgment of the strange, dignified Roman before choking on a laugh as he spotted Selenia attempting to flirt with the man that had several years in age on her own father.

At the word of Felix, Vitus began his attack with a vicious slash at Cassian's chest while stepping towards him aggressively, attempting to make Cassian back down.

Vitus grinned when a few of the women in the crowd gasped at his boldness, he obviously intended to impress them all with his skill. They had discounted him as a spoiled son of a merchant that was softer than all of them, but with each stroke of his swords that drove their champion backwards, he thought to gain their respect.

It was simple but nimble footwork that allowed Cassian to dodge to one side, spinning around to allow himself the opportunity to return his attack with a deadly speed unlike anything he had done in months. He thrust the point of one gladius towards Vitus' midriff while using the other to parry his attack.

Vitus pulled back at the last moment to avoid the pierce of the blade. He disengaged to step left, tightening his grip before swinging his arm in an arc that brought the gladius down towards the gladiator's shoulder. The spray of blood would have covered half the room and Cassian would have been crippled forever if it had connected.

It was easy to move his body away from the falling blade, the attack was like that of a recruit upon the ludus sands. He crossed his blades against those of Vitus and used his greater strength to force the man's arms upwards thus bringing the tips of his own weapons towards his throat. Their eyes met and flashed with rage though any Roman in the room would have been hard pressed to determine who bore the greater hatred; the champion or the man who wished to defeat him.

It was with a snarl of frustration that Vitus pulled his head back away from the deadly steel. Moving quickly, he brought his foot up to plant a heavy blow on the chest of Cassian, meant to throw him off balance and give the Roman an opportunity to get out of his reach and prepare for the next blow.

"Slave scum. You think you can really win? Even IF you are victorious in this match you will still lose. Her, your life, your title, will all be stripped from you eventually and I will be there to see it."

He reeled from the kick, his balance thrown by the unexpected move, but it took only a breath to see it restored. "That took some skill." He growled at Vitus. "But you do not have what it takes to see your greatest wish fulfilled. Come at me again in attempt to impress." His lips spread in a grin. "If you think yourself able."

He lunged forward with a grace and precision like a lightning strike and just as deadly. His blows fell upon the opposite shoulder and the steel found its mark between Vitus's shoulder and the armor protecting it. Blood was the evidence of the success of his blow as it began to seep from the seam.

Vitus cried out with rage and instinctively brought the back of his hand across the other man's face which brought a snicker of amusement from a few men in the room. Cassian did not care but had to hold back laughter when Vitus snarled. "I have skills and strength that would surprise you, were you to live long enough to witness the fullness of my power." He prepared his sword for another attack, but the pain from his injury made it impossible.

A grunt of disgust escaped Cassian's lips at Vitus' reaction to the pain. The man showed his deficiency with such a blow and he was not the only man who was aware of it if the noise of Vitus' peers was any indication.

Thinking quickly, the gladiator let go of the blade in his left hand and spun on his heel, giving himself the opportunity to duck low and roll towards the discarded weapon and returning to his upright stance behind the Roman before he had a chance to understand what had happened. Closing his free hand over his shoulder Cassian drove a knee into the base of the Roman's spine. "Which of us stands surprised now?"

The room was silent at the boldness of the gladiator and more than a few heard the gasp from Violetta when he dove to the ground. She had taken a step towards them, but the warning hand of Meridius was on her shoulder stopping her before it was noticed. He could not risk even a gesture to calm her in a room that was silently staring at the battling warriors. When Cassian delivered the blow to Vitus' lower spine, she looked like she would have cheered aloud but managed to cover her mouth before the sound escaped.

With a dark grin Cassian gripped Vitus by the hair and wrenched his head back. Bringing the edge of his blade to rest against his throat, pressing hard enough to draw blood if the man moved too quickly.

"Beg Missio." He growled. "Raise hand or see yourself to the gates of Hades before you draw your next breath." He turned his eyes to look at Felix while waiting for the man on his knees to make the choice that they all knew he would: life.

Felix raised his brow and glared pointedly at his son who knelt, gasping against the steel pressing the vein that could send his life blood spraying across the floor. He was not pleased to have all his plans threatened because his son was pathetically stubborn.

"Fucking slave." Vitus snarled, dropping his sword and while the rest of the company gasped at the sight, he raised his hand in the demanded gesture.

Cassian could tell that he was angry at being defeated but it would be worse when he realized that, to a man, those gathered had expected and perhaps hoped that he would die at the hands of their champion. They had never wanted him to win. "Remove hands from my person and return to your master, dog." He spat, struggling to try and stand while Cassian's iron grip held him firmly in place.

"I am no dog but perhaps a wolf." Cassian smirked, standing tall. "My name is not slave but Cassian, champion of this city and future champion of all the Republic if granted the chance in Rome itself." His eyes were locked with Tertius' as he issued a challenge to the lanista to see him to the capital and give him the chance to prove his boast.

Returning his attention to Vitus he added. "There was once a time when I was a man of greater standing than you shall ever be. You would do well to remember that." With a bow of his head in the direction of Felix he stepped away to the side of the room, behind Tertius, where his eyes could rest on Violetta unhindered.

Vitus turned to look at the man who had held his life at the edge of his swords, hatred dripping like wine from his tongue as he spat. "You stand a slave and will be so until Hades takes you." He rose to his feet and put his hand to where the blood was flowing freely on his arm and barked in Violetta's direction. "Attend. You will see this stitched, bring wine. Now."

"No!" The protest was a reflex, the instinct to protect her powerful in its need. "She is not yours. Is there no medicus in this house?" He looked around the room, fighting to keep the fear he felt growing inside his chest at bay. Cassian knew that if Violetta left the room with Vitus it would be her that would carry the weight of the Roman's defeat.

When no one moved or spoke he stepped from the wall, past a glaring Tertius, to face the merchant. "Fuck the gods, Dominus. I did as you asked and spared the life of your son. He will bring her to harm and every person in this room knows that to be truth." His dignity set aside he lowered himself to his knees before Felix in the hopes that his plea might be considered. "Please, see her spared."

Felix looked at him upon his knees and then at the back of his departing son before nodding at Tertius. "Rise Cassian, it does not suit a champion to kneel the night of his victory. Meridius will be the one to see Vitus to the medicus." He stepped towards Cassian and put his hand on his shoulder. "You have my gratitude for the life of my son, and it will be shown." He turned his head to look at the woman whose protection humbled a champion. "See wine brought to a man much deserving of it so that we may all raise cup in a toast to the champion of our city." Felix called to the crowd that raised their voices in response to his suggestion before returning to their talk of what they had witnessed.

Coming to his feet and standing to his full height Cassian offered a tense smile and nod.

"Gratitude. I pray that the gods see this as an end to the discontent of your son and his enmity towards me, but I fear that it has now only been increased. Faced with a loss before his peers and his noble father will he not find another way to win in his own eyes?" He looked at Violetta. "Will he not continue to attempt to destroy innocence for his vengeance?"

When his words were met with nothing more than the turned back of the man he spoke to, he knew that little else would be done. Raising his head once more he found the eyes of the Roman all had deferred to watching him carefully. The man looked about to approach him when he felt a soft touch at his elbow, and he could not help the smile that spread across his face when he turned to greet her.

"I swear to the gods I can almost taste you." He whispered, wrapping his hands over hers as they held out the cup of wine. His lips spread in a wicked grin, the aftermath of the fight left him hungry for her and there was only one way to appease that desire. "Your hands shake, do you find yourself fearful in the presence of a god?" He teased, a softness in his voice saved for her ears alone. "He will not hurt you again, I will find a way to make it so. Put fear aside, I would see you smile."

Violetta smiled briefly, his teasing having the effect he intended. "The taste of you still lingers upon my lips, keeping sweet memories close to thought." She whispered in return, looking around the room, her eyes lingering on the doorway that Vitus exited through. "I have no fear of the god but find the excitement of his blade at the throat of my oppressor to be more thrilling than I have words to voice. It makes the hands unsteady but trust that the heart soars."

He felt the eyes of not only their respective Dominus' upon them but the stately Roman that still sparked his curiosity. She must have felt it too for she asked softly. "They watch, for what?" He fought the urge to curl her to his chest and take her anywhere but that room and make love to her until they both could do nothing but sleep. The press of those around them impressed upon him the impossibility of both those thoughts but he wanted them nonetheless.

CHAPTER 21

"That is a joy that is as satisfying as it is short-lived." Cassian said, taking a deep drink of the wine she offered as he watched where she was looking. "Do not worry what they look at or why. I have learned to give no care for their interest until it forces itself upon me." He did not think of how often that had been the case when a woman of some standing had taken it in her mind that she wanted to bed the savage gladiator who refused to allow himself to be groomed to the likeness of those around him.

He had no way to know if Tertius would remove him from the villa and return him to the ludus that night or if this brief encounter in the middle of a room full of Romans would be the last time that he saw Violetta. Determined to make the most of the moment that they had he slid his arm around her waist and pulled her gently against his muscled frame, not caring that the sweat from his efforts would dampen her dress. "Kiss me Violetta, here and now, I need you." His voice was a blend of command and begging, his lips teasing at the edge of her own waiting for her permission to go further and take what plunder he wished of her in that space.

A quiet laugh broke from her lips when he pulled her close. "I care not if the rest of Velletri sees us but if Felix or your Dominus learn the truth will we be safe from their use as pawns?" Returning the passionate kiss, she whispered. "My thoughts turn from Romans to the deity who owns my heart and my devout desire to worship him and him alone."

He knew that it was bold and perhaps foolish, to embrace her in the presence of the elite who were whispering and muttering as they stared at the lovers locked in their embrace.

Would they suffer the wrath of their masters in the morning for this display of unbridled affection? His lips fell to her neck and she moaned, and his care for the next day disappeared while he held her, stroking the demand rising between them. If only there stood a chance at a more private joining but it would not be allowed.

Felix turned his head at the same moment the two slaves pressed their lips together and raised both brows in amusement and a small amount of agitation. Stepping closer to speak to the lanista he asked in a quiet voice, not to be overheard. "It seems your man is one of honor. Though I do not think it was easy to grant the missio to my son. What thoughts do you have towards the pair?" He gestured towards Cassian and Violetta, causing him to hold her tighter. "He spouts words of no affection between them, yet he bends knee to beg for her safety. What kind of man does that for a woman he holds no affection for?" He took a long draught of his wine while awaiting his answer.

Taking back his glass of wine from Jovian, Tertius answered. "Cassian is a man of the highest honor. He has always been that way though it has not always been to my advantage." With a deep breath, the lanista added. "He loved a woman once, the wife of my Doctore who manipulated his affections in an attempt to sway him from showcasing his best skills so that her husband could remain the champion of my house after receiving injuries in the arena."

He shook his head and turned so that Cassian could no longer see his lips or hear his voice clearly as he continued. "She died in his arms, after drinking a poison meant for Cassian that was sent in a jug of wine from a man enraged that I would not sell him. The man carries the guilt as though the fault was his own. He was never told that she was a part of the plot to end his life and had she not died that night she was to have been put upon the cross the next day." Turning back to look at Cassian he added. "It nearly broke him. There were nights that I heard him myself, begging his gods, in tears, to forgive whatever sin it was that had caused them to take her from him. Never did I think to see him hold another woman with affection but if his actions today are to be believed I think he would give anything in sacrifice for your girl."

"So it would seem." Felix replied with a smile that bordered on devious. "All the more fortuitous for profitable ventures." His eyes shone with the effects of quality wine while scanning the guests and landing upon the strange Roman Cassian had not recognized. "Titus Claudius!" He called from across the room, unknowingly alerting the gladiator to the mysterious man's identity. Sweeping towards him, dragging Tertius by the arm and obviously eager to introduce the pair, Felix was not about to see this solitary chance wasted. "The gods favor me with your presence Titus." He said, passing Cassian and Violetta as though they did not exist in his hurry.

The steely blue eyes looked up from the inane banter of the magistrate when his host greeted him loudly by his name. "Felix, gratitude for the invitation. I had been searching for an excuse to come to fair Velletri. Had I known your celebrations boasted such quality entertainment I would have made a point to spend the summer here." He sipped his wine carefully before continuing. "Interesting wine, from Germania?" His brow arched as the merchant began to sweat as though caught in some grievous error. "It is a change from the Falerian I usually favor. Always good to cleanse the pallet is it not?"

Felix smiled nervously. "Had I known that you would grace us with your presence I would have secured more but what I have is at your disposal." He looked around the room, from the gladiator to the doorway that his son would soon return from. "I only wish it had been a better match than my son. I had intentions towards a different showing, but the circumstances of the day saw it changed." He snapped his fingers towards Violetta. "But let me see that your wine, at least, meets expectations. Violetta. Attend the senator with the Falerian wine and see his cup well filled tonight." When Titus nodded his gratitude Felix smiled, much more relaxed to the observant eye of the gladiator who was studying them both. "Tell me what you think of our fair city now that we have managed to bring you here at long last."

Cassian wanted to lose himself in the complete bliss of holding Violetta in his arms, kissing her with passionate abandon despite standing in a room surrounded by Romans. It was like a dream that he was rudely woken from by Felix and Tiberius' scheming and then they commanded that Violetta leave him to serve the Roman that he knew by reputation alone? This was the man that had possessed Proximus?

He slowly loosened his hold on his woman and whispered. "Go, I will be here. You are safe." No sooner had she stepped to obey her master than the voice of his son could be heard bellowing the announcement of his return. "The shit returns." He murmured and angled himself to shield Violetta from immediate sight as much as he was able though there was little he could do to stop his wrath should it be directed at the innocent target.

Vitus scanned the room as he came to its entrance, in no mood to deal with his father's most favored 'pet' Spaniard.

"Bring me wine and be quick about it." He snarled over his shoulder to Meridius and strode down among the other guests, many of whom smiled smugly then looked away in their amusement at his defeat. He stopped in his tracks when he saw his father and Tertius conversing with Titus Claudius, his face showed the realization that he had been bested, by a slave, in front of the greatest commander of the Roman army.

A dangerous rage flooded his face that caused Cassian to shudder. Someone would pay for the man's humiliation but how could he prevent such an action? How could he protect what would hurt him the most, his heart?

Cassian stood still as a statue while Violetta carried the jug of expensive wine in one hand with an elegant cup in the other. He watched when she offered the cup to Titus Claudius as he spoke with Felix and Tertius. His ears strained to hear each word, grateful they stood not far from him. "The Falerian as you commanded Dominus." She said softly, her eyes cast to the ground aware that the fabric she wore was sheer and that the men she served could see every inch of her body. Her cheeks flushed, as though she could feel their eyes on her like hands, and all she wanted to do was to run and hide. It would not be allowed, so he watched as she gathered the strength to ignore her exhibition and do as commanded, serve the expensive wine to a guest he feared could be just as costly to them both.

"Would you have me bring a plate as well, Dominus?" Violetta looked at Titus instead of Felix and found him staring not at her body but into her eyes as he nodded for her to bring the food. Cassian was on edge until she stepped away to find Jovian beside her seeking the same food for their master.

"They watch you like eagles watch a dove." The Syrian said with a smirk. "It is as though they cannot decide if they will devour you or protect you." He helped her pile the plates for Felix and Titus before turning to return to their masters. "He will sacrifice anything to save you, know that in your heart. There is little he would not do or give to see you safe, if it is in his power." The boy glanced towards Cassian who was still watching every step they took. "Do not doubt him, he cares more than he should."

"What do you mean?" She asked in a whisper, throwing her eyes towards her champion then back to the man beside her. "More than he should?" Did Jovian think that she would hurt him? That she had the power to break the heart of a man that had stolen half the hearts in the city? "I do not doubt his desire or intent but the capability to carry it out is near impossible." She shook her head sadly, they would never be able to be together as they wished, not while she was owned by Felix. "I too have a care for him, he holds my heart."

Jovian's expression softened. "Then be careful and pray that both the Roman and gladiator have enough sense in them to see that you are the best thing that has ever come into his world and he needs you as much or more than you need him."

They returned to the company of the Romans and Jovian returned to his fawning flirtatious persona, feeding his Dominus while silently flirting with Felix with his kohled eyes and painted lips. The boy was incorrigible, but the distraction was working; Felix smiled with an unmistakable light in his eyes.

Violetta was pouring wine for the men and cast a fearful glance in Vitus' direction as he entered the room. He stepped towards the lanista, calling in a friendly voice. "Tertius, your man is a mad shit but, as all well-trained dogs, he performs well to please his master." To the casual glance he was smiling and happy, but she could see the rage simmering below the surface in his eyes. "Though with such skill must come pride. Do you not think it would be good to see him humbled? Before he becomes a danger."

If he had disliked Cassian before, surely, he now hated him and would pray that he found himself on the wrong end of a gladius or even better; the cross. She wondered, if he hated the gladiator, was his master covered with the same blanket? Violetta had heard that Tertius sought to rise above his station as lanista with dealings and flattery for those he was trying to impress. She knew that if Vitus was determined to put a stop to whatever small rise for Tertius and Cassian this night could achieve he would do anything, even faking laughter at his own expense, to see his father stopped from furthering the deal.

"A mad shit?" Tertius asked with a tilt of his head, meeting the younger Census' statement with a barely hidden disdain as he turned on his heel to face the defeated man. "Why would I seek to humble the champion of our city when it is his pride that sends him to the sands assured of victory?"

Violetta thought he was being careful with his words, so he did not risk the displeasure of Felix and put into jeopardy the plans that they had been working so hard towards. "The man met your challenge and yet you still breathe. There is no need to attempt to see him put down for doing as he was trained."

Vitus seemed dangerously on edge but there was no fault to be found in the gladiator's actions except perhaps that the crowd had wished for blood they did not receive. She still thought it was a miracle that Cassian had been convinced to allow the missio for it would have been easy for him to find a way around it and end the younger Census' life.

"You are not the first man nor the first Roman to fall to his skill, there is no shame in such a thing, except in your own mind." Tertius said with a finality Vitus was not likely to accept.

Vitus' lip curled in disdain, making Violetta cringe at the memories it invoked. "Apologies if I am a man who likes to make sure that a slave knows its place and use." He emphasized his point when Violetta refilled the lanista's cup by running his hand down her back to cup her bottom. "The man sought to impress upon me that he and I were of equal quality but for his brand."

He laughed as did a few others around him, ignoring the flush of embarrassment on her cheeks.

"Though you are right, perhaps I should break words of congratulations to him. I am sure that he will expect a reward for his victory," He addressed his father. "Do you intend to award him the same prize as his last victory since his loss in the lanista's villa was treated as such in your agreement? Perhaps he has tired of her and would like something new and fresh in his arms." He smiled to himself while the memory of that night made Violetta want to weep at the sweetness. "What say you Tertius? Should I speak to your man, your champion?"

Tertius glanced at Cassian and waved his hand dismissively. "Break what words you will. I stand certain my man will see you treated with all respect due to you. I had given no thought towards reward but yes, perhaps you would like to be the one to present it to him. If your father is finished with her services with the wine?" He looked at Felix with a conspiratory smirk on his lips that the merchant returned with a smile and a nod of agreement that sent a thrill through Violetta.

Smirking, Vitus drank deeply from his cup and took Violetta by the arm. "I shall most assuredly bring the man his due." Crossing the floor to stand before the night's victor he noted the untouched wine at his side. "Do you spurn my father's generosity Cassian? Is his wine beneath the great gladiator?" He pushed Violetta forward. "Or is it simply his slaves that you wish to partake of?" The taunt hit its mark. She saw the anger flash in his eyes that she was once again a pawn at play in his games. Eventually he would snap and then Vitus would demand that he be put down like the dog he thought Cassian was.

"Dominus." He bowed his head slightly to the man. It took all her control not to pull from Vitus and hide behind her lover, using him as a shield to keep her protected. "The wine is above such simple tastes as mine. The vintage is rare and should be given to one who can appreciate its quality. That is not me. Though its offering is much appreciated I am unworthy. Your father has my gratitude. For many things." She prayed he could see the fools' game and would not fall to such obvious folly. "You bring with you that which I stand most grateful for the giving of. Am I to be granted the reward promised then?" He asked with a grin that she could not help but share for a moment.

Vitus's laughter sent a shiver down Violetta's spine as he moved closer to his target, letting it appear that he was in the best of humors while breaking words with the gladiator. "You are unworthy of it, as you are unworthy of so much else

Cassian." He said pointedly, moving aside so that both of them could see the woman standing behind him, nervous and fidgeting.

When she turned away from his stare Vitus hissed with pleasure at the sight of the healing wounds on her back, the memory of her pain bringing him back to the edge of pleasure. "You will return to your ludus soon gladiator." He said in a whisper as he put an arm across the man's shoulder and picked up the cup of wine. Pressing the silver into his hand he added "I insist, enjoy what luxuries stand available to you now for it will not always be so."

CHAPTER 22

Vitus watched the realization of his veiled threat sink in before he stepped away, his hand caressing the woman who stood frozen at his closeness. Leaving them, he rejoined his father and the imperator who stood discussing matters of the senate and those they were both familiar with.

"There are so many among the senators that do not have your head for business Felix. Yet I must suffer their attempts and those that seek advice as though I am a councillor instead of a commander and politician." Claudius laughed as he drank deeply of the expensive wine. "Though there is one, Julius Textus, you may have heard of him even this far removed from the capital. He stands alone as a man that I watch with greatest interest though he does not yet bear the rank of Legatus."

Felix laughed and nodded. "I have often found those of the senate to be, at best, small minded but you are a man of a different sort and impossible not to respect." He replied, sipping the fine wine to savor the tart flavor before he held out the cup for Jovian to refill since he had taken the place of Violetta when Vitus had taken her to be given to the night's victor. "The name of Textus has reached my ear in more than one conversation in recent months." He smirked and added. "But I had heard that he was more of a wild dog than a man for such hallowed halls as the senate. His results in battle are something that cannot be contested though."

It was Tertius that joined the conversation then, much to the disgust of Vitus who thought the same as many others in the city: that the man had no business attempting to raise himself so far above his station. "I have heard of the man even in my humble trade. They call him 'The Wolf of the Battlefield' and even now I have a man training to show the good people of Velletri the story of one of his victories over the Thracians. Such a man would be wisely kept to your side, even a mad dog has his uses does he not?" The lanista grinned as Felix and Titus Claudius both laughed and Tertius pressed his luck just a little more. "Come Titus, you must meet the man behind the night's entertainment before he is whisked away to enjoy the baser pleasures of a gladiator's victory."

Felix nodded as they began to walk across the room, Vitus walking just behind them as he added. "You speak truth good Tertius. One can never know when the aid of a savage may be what is needed the most." Census and Claudius shared a brief smile over that subtle dig to the lanista and his push for advancement while Vitus chuckled out loud. He had been about to suggest an introduction himself when the lanista beat him to the words. His father obviously hoped that this meeting might blossom a need to further the union between the two houses. The knowledge of the Imperator's love of the games was what Felix had planned to use to bring himself to

Rome itself and thus place him in the position to further his wealth through the coin lined pockets of the senate.

"Be wary Titus, the man Cassian is a savage that would rival even your wolf Textus." Vitus said, forcing himself into the conversation and making eyes with the man he mocked. Noting that the slave still had not consumed the wine he forced it back into his hand

"I have been called much worse by lesser men than yourself Dominus." Cassian quipped before drinking the rich red alcohol. "I offer my gratitude for fine drink and the training, both are well received, I hope to your pleasure." Vitus noticed that a few others of the city's elite had joined the small group. "My only apology is that the match did not last as long as I had hoped though I cannot claim the fault for that."

Vitus chuckled, using the sound to give him a moment to hide his true feelings of anger as the others enjoyed the laughter at his expense. His eyes met the Imperators before locking with the mirthful eyes of Cassian. "If ever a chance is afforded to cross blades with you again trust that it will end differently as my greatest wish would be realized." He nodded to the slave then returned his focus to his fellow Romans, forcing himself not to look around the room for Violetta, who was not next to the man he had left her with. His instinct was to find the woman and force her to his side, attending to his every need, but he would not lower himself again just to find her.

The Celt smirked. "Your wish for death is well noted Dominus. If it is truly your desire then if we find ourselves crossing blades again, you would be better served to see your father stayed from making bargains that see your life spared, again. With hands unfettered I would gladly see your wish granted with true contest."

The amused look on Claudius' face coupled with the shocked outrage on Tertius' sent the slave's head to the expected bowed submission when faced with the men who could control his life and his death which Vitus still wanted more than his next breath.

Vitus held his father's wine when Felix threw his arm about Claudius' shoulder and drew him nearer to the gladiator, Tertius hovering, anxiously watching for trouble.

"Come Titus, let me present to you the champion of the night and of our fair city, Cassian. The Celt stands a god of the sands, his training seen to by the man behind you: Tiberius Tertius. He stands a lanista for now, but I can tell you he is a man of loftier ambitions." The merchant leaned closer to whisper loudly "He is a man that I call partner in some ventures. His stable of gladiators is most impressive, though I am told he is not easily convinced for their sale I had thought towards bringing some to Rome and perhaps engaging them against your own?"

When the Imperator raised his brows in thought Felix quickly turned to Vitus, likely hoping to stop him from making a statement that could jeopardize the deal he was negotiating.

"I trust the wound brought by vanity does not sting beyond bearing or beyond the grasping of the lesson delivered with it."

The question was weighted, as was the look he gave, one of scolding command to play the part of obedient son no matter his personal feelings. Vitus obeyed but there would be a price to pay later.

Claudius smiled, nodding to the lanista and merchant but ignoring Vitus, to his irritation. "I can see that his reputation is not inflated, his skill is unrivaled in the city though perhaps Rome would find something to offer in challenge. Our own champion against your own perhaps?" He looked at Tertius. "It would be at my invitation and you would be my guests in the city. It would be my honor to host you both." Vitus wanted to laugh. They all knew it was unlikely that the lanista had the coin to stay anywhere that would not come with an infestation of fleas.

"You are too kind, Claudius, and I would be thrilled to accept your offer. Cassian shall return to training at dawn to see him prepared for the match to be set at your leisure. I would ask a month to see him and a few others of note into top condition to give the best performance possible." Tertius said, giving the gladiator a nod that he had done well with his boast. "Is there a man to meet him? I do not know of any that hold such distinction."

The lanista grinned at the people of his city, encouraging their belief that their champion could best all others though Vitus was already planning a celebration of his death.

"I know just such a man, Tertius, as to give your Dimachaerus a test to his skill unlike anything he has yet faced. Finnicius is a Retiarius champion of Rome and many would put coin forward in wagers between the two great fighters." Claudius said with a look of utter surety on his face that Vitus envied for its confidence.

If the man was as good as the rumors about him, he might be more than a proper challenge for Cassian. He might even be good enough to end the Celt's life.

"Soon this match shall be heralded throughout Rome and the great Circus Maximus shall be filled with those who wish to see the match play out between the greatest champions of the Republic." Titus raised the gladiator's head until their eyes met. "What say you to that challenge Cassian? Do you wish such a match?"

Vitus watched as from beneath hooded eyes Cassian studied the great Roman. Everything about him spoke of wealth and refinement but it was hard to determine the true depth of his intention. Titus's gaze was guarded though it scrutinized every breath taken by those around him. Claudius was a predator of the highest standard and it took a man of equal nature to see it and Vitus was just such an animal.

This match had the potential to make Cassian the champion of the entire Republic, a man sought after by many, the elite fighter and perhaps a man of enough influence that he could convince Tertius and Felix to see Violetta purchased if not freed entirely. There had never been a Retiarius in Velletri, but the man looked determined to face this new enemy. Finally, he answered Titus.

"I stand and fight at your will and that of my Dominus, should he wish it." Cassian said flatly, keeping his eyes locked with the Vitus.

"You think the man is worth that kind of time and investment? From this small match alone?" Vitus said in confusion before he realized that he sounded the petty child his father expected him to be. Quickly placing a near mocking smile upon his lips while he sipped the Falerian wine he continued "It was not a proper showing of skill from either combatant, I would hate for not only your coin but the time of the people of Rome to be wasted on a man destined never to rise further than he stands now. The blemish on your reputation is something else to be considered."

His eyes danced back and forth between the lanista and his gladiator, his words carrying meaning for them both. "Though it is hardly my place to comment on such things for a man of your standing, merely an observation."

His father glared at him as Claudius drank his wine, ignoring Vitus who realized he had made a fool of himself.

"Indeed, it is not your place." Felix growled. "Go and find other ears to hear your prattle. You have no concept of the arena or the men that fight within them as your demonstration tonight shows us."

As soon as he had removed himself from the immediate area Vitus watched as his father returned his attention to the important guest ignoring his son completely.

"It would be a glorious match between the Retiarius and Dimachaerus, would you not agree Tertius? We should make it so and have your man returned to his training as soon as is possible."

He could see his father was eager to close the deal with both men; Tertius, who looked to the care of his man above all and Titus Claudius who was known to have a softer hand regarding the care of his slaves.

"Cassian," He addressed the champion. "You should go and have armor removed. I will send Violetta to attend your needs, whatever they may be." Vitus downed his drink and turned away, his face a mask of anger.

CHAPTER 23

Violetta could hardly believe what the merchant was telling them. After they spent the day in isolation due to stealing what the man considered his own, he now offered it freely as though the most natural thing in the world.

"Gratitude Dominus." Cassian said, hiding any surprise he might have felt. "Given the chance I would see your eyes filled with a spectacle the likes of which you have never seen before." He bowed his head and stepped away, walking slowly as though he waited for her to follow him.

She would be in his arms within moments and there stood the chance that he could stand the champion of all the Republic. She was baffled at how the day had led to this, all seemed to be aligning for the greatest things she had ever dared to desire. Would the gods allow it or was there something more that they hid to see that her joy was not perfect?

Jovian made his way to her side as Cassian kept walking from the room. He made sure to deliberately get in the way of Meridius so that the leanly muscled Spaniard crashed against his slender body and gave him the perfect excuse to rub his hands across his sculpted chest before insisting on his leaving him alone with her. Meridius' eyes and the set of his mouth protested but, in the end, he left the two of them alone in the shadows.

"You watch him, he watches you and the Roman watches you both. What did you do to make them both lust for you so strongly?" He asked, leaning languidly against the wall like a lazy child, avoiding a task that he must do. "I have never seen men like this over a woman, let alone a slave. Tell me the secret and then I will take you to Cassian. He will soon remove his armor and I promise he would rather have you do so than to do it himself."

He moved behind her, and Violetta could feel his breath on her neck as his hands slowly came to rest on her hips. "I have no secret except myself." She whispered, forcing herself to calmness under his unwanted attention. "I play no games, do not flirt with others and then deny them. I am only myself, always, to the men who stand my Elysium and Hades both. There is no victory in this, nothing for you to learn or envy." She turned her head to look at him. "You have the eye of all upon you. You flirt with slave and Roman alike and yet you want what you think I have?" She shook her head, her hair brushing against his chest. "I do not think you know the cost of your desire nor do I think, in the end, you would pay it."

She left him to make her way through the door that Cassian had used for his exit, hoping to be able to make her way to him in time since it seemed that Felix had given her to his arms once again. She did not look back to see the troubled expression on her young friend's face, but she knew that he was confused in more ways than just one.

Now that the match was over his armor must weigh heavy upon his shoulders, chafing his skin with each move. Rarely did a gladiator wait before removing the heavy leather protection but she knew that if it was not done soon the rub would turn to blisters which could make the next match dangerously uncomfortable.

The hall light was dim, but she saw him reaching the door of the room that held the casing for his armor, his entire body moved with a sigh. Perhaps he thought it had been a lie that she would be allowed to come to him? Words to placate the gladiator and make the merchant look indulgent in the eyes of his guest?

She snuck to the doorway to watch as he stepped towards the empty cases to begin removing his armor so that he could return to the celebration and gaze upon her even if he was not allowed to hold her.

"If I had her here there is nothing that could take her from me before I made sure she knows what she means to me. The very beat of my heart is for her."

"As hers is for you." Violetta said softly stepping into the room.

She had been awestruck by his silhouette against the dim light of the candles, the outline of a god in her mind. Her journey to join him had been delayed by her care in making sure that she was not followed or summoned to return to serve the others in the room. She had ensured that Felix, the lanista and the honored guest had full cups before she left, remarkably both the lanista and Imperator had looked at her kindly, Claudius had even thanked her with a smile. What it would be like to be owned by such men, ones without derangement, that did not take pleasure in the emotional agony they could cause those that served them. The moment that her champion turned to face her all other thoughts disappeared completely.

"I should help to remove what I put in place should I not?"

CHAPTER 24

He watched her so closely he could see the flutter of the pulse at the base of her neck. The soft scent of her was intoxication and engulfed his senses until he thought he might be drunk simply on the smell of her. "I would welcome the soft touch in its removal but, feel as though I should return the favor by removing the barrier between our flesh." He whispered, reaching a hand to her hip to draw her close and press himself against her softness, to drink her in with his eyes, his nose and lips.

A smile teased his lips as he bent his head to capture hers in a kiss as soft as the rose petals in the water basin beside him. His blood ran with need for her, like a fire in his veins but he would not risk frightening her with the intensity of his need. Slowly he brought his hand to loosen the knot at her shoulder. He slid the fabric aside as his mouth moved down the slender column of her neck until he brushed aside the sheer material allowing him access to taste the sweet berried peak of her breast.

Her breath caught when his lips touched her skin and when they closed around the sensitive bud, he felt her shiver with desire. Cassian smiled as her fingers worked quickly on the buckles at his shoulders, soon pushing away the heavy leather armor to let her fingers dance across his flesh. She stared at him as though memorizing every inch of him, leaning forward to flick her tongue against his chest.

"All barriers between us should be removed Cassian. Slowly and deliberately until there is nothing between us." She whispered

Soon he would be able to hold nothing back; every touch of his fingers, kiss of her lips was like lifting of the weight of chains. The physical proof of his need to claim her rising between them to strain against the leather covering his subligaria.

"Violetta…did they touch you? Did Tertius lay his hand upon you?" He whispered, holding back the groan of pleasure. His chest squeezed with the longing to join with her, to complete the union his heart ached for. The things she made him feel, with an innocent brush of her hand, were unlike anything he had ever felt before and for the first time he welcomed the change and the vulnerability she brought to him.

She shook her head in answer to his question, no one had laid hand upon her. The knowledge set his heart as free as his desire. His hands were like velvet covered steel, skimming up her sides to cup her curves in his palms. She was his personal Elysium, a shelter from the raging storm of agony and blood that was his life as a gladiator and slave. He could taste her need in the urgency of her kiss. The hunger building between them was like a spark catching the edge of a paper and bursting to life when he pressed her to the wall. His chest and shoulders were finally bare. The leather coverage at his waist soon joined the armor to leave only his legs covered beneath the knotted linen around his waist that barely contained the eager column of his masculinity.

"I need my woman, I need…you." He rasped, voice tight with the strain of holding back his eagerness while he gripped her breast and raised it higher, sucking it deeper into his mouth, drawing his teeth across it to make her whimper.

Her back against the wall Violetta quickly wrapped her legs around his waist, leaning back to let the wall take her weight while she licked and nipped at his ear and neck. Her hand slipped down to cup him through the linen, stroking, encouraging him to find a way to join their bodies the way their souls had come together. He raised his eyes to meet hers and his breath caught in his chest. He was danger and safety combined for her but there was nowhere else he would have her than within his arms feeding the fire that burned between them.

"Cassian. I need you as you need me." She whispered to him as she brushed a sweat soaked strand of hair from his temple. "Do not make me wait longer."

He wanted her, needed to bury himself inside her and feel her walls clench around him to complete their union again and again until there was nothing between them but the breath of the gods themselves.

Using the hand that was not supporting her Cassian raised the material of her dress then dropped it to push aside the cloth at his waist that stood as the barrier between their joining while his fingers slid around the curve of her thigh to tease her entry as he eased her closer to him. Carefully lowering her, he sheathed himself in the core of her passion. Feeling her tight, wet, heat a fulfilled moan slipped from his lips. The bliss he felt was like a delirium, fire and ice washing over him with waves of their passion. He met every move of her hips with one of his own, the taunting rhythm of her body calling to him and building the pain of his need. He sought to fill her, to empty his soul and his body into hers.

A whimper of rapture broke from Violetta's lips which she pressed to his temple in a silent plea for more. Her body rocked to match the rhythm he started; her own fire kindled by the sounds that escaped her lovers throat. She closed her eyes and gave herself over to him. She completely and utterly surrendered to the boldness of his possession.

He could feel the thundering of her heart against his chest and hear how her breath caught and hitched in his ear with each thrust. From the very moment he had entered her body he had felt nothing but bliss, known nothing but pleasure that sent his senses spiraling. He felt free, a true warrior in the throws of primal euphoric bliss. He thrust harder, reaching deeper into her soul. The ecstasy of their union brought his breath faster than ever before, it was rapture like nothing he had known in his life as they moved together in tandem towards the oncoming call of the heights of orgasm. He could not find words to express the depths of his feelings when she opened her eyes to lock with his, so he took her mouth with his in a kiss of possessive passion.

Her body tightened around him, so close to release that she could not keep her hands from moving frantically across his shoulders, clutching to pull him nearer. Her moans turned to ecstatic whimpers as he moved to take her harder, his cock touching the very mouth of her womb. In the flash of a moment he moved across a hidden nerve within her and she buried her face at his shoulder, his name ripping from her lips in a cry of euphoria.

Cassian's heartbeat grew near frantic, jarring in his chest like the blow of a hammer. He shuddered with the pleasure spreading through his entire body in waves of overwhelming power, the sensation exploding through him was a sweet ravishing of every sense he possessed, and he could not stop the low cry deep in his throat. It was infinite, an eternity of pulsing pleasures that he did not want to think of ending. They were straining together in an ever-escalating fever, blind with the deep satisfaction of this shared moment with her, a true cataclysm of pure bliss.

Violetta collapsed against him in the ebb of their shared orgasm, her lips fluttering across his flesh with a tiny flick of her tongue. She looked up at him with a lazy, dazed smile on her lips.

"You stand a triumphant god once again and have rendered me unable to even stand upon my own feet." Her body trembled in his hands, but his hold was secure and kept her close, safe, while she leaned her back against the cool stone of the wall behind her.

He stood, holding her close and inhaling her essence, content to his soul in the wake of their shared passion. Slowly he set her on her feet, helping to hold her up until she was steady enough to stand alone. He sucked in a deep breath, silent and thoughtful for a long moment before he cupped and raised her chin until their eyes met. Pressing a soft kiss to Violetta's forehead, he stroked a strand of hair away from her eyes.

"I love you Violetta and I will treasure you for all my life. You are the peace, the only peace, in my soul."

He pressed his lips to hers and pressed their foreheads together. Her innocence had been the greatest gift given to him. He had been the first man to teach her of love and passion which was something that would please him always, something he would enjoy teaching her more of as long as he was able to. A soft smile lit his eyes, chasing away the darkness that had started to claim them. "You have been the greatest gift of my life and I have never known such happiness in my life until you were brought into it."

She flushed slightly at his words. "It is I who holds the greater debt of joy between us Cassian. That you would return my affections was a thing I could never have hoped for. You stand the solitary light in my existence."

Had she ever known that there could be such emotion between a man and a woman? What had her parents showed her in the memories she had of them both as a child before slavery? "I would have you know that you possess me, heart and soul, in a way that no Dominus of Rome ever could, and I will stand yours and yours alone until Hades himself takes me." He nuzzled against her neck, hiding a smile as he kissed her down to her shoulder. He could not stop nipping and sucking, the taste of her was too sweet and his hunger for her was insatiable.

Her head bent, letting her long hair fall around them both in a curtain that tickled his bare chest, but it was not laughter that the soft touch sparked in his heart but rekindled desire. With an overpowering clarity, he realized that he wanted her again. Though not usually so impatient, all he could think about in that moment was sinking into her and taking her again with a mindless passion and power until oblivion overcame them both. His shaft throbbed near to painfully, his body responding to her words on a basic and primal level with a lust so pure and raw it threatened to make him the savage some made him out to be. With a groan Cassian fought his driving urges but instead he merely teased the outline of her lips with the speared tip of his tongue.

Violetta leaned into him, her arms entwining around his neck, then her lips parted at the urging of his tongue and her eyes opened briefly but the cry that came from her lips was not one of passion but of fear. A quick turn of his head revealed, leaning in the doorway, stood Vitus a vicious smile spreading across his face.

Pg 228

"Only a whore to serve the beckoning of your cock? I think not, gladiator." Slowly Vitus paced towards them, his smile turning to chuckles as Violetta curled against Cassian's chest. Her fear was evident and almost palpable.

"I think there is much, much more going on here." Vitus beamed, as though he had the pair just where he wanted them.

Had he heard their declarations of love to each other?

"You may fool my father's eyes, the old man does not see through the lies you spew from forked tongues, but I do." His eyes raked over them both, Violetta flinched from his gaze, but Cassian glared with a challenge that had nothing to do with the arena and everything to do with the viciousness of a man whose woman was under threat from another. Vitus might expose their affections to his father, or he could use them now against them both in a way that would devastate what they had built. They might fall apart in the wake of his actions and he would revel in their misery.

Cassian's hatred for this man above all others uncoiled like a snake. It filled his veins with venom, but instead of destroying him the poison made him bold, fearless except for her safety. "Then your sight is as flawed as your techniques with a sword. I but take the prize given to the victor of tonight's match." He wrapped his arm around her waist, pulling her close, keeping her safe from the hand of the Roman as she was his to protect.

"She was given to me for such purpose and I would see such a wondrous gift used as intended, to do otherwise would offer insult to your father." If it was possible to slay a man with just a look then Vitus would be taking his last breath upon the floor that moment for his glare was as sharp as a dagger. He appeared calm, undisturbed by the interruption, but there was little else he could do when faced with the intrusion on passion's indulgence but deny it, though it hurt him to do so with her in earshot.

Vitus moved closer, until they were eye to eye. "You lie. Do you think me deaf as well as blind? That I did not hear words broken of love and affection?" He slammed his forearm across the gladiator's throat, surprising him by pushing him to the wall. He was hoping to force him to release Violetta. "That she was given to you as a gift does not stand as a question. However," He brought his hand up to caress her cheek, growling at her instant recoil. "You deny the rights of her Dominus upon her body. Gift or not she is not yours and that is a lesson you will learn swiftly or see her put to pain for your ignorance."

Pain and shock shattered the composure he had fought for, just for an instant, but it brought his rage back to its peak. Perhaps the fool thought that he stood against a weaker man or that he would cower after being caught in the lies, but he would soon find that he was wrong, deathly wrong. He maintained his hold on Violetta, fighting through the asphyxiation and made use of his free hand to grab the arm that had struck without thought of his retaliation. Pulling Vitus even closer, he twisted his arm until it was pressed hard against his back.

"She is as much mine as she is yours for her ownership, her 'mastery' lies in the hands of your father and not you." He growled, increasing the pressure on his arm until it was near to breaking from the pressure.

Vitus' lip curled in an agonized snarl as the pressure and pain in his arm became near dizzying. "Slave dog!" He spat

"I would see you to the cross for this if not for the bargain between Tertius and my father." Sensing the man would not easily release his arm Vitus slowly moved the arm that had been at Cassian's throat to grasp the jaw of the woman at his side, clenching hard as his hand slid down further to encircle her slender throat. "If you break my bones you will die soon and in great agony. If I choke the life from a worthless used slave whore, I might only receive angry words from my father and perhaps even Tertius for upsetting his prized hound. Either way, you lose everything." He met the angry glare with one matching in hatred as Violetta began to cough against his grip.

Cassian drew a deep breath, holding it in his lungs until they burned. Instead of sighing in defeat he used the fuel to further his purpose and forced the Roman tight against his chest.

"Release hold upon her or die by my hands where you stand." In a move too quick for Vitus or his guards that had entered the small space to stop him Cassian released the pinned arm and gripped the man's throat instead. It forced Vitus to bend his arm, but he still did not let go of Violetta, who was now fighting to loosen his hand at her throat.

"Release her!" Cassian snarled. "I have no fear of death upon the cross if it stands as the price to see her free of you for the rest of her days."

CHAPTER 25

It took a moment, but Vitus released his grip. Violetta fell back against the wall, her hand to her throat as air filled her lungs once again causing her to cough as he laughed. She realized her distress was going to cause him amusement until the day one of them died. Shaking her head, she stood tall and managed to whisper "I am fine. It is fine now, Cassian."

"You think so? Little flower? Your lover betrays his heart." Vitus turned his attention to the gladiator who held him tight still. "You betray yourself with such words champion. Do you not think she would be swift to join you should my father find me dead by your hands?"

His actions had brought to light exactly what the Census' had suspected and now he would make use of their affections to cause them pain.

"She breathes freely now. Release hold or see her pain worsened again."

The next few seconds were a flurry of action; the pair of guards, that had not wanted to push him to deadly force, rushed forward, instantly seizing Cassian's arms to allow Vitus free from his grasp. It was only seconds longer before he was gripped and turned, his face shoved hard against the wall. Steel pressed to his back, Cassian's wrists were shackled together once again, and a guard growled harshly in his ear promising death should he dare to even twitch in the Roman's direction. It would have taken next to no effort to see himself free of their hold but anything he did, any action he took, would have a direct effect on Violetta and she knew he would not see her harmed again due to his actions.

This night was becoming agonizing for them both. Determined not to add to his torment Violetta released the breath she was holding and focused her gaze on him. She hoped that they could find strength together to survive whatever the sadist had in mind for his vengeance.

Breathing deep at the release of his throat, Vitus seemed determined not to give the gladiator the satisfaction of seeing him cough or struggle to regain his normal breathing, so he laughed as he watched the bonds placed upon him. He would try to break her lover now, tonight.

Violetta knew he would not accept that he was bested by a slave even if the man held the superior skill with a blade. If there was a way to see himself the victor, then he would find it. Glancing at Violetta, Vitus beckoned her to his side with a simple gesture. "Attend."

She did not hear him. She could not hear any sound but the shackles locking around the wrists of the man who loved her and the breaking of her heart for what this meant. Only the will of the Imperator could save them now and who knew if the man would still wish for him to fight in his Primus after the reports of such behavior reached his ears. Her eyes met those of her lover and tears began to stream down her cheeks. She took a step towards him but was shaken from her agonized stupor by the sound of Vitus once again barking her name. She turned her head just in time to see him start towards her, instinct kicked in immediately and she curled her head down into her chest in hopes to escape the blow that was coming.

Instead of a strike Vitus gripped a handful of her dark hair and began to drag her from the side of the gladiator. "You will attend, slave, or give cause for pain." Once he had her in the center of the room, he pulled her upright, facing the man she loved and commanding that he be turned to face them both while still pinned to the wall.

"What punishment would seem fitting for this offence in your mind?" He smirked as he asked, flicking his tongue against her cheek. He was going to taunt Cassian with each move until something inside the champion snapped and he turned into the mindless beast he was accused of being.

Violetta looked at her lover; his jaw was tight and sweat pearled on his brow before sliding down his face. She could see that it was taking every ounce of his being to hold back. There was little he could do that would not end in a catastrophe for her so there was nothing to do but admit that control was now in the hands of the monster who reveled in his cruelty and its effects.

Her breath sat frozen in her chest and her gut filled with loathing for the man who stood beside her. When Cassian saw the scene that Vitus intended to play out for his own amusement and their shared torture the unfamiliar expression of defeat washed over his handsome face. He was defenceless except for his words. "Her actions are nothing more than what I forced upon her and done in obedience to your own father who gave her to me this night, once again. If there is blame to be carried it should be mine. She should be left untouched in this feud between you and I." He growled.

Vitus grinned and burst into a dark laughter. "You are under the protection of Tertius and the Imperator has a desire to exploit your skill to his glory in Rome's games. As much as I would like to injure you, the lash against such proud flesh would please me more than any number of whores, it stands forbidden. This way you stay uninjured and yet will still be brought to knees to beg for my mercy." He tilted his head towards Violetta. "This means of discipline will have to satisfy in the absence of freedom to treat you as the common slave you are." He trailed the tip of his finger down her arm to emphasize his meaning and how he meant to make use of his victim.

Violetta's mind raced as she listened to their words, trying to think of a way that she could delay the actions of Vitus and give a chance for Cassian's Dominus to find them and put a stop to things before they got out of hand. "Dominus, please, he speaks the truth." She pleaded, trying to loosen his grip on her hair as he wrenched it painfully. "I had no choice in this. Your father commanded it."

"You stand the greatest coward I have ever seen Vitus Census." Cassian growled from the wall. "You would take vengeance upon an innocent woman instead of the man who truly brings you offence. You fear what your father would do to you and you know that you cannot best me in a fair fight, so you bring harm to the one I care for since you are not allowed anything else that might harm me." He was reaching now, trying to antagonize Vitus to the point where he would snap and forget that he was not to injure him. It was foolish, making himself the target, but if she were freed of the Roman's hands Violetta might be able to try to find Tertius or even Felix to tell them what went on here.

"Do not lie to me bitch!" Vitus roared at Violetta the same moment he brought his hand down in a ringing blow to her face that knocked her to the ground. "I heard you break words of affection between you." His head turned slowly to look at the man his father's guards were now struggling to restrain.

"A man who possessed decent sized balls would not use a woman to show off his supposed strength but would stand and fight those that challenged him. It is no wonder Felix Census stands ashamed of the man he is forced to acknowledge as his son, any father would feel the same if you were named their offspring and heir." Cassian called again from his position at the wall.

"You think me a coward gladiator?" He stepped closer and put a hand to the straining shoulder. Every muscle in his body tensed and his other hand closed in a fist. "You wish to be the one to receive the brunt of my anger? Of my vengeance?" He drove his fist into his stomach with surprising force. "Do you think me weak now?" He laughed, repeating the blows several times before raising his target to connect his fist to Cassian's eye, which sent the gladiator's head whipping back.

Violetta could not stop the tears on her cheeks or the agony she felt watching him be beaten like this because of her, for her. She slowly rose from the ground, her head ringing from the blow and the familiar sting of a bruise starting to burn on her cheeks but she could not let this happen for her. She reached towards Vitus to attempt to grab his hand and stop him from continuing his assault but before her hand could make contact the guard from the doorway came behind her and looped his arm about her waist, growling in her ear.

"Stay hand little shit or find it broken."

She stilled and let him pull her back, ignoring the fact that his armor pressed hard against her back while she stared helplessly at her lover's fading consciousness.

Vitus glanced at the guard now holding her then back to the bruised and bloodied man before him and laughed. "You wish to bear witness to the size of Roman balls gladiator? I will gladly make it so." He threw a final hard blow across his jaw before straightening his robes and instructing his men. "See her to my chamber and this shall be settled soon." He turned to face those holding the gladiator. "Chain his hands before him, they will find use before long."

"No!" It was an instinctual reaction, instant and savage, as though his soul was wrenched towards complete madness. She watched as Cassian pulled against the restraining arms, absent all thought except the primal need to see himself free. He stood near to a titan, possessing the physical power to destroy his opponents, he had the skill and cunning to see himself free of similar grips while fighting unarmed, yet his face was filled with hopelessness.

Cassian kept his eyes locked to hers, the golden amber pulling her into his soul, hoping for shared strength. He cried aloud as something snapped with Vitus' next blow and his head fell to his chest, with awareness now floating as though just beyond his grasp.

Violetta watched helplessly when Vitus took Cassian by the roots of his hair and lifted his head, leaning to hiss with a gleeful deviousness. "You will see both cock and balls of Rome tonight. Then let Jupiter judge which between us stands the victor." He released his hold and nodded to both guards. "See him wakened and washed. Then deliver him to my chambers as commanded with his hands shackled in front." Walking past Violetta and the man that held her from running to her lover he chuckled and made his way towards his chamber to await the fulfillment of his command.

The guard stood watching Cassian struggle for consciousness, his arm looped easily around the waist of his woman, with a hand grazing her hip and thigh where the dress was slit. "Is she worth this to you gladiator? You say she is nothing but a whore to fuck. You could have any woman in the city, but you risk Hades and the wrath of Vitus for her?" He put a hand under Violetta's chin, forcing her to raise her head to look at the bloodied face of her defender. "Is she truly such a prize?"

The man's question seemed to reach through the haze of pain and complete confusion from the assault. Cassian eyes were barely open, he was losing the battle for consciousness. "Is she a prize? Worth the fight?" He groaned and shook his head to try and clear his ringing mind. "I would risk all for her, now and always." He whispered as though to her ears alone. "What plan does he have for me to see cock and balls? I cannot understand his words." Blood from his bleeding nose dripped to his chest as he tried to raise his head to lock eyes with her before he sank to darkness.

"You shall see his intent soon enough, dog." The guard said with a laugh before addressing his comrades. "See him washed, Vitus will not want blood on his floors." He walked away from the semi-conscious man, pulling Violetta with him. "Come, little flower." He said, almost kindly, as he raised her eyes from the floor to look into his. "Vitus wishes some time alone with you while you await the arrival of your...champion." The word was a laugh as his eyes raked her body beneath the sheer dress. He brushed his hand from the base of her neck down her torso until he caught the chain that hung between her hands and pulled her against him. "We go now, regretfully."

Violetta cringed inwardly, wanting to run to Cassian and wash the blood from his face, kiss his lips and sooth the pain of his soul. That he endured this for her and still broke words that he would risk all for her, to save her, was unimaginable. She could not tell if her heart was breaking or soaring to the heights of the heavens on the knowledge that his love for her was strong enough to withstand the monster's plan. Vitus was going to use what he had learned that night against them both. She knew that there was nothing to be done but endure it, he would not break them, his power was not enough.

"Cassian…" She called to him before being dragged from his sight at last, hoping that her voice might give him some hope, carrying with it the strength of her conviction.

Cassian had been led away while Violetta had been taken in the opposite direction, half dragged, and half carried to Vitus' private chamber. The guard had skirted the scene of the festivities to roughly deposit her on the floor at his feet. "Leave us." Vitus said, crouching low and stroking a hand across her hair in a gesture that might have appeared kind and soothing, but it was a mockery and meant to bring terror to her. For she knew better than anyone in the house that when he was calm in the face of irritation, he was the most vicious. He had shown her on more than one occasion the true monster beneath his façade of calmness.

"You and I stand alone now Violetta. How about the truth hmm?"

He stared down into her fearful eyes as his hand slid to her throat, suddenly squeezing until her jaw fell open.

"Let there be no lies between us now Violetta, those sweet lips were meant for so much more." His lips spread into a smile that sent shivers down her spine as he revelled in her fear. "Do you still say you are nothing more than a prized whore to the gladiator?" He rubbed his thumb across her chin, running his eyes over her body.

Violetta's pulse raced as she bit back a cry of agony. She was sure that he meant to bring her pain, but she still thought to attempt to stave off his anger. "I swear Dominus, there is nothing more between us. What small affection there was fell as passing fancy to one who…" He stopped her words by sliding his hand over her mouth with a shake of his head.

"I commanded there to be no more lies and you seek to mock me with simple falsehoods that a child would not believe? I stand disappointed." Vitus' hand began to tighten, and her eyes widened in fear that he would end her life that moment and she would never get to see Cassian again.

CHAPTER 26

Cassian came back to awareness in the tub and surged to his feet, the water cascaded down his back as it splashed to the floor. He stood still for a moment before shaking his head, the wet strands of hair clinging to his shoulders and letting drops run down his back and arms to trickle down the thick pillars of his legs. His body glistened with the lingering moisture as he stood utterly naked while he attempted to gather his thoughts. The realization that he had not dreamed the events of moments before dawned slowly on his mind as he bent with a groan to pick up the cloth that had been left for him to dry with.

Staring at himself in the mirror the champion sighed at what he saw; the bulk of his leanly muscled body were impressive, and well he knew it. His body had the symmetry of form that came from years of training and the strength to match it. Despite the beating he had just endured, the bruising on his eye was deepening, there was no denying that to the naked eye he stood like a statue bronzed to perfection. Like the many titans and warriors of Olympus he was compared to, the supposed perfection of his body was marred by scars, the tokens of his victories. All of this meant less than nothing if he could not keep Violetta safe and alive.

His head cleared, and the words of the guards and Vitus came back to him, the thought of his woman in the arms of that savage brought him back to the height of his rage. He tied the linen left for him to wear about his waist and raised his burning eyes to meet the man who waited for him. "Take me to Vitus." He said, his voice deadly and toneless. "We will see this to an end tonight." He stepped free of the bathroom and followed the silent man hoping that he was not too late to spare the woman he loved from further pain. He would do whatever was needed to ensure Violetta's safety.

Cassian walked into Vitus' room, his escorts at his side, in absolute silence. The shackles were now binding his hands before him while his bare feet were soundless. A shove forced him inside the room where his eyes fell to his Violetta crouching on the floor, her eyes were wide and shoulders trembling within the Roman's vicious grip.

He tightened his jaw and, before he could stop himself, he growled. "You stand less a man with the passing of each moment and never less so than in this one. Only a coward uses violence and intimidation on the helpless."

"And you stand more the fool, a mere slave. Were it not for your skills in the arena you would be as worthless to the lanista as you are to me." Vitus said as he rose to his feet. "You think to stop my taking of her by crossing blades? By your manipulation of my father into bidding that she never be brought to the lash again?" He smirked with a shake of his head. "Your own Dominus and his pact with my father to earn small coin in return for introduction to those of note from Rome are all that protects you from the fate you deserve. The whip now stands too good for one such as you." He still held on to Violetta as he stepped towards the gladiator. "Despite all that, do not dare to think that you can rob me of my deserved retribution. There are other ways I would use to see the debt satisfied. What are your thoughts towards that? Do any thoughts exist within your mind that are not fighting or fucking another man's property?"

He felt a twitch of his eye when he clenched it tight, pain radiating from it with such intensity that he was convinced that the socket had to be fractured. Regardless of the pain he refused to acknowledge the agony that was beginning to creep into his consciousness. His heart was beating faster than the drums that thundered in the arena and twice as loud. Every muscle in his body tensed but he faced down the Roman, fully resolved towards his own victory.

"I stand without the need of any man's protection. As I stated before, it is you who cowers in fear of your father's wrath." He risked a glance at Violetta then to Vitus. "There is no debt owed, Dominus, and certainly not by one who stands innocent in all of this."

He watched the words sink in and continued with a growl. "It was your choice to cross blades with a man of greater skill. I did not press for it. The contest was fair and your chance to prove your worth. It is the fault of only yourself that you were found wanting in all regards, certainly not the fault of a girl who has never held a blade so why punish her?"

His eyes flickered to the terrified woman that Vitus still gripped tight. He was not worried for himself, as soon as Tertius and Felix laid eyes upon him they would know what he could not say. His own pain would be avenged but what about hers?

"You stand a fool to think that this will go unnoticed, stop it now and have done with it all." Cassian squared his shoulders and hoped that if the gods existed that they had some mercy left in their hearts for her even if they turned from him.

Vitus shook his head. "You will say no word of this. If either of you seek to bring this before my father or Tertius I will state that I came upon your savage ravishing of the girl and applied the needed force in attempt to spare her life since you seemed intent upon ending it. Your rage over her putting you in the position to have to fight me had overcome you and I had to save my father's property." He looked down at Violetta, she was quaking at his feet, bruises from his grip appearing on her throat. "You will both do my will in this or see my every action set upon seeing the two of you separated for the rest of your days." He smirked, watching his words hit home while he continued to stroke Violetta's hair with his thumb. "As to the debt, you freely partook of my most desired toy when it is denied to me. To add to that insult you threatened my life, therefore you are the one who will aid in her lesson, while learning one of your own."

'And in this you prove yourself even more the fool.' Cassian kept the thought to himself, but the glare of his eyes left no doubt to the contempt he felt for this man and the underhanded manner of his attempt to placate himself. The idea that Felix or Tertius would believe Vitus's falsehood was almost laughable, both men knew his heart despite the words of lies he had been forced to utter to keep her safe and the merchant's pride intact.

He could feel the break near his eye, though he was able to see for now come dawn he would be lucky if the swelling allowed him any sight at all. He would be leaving this house tonight and it would be with Violetta at his side or else he would never raise a blade in the arena again. The lanista could surely be reasoned with to bring her to the ludus, especially when he saw the injury done to him by Vitus simply because the man could not abide to lose to the city's champion.

"What tale you attempt to ply their senses with had best be well told, Dominus." He growled before shaking his head. "How your father chooses to reward me with his own property is not your business, though you take great pains to make it appear so." He took a deep breath and allowed his tone to change when his eyes fell to Violetta "Nor is it your business what or who my hearts treasures, nor how such affection is consummated."

Vitus smiled viciously at Cassian's admissions. "Finally, one of you breaks words of truth in this." He reached down to put his hand under Violetta's chin to raise her to her feet. "It changes nothing but to make sweeter the lesson which you will aid in teaching." He ran his hand down the girl's side, caressing the bare skin while he perused her flesh beneath the sheer fabric.

"The truth is always best, is it not Dominus? In all things?" Cassian sneered, his steps taking him close enough to touch her, his eyes were soft with love and apology for whatever his part was to be in what was coming next by the Roman's command. "I would not suppose it is a thing that you are accustomed to considering."

Pushing her forwards until she stood between them Vitus' smile grew even more ruthless. "To task then, remove her dress. I have no wish for it to be sullied when we return to the feast of my father."

His eyes focused only on Violetta, caressing her with his gaze where he wished he could place his hands. He tried to calm her as though he could command a soft breeze to surround her and ease her fears and pains.

"There is only us." He whispered, "Us alone."

Taking a deep breath, he realized that he was distracted by the trust in the eyes of the woman beneath the sheer fabric barely covering her. Her breasts, as pale and perfectly round as pearls, strained against the cloth as his cock swelled and did the same. He choked back a groan while lifting his hands to untie the knot at her shoulder, His eyes locked to hers without moving while he guided the dress away and let it fall to the floor.

He could tell that Violetta was working hard to ignore Vitus while he watched them as though they were performers in his private amphitheater. She stared longingly into his eyes and trust shone there, trust he worried he would not deserve at the end of this night. Her lips formed the silent words to match his 'only us' as her breath slowed from its frightened, frantic pace caused by Vitus' cruelty. The sigh that slipped past her lips as the fabric slipped to the floor was as peaceful as it was aroused, and Cassian smiled. Though Vitus had his eyes upon her now, her eyes held the memories of the night before and all the nights since Cassian had come here to this house, the nights they had been locked together for hours in the escape their passion brought them to.

Vitus watched them lustily for a moment before speaking his next command. "Well obeyed. Now let me see your hands upon her. Turn her to face me and show me how you can do what I cannot. Bring her to the peak of arousal before my eyes."

He sat down in his chair to observe the acting out of his lewd commandment with a blank look on his face daring either of them to protest.

Cassian's smile fell to a hard line at the Roman's command. He had his suspicions as to what game it was now that the man was playing at and the perversion of it sickened his soul. There was little choice now except to do as he was told and try to make it less like a nightmare for Violetta. Leaning with a deliberate slowness he pressed his lips firmly to her temple. He let them melt there for the space of a breath then dusted a line of more delicate kisses to the lobe of her ear before slowly turning her to face Vitus as he had been ordered. As he turned her, he cupped her shoulder with his palm, kneading his fingers into her flesh in circles that expanded in slow sensuality. He swept his fingers down in a long, soothing stroke before resting his palm on the gentle swell of her hip, leaving it there he teased the tip of his tongue at the side of her neck, a soft moan escaping him before he could catch himself.

Violetta's breath caught and hitched as she gave in to the sensations his hands brought to her body while the Roman watched, growing hungrier for her with each second that passed. Rising to his feet Vitus stepped towards them slowly, the hate in Cassian's eyes growing with each step. Standing before Violetta the Roman reached out to take a breast into his palm, weighing it carefully before squeezing so hard it brought a sharp cry from her lips and a deep growl from Cassian in a sound of defensive rage.

"You will prepare her for me gladiator." He said, his teeth flashing in a sinister grin of glee at Violetta's fear. "It will be your hands that hold her body still as I take my pleasure within the slick heat you will bring her to." He licked his lips and turned his eyes back to Cassian while his hand wandered down Violetta's torso, grazing fingers across her stomach before dipping to the apex of her legs where he pressed a finger against her. "You will cry out for me little flower and it will be your champion that holds you captive until I have had my fill of you. Then we will see what lies you weave for his protection."

"You must be mad to think I could…" The words were a harsh whisper that he had not intended to voice but his shock at the brutal command was uncontrollable. It could not be real, it felt like a blade had been pressed through his heart. "Prepare her for you then hold her down for your cock?" The gods could not be so cruel as to let this happen, he would not be a part of that and yet he had no choice for if he refused the result would be worse than this rape. Years of training and stone-like self control were no match for the despair he felt, he was unable to hold back a groan of misery. "Apologies." He whispered in her ear before raising his hands to play over her breasts, his lips burning small kisses across her bare shoulders as he turned her to face him, praying she could see the torment he felt in his eyes.

"No, please no." Violetta whispered, unable to do anything but respond to his touch.

He hated Vitus for this, to take the only thing of solace in her life and twist it to his liking, warping its beauty until there was nothing left of the playful intimacy was one of many things that he hoped Vitus would one day die for. When his kisses inched downward Violetta whimpered in desire and the moment hiss lips brushed intimately between her creamy thighs she looked as though she could weep. Her body wanted to surrender to the pleasure he brought her, to relax and give in to his skillful demands but the eyes of Vitus watching, filled with savage expectations, stilled her in terrifying agony.

"Dominus, please do not do this." She begged, her hands gripping Cassian's shoulders to keep herself standing while he skillfully brought her to a state of arousal that he knew she could not fight.

Vitus watched Cassian kneel to devour the sweetness of the woman he held dear, but the man barely listened to her plea for mercy. Circling behind her he brushed her hair off her neck, so he could whisper in her ear, enraging the man on his knees before her. "Oh yes Violetta, you will learn to do as you are bid or pay a price higher than you can imagine." He moved his hands to grip her hips, settling them over Cassian's, and pressed his robed arousal against the hollow of her back. "Oh yes you will learn little one and it will be a beautiful lesson to teach." Releasing his hold, he walked back to the edge of the bed where he began to remove most of his robes. "See her ready soon gladiator. I grow impatient."

Cassian's mind swore oaths of vengeance as he stood, one hand brushed the outline of her hips downwards while the other raised her chin so that their eyes met and locked until the length of chain between his wrists forced the other hand to follow. His fingers entered her gently, Cassian stroking her heat without breaking the eye contact that was the only thing keeping him sane in those moments. His hand worked lazily between her legs as if his blood did not thunder through his veins, screaming with yearning.

All he wanted was her; in his arms, moaning her pleasure while he filled her with firm strokes until every muscle in her tightened around him, milking his body with the strength of her climax. Unfortunately it was not to be, not this night or any that he could see on the horizon and the pain of that knowledge was the only thing piercing the veil of his lust and bringing him back to the present where all he could do was strive to give her as much pleasure as possible before handing her over to Vitus.

Even though they both knew that he was preparing her for the monster in the room Violetta could not help responding to the sweet passion between them any more than Cassian could himself.

His touch teased her to the very edge of reason, her hips rocked against the heel of his palm hungrily. Their eyes shared the longing they felt for each other blending with his anger and her fear of Vitus' plan. He let himself believe for a breath that it was truly just the two of them and that any moment he would scoop her into his arms to take her to his bed. Her eyes closed, her body getting closer to that edge of bliss that she needed, but he withdrew his touch and let his words bring them both back to the truth like a douse of icy water.

"It is time, my love."

CHAPTER 27

Cassian's voice was rough with charged emotions when he stepped back "She is ready now Dominus, for you." He felt like a monster to match Vitus but what was he to do? If he disobeyed it would end in death, but obedience destroyed his soul. Either way he betrayed her but this option, heinous as it was, made sure that she would live even if she never wanted to see him again. "My task is done."

Vitus beckoned Violetta to the bed where he stood, his hand beneath his robe in self stimulation, panting near his own release. Cassian could see in her eyes that she hoped, as he did, that the man would not last to penetrate her while he watched helplessly. When she moved to stand before him Vitus sucked in a deep breath that released as a hiss before he reached to grip her slender hips while Cassian growled from where he stood. Vitus pulled her tight against him, one hand dropped to probe the dampness between her thighs with a rough thrust that brought a yelp of surprise and pain, opening lips pressed close to avoid a kiss should he attempt it.

Absolute hatred filled Cassian and blurred his vision with a haze of red. 'Do not succumb to it.' He told himself. He had to focus, this was a battle like any other he had fought in the arena and his opponent had already made a grave mistake, trying to prove himself the stronger man. It would not take much for a discerning eye to see the damage done by the Roman's temper. All who did not already know would soon see that the man stood weak in the presence of his betters and feared anyone that would defy or contest his will.

Cassian knew that Vitus was simply behaving as a child, a malicious and dangerous child, that had been refused what he wanted and so was lashing out at all those around him. Like a toddler who broke his toys out of spite so the Roman saw himself and Violetta, nothing more than toys to be broken. It would be a deadly error on his own part if Cassian lowered his guard by allowing his emotions their true expression and so he removed himself from them, turning as cold as stone. To be distant and uncaring in outward appearance was the only way he could make it through this.

"Stand opposite." Vitus directed Cassian, "And hold her arms near to her shoulders." He had not yet taken his eyes from Violetta before him, his hand continuing to explore her wetness while his mouth bent to press to the flesh at her neck, his teeth dragging cross her rapidly thundering pulse, causing Cassian to tense. He wanted to kill him, to stop this horror.

When she whimpered in fear, Vitus laughed and shoved her roughly to the bed. He licked his lips, his eyes drinking her in while he struggled drunkenly to remove his remaining robes. Finally casting them aside he stood before her closed thighs and turned his head to glare at the gladiator who had not moved to obey him. "Do you stand deaf? Take position." Looking back at Violetta who lay, arms above her head, closed to him still he stroked himself in anticipation, lust filling his eyes as he growled "Open."

Cassian stilled, his entire body tightening with his forced restraint. "Your will, Dominus" He replied flatly, his tone like ice and his body language firmly devoid of emotion, he moved to the directed position and clamped his arms in place as commanded. He could not let himself worry about the pain his hold might cause, it might even afford her some distraction from the actions of Vitus, but he would keep her still no matter what. He was not Cassian now, not a lover or a titan of the arena, but a guard to her safety whatever the cost to them both. If Vitus made a move that would bring her to greater harm it would not matter that his life would be forfeit, he would see the Roman dead upon the ground as he would be now if he thought it would save them.

He could not meet her eyes. His sense of having betrayed her trust was too great. He also refused to meet the eyes of their tormentor and see the flashes of victory he was certain they contained. Every sense he possessed was on focused alert should his defense be required to save her from a greater harm.

She stilled when his hands took hold, her eyes filled with confusion by the iron grip that was as unfamiliar as his apparent indifference was. He could see she was fighting panic when the chain between his shackles came to a halt just barely above her throat. Her breath and pulse quickened with the realization that fighting this would now be impossible. It was when she turned her fearful eyes up to meet his gaze and he had to turn away from her that she made a solitary wail of despair.

He felt her fight as the Roman pried her thighs apart and cried aloud when he forced himself into her body. After that he turned off his mind, forcing it to ignore all feeling except that of the soft skin that would be bruised beneath his grip, because of his touch. He still could not meet her eyes and so she turned her head away. Her tears streaming down her cheeks to land, scalding hot, on his whitened knuckles where he gripped her tight, the water burning through to his soul.

He forced his mind to dream, to place his thoughts on memories, anything he could to make what was happening bearable until he could offer comfort to his woman, if she would let him.

In his dream, Cassian could taste her need on her lips, the hunger in her touch and he felt the urgency rising between them like a fire burning through his muscles. His control was being chipped away by the sweetness of her moans, the pleading in her whimpers and he was ready to give in. She was pulling him as close as she could, clutching his arms and shoulders, threading her slender fingers through the length of his hair, trying to satisfy her need. He kissed her deeply, his palms overflowing as he cupped and kneaded her breasts. He worshiped her body as only a man who knew it, who knew her, was able to do.

Their passion was pure carnality, fueled by a primal need that grew each time he drove himself deeply into her. The pressure was building, it was excruciating bliss to be so close to the edge but just before he could slip over, he forced himself back to the brutal reality and the rape playing out before his helpless eyes.

His mind screamed in soundless agony, wordlessly begging the gods for aid or at least the permission to release her from the hands holding her down to endure the barbarity forced upon her, his hands that held her captive to a pain they would forever share. He commanded himself to feel nothing, to stand as stone, to not give Vitus the chance to crow his victories further, but he could not seem to stop himself from lowering his eyes just once to look into hers

Cassian was devastated by what he saw; fear, pain, helpless panic, but as she seemed to register that it was his eyes that she saw he was amazed to see trust and sympathy shining back at him. He was so moved by the emotions in her eyes that a single tear slipped from his to land at her temple, revealing to her alone that the champion's heart broke for the woman he loved.

When their eyes met Violetta looked shocked to see and feel the tear that he shed. Quickly blinking back further tears she turned her head to the side, touching it to his wrist above the edge of the shackle where she could feel the rapid beating of his pulse. Eyes closed he hoped she was able to find solace in the last moments while Vitus roared his false triumph in his climax.

In that moment the claws of defeat sank deep into the champion's shoulders. A sickening dread took hold in his stomach at the thought that the seed might take hold within her. He felt as though his insides had turned over when the image of her with the Roman's child flashed before his eyes. It was possible, but he would plead with her gods that it did not come to pass for her sake as much as that of his heart.

Gently Cassian loosened his hold and carefully lifted the chain away, ensuring that the rough metal did not scratch her delicate skin. He flinched when he saw marks already forming where his hands had been. They would continue to darken in coming hours and by dawn would be undeniable reminders of what he had done. "I would lend you assistance." Was his guilt filled whisper at her ear while he held out a hand to cover hers and help her, slowly, to stand.

"Gratitude." Violetta whispered in return, her words catching in her throat, which sounded raw from holding back her tears. She looked shocked at the sight of the bruises on her arm, as though she did not feel the pain from them. Was the other pain she had to be feeling a distraction from her arms? He hoped that was the case. Her hand was shaking in his while he helped her to her feet, the gentleness of his touch offering comfort in the wake of Vitus' brutal assault. "It was not needed." Was all she said to him before rushing to where her dress lay in a pile upon the floor. Clutching it to her chest like a shield she wrapped the sheer material back in place, fighting fresh tears at the back of her eyes.

Vitus stood straight, panting with the effort he had exhausted. "The lesson is well learned I hope." He stated with a chuckle as he ran his hand through his hair and looked at Cassian. "Attend my robes. I would return to my father's celebration where I expect to see you both within minutes." He pointed a finger at Violetta. "You with dried eyes. I do not want to be questioned about your appearance, so you will correct it."

He had been about to whisper more assurances in her ear when the voice of Vitus stopped him and caused his head to turn, wondering at the absurdity the man had uttered. "Impossible."

A flicker of anger in his eyes Vitus arched a brow and barked at the lovers when neither of them had moved to obey his command. "Was I unclear in command? See to robes as I have words to break with the Imperator regarding his games."

He laughed loudly when Violetta ran to clutch the dress to her body, attempting to find some traces of modesty that had long been lost to her. "I do not have all night. Attend, now." He commanded again, snapping his fingers at the gladiator impatiently. "And remember that neither of you are to break word of this to anyone."

Letting Violetta have a moment of peace, of quiet, Cassian obeyed the insane command of Vitus. Each article of clothing he aided the man in donning brought with it a fresh wave of loathing for them both; Vitus for what he had done and himself for continuing to play the part of a mindlessly submissive slave when all he desired was to tear the man's throat out. Though he forced himself to this state to keep Violetta safe from further harm he swore to himself to find a way to bring vengeance down upon Vitus' head, revisiting the pain he had brought to Violetta ten-fold.

Tearing his eyes away from Violetta's heartbreaking grief he lifted a hand to his eye, the swelling and dark bruise would be more visible as time passed. Grinning painfully, with a scoff at the man who thought himself a clever victor he responded. "No words will be needed for your actions this night have a voice all their own which will be clearly understood when I stand before Tertius and your father."

His voice had been as cold as the steel of the weapons he wished he held in his hands but when the Roman left the room Cassian put aside his rage and did what most would not have dared with the appearance of guards at the door; he approached Violetta. She was still weeping on the floor, and so he crouched before her with a gentle hand on her shoulder to alert her that it was only him.

Looking deep into her eyes he brushed the pad of his thumb down her jaw and gently pressed his lips to hers. He kissed her with the tender apology that he could not find words for. He hoped that she held some feeling for him still, that she would not fear his touch now as he knew she feared Vitus. "It is done now. Violetta, he is gone." He whispered softly.

There was a tremble in her lip when his mouth pressed to hers, a soft cry escaping her as she accepted the solace he offered. Her hands clutched his arms with a strength he did not know that she possessed. She broke their kiss to bury her head at the base of his throat, shaking it back and forth in silent but late protest to the actions of the night.

"I do not know if I can bear it." Violetta whispered to him. "Stomach churns inside a body defiled, tainted."

She looked up at him with a silent plea that she had not been lowered in his eyes due to the horrors of the night. To ease her mind, he leaned to kiss her forehead, trying to show her his heart through the soft touch. "It is done, Violetta."

"It is done." She responded with a soft whisper and a weak smile before lifting her hands to attempt to finish tying the fabric of her dress back into place.

Suddenly, as his hand reached to help her tie the knot he had undone, a hand cuffed him across the back of his head. Cassian turned to look, trying to keep his breath even as he fought to keep his balance. Had the blow been meant for him or was it a strike against Violetta that he had blocked by chance. His eyes flicked to meet those of first one guard and then the other, but it was impossible to tell from their expression what the intent had been.

"Stay hand!" Barked the senior guard to the one holding a whip, ready to strike if he thought it needed. Reaching quickly, he grasped his wrist to stay any further blows. "He has done nothing to deserve that."

The other guard looked at his companion and shook his head. "He takes liberties with a woman not his own. He stands shackled and chained even if he is a champion, he still stands nothing but a slave."

"He stands a man pushed beyond bearing." The senior man replied firmly. "Return whip to belt. Any man is more likely to cooperate if he is treated with a little dignity." He turned to nod at Cassian. "The man does stand the city's champion. Slave or not, he has stared death in the face more times than you or I have and deserves some respect for that alone."

"He took no advantage." Violetta said mournfully, her hand reaching gently around his hair, flinching when she touched the blood trickling down from the blow. Now words with Tertius were unavoidable and the likelihood that he would permit his prized gladiator to reside under this roof another night was gone. All hope of finding comfort in each others' arms in the dark of night had been snatched away by the violence of the Romans.

While the two guards debated what he did or did not deserve Cassian put them from his mind and masked the pain burning through him. A soft smile on his face he cupped Violetta's chin and brushed his thumb across it with his eyes locked to hers, trying to say without words what his heart felt. He wished that there was some way he could have spared her what she was feeling, the shame in her eyes and the tear stains on her cheeks pulled at emotions he had forgotten he had.

If time was permitted, he would have pulled her into his arms and soothed her tears until she fell asleep with her head above his heart as she had done since his first night in the villa. He wanted that again, tonight and every night. He found himself staring into the oceanic blue of her eyes and realized, in the agony of the night, that he wanted her forever and would do whatever it took to deserve the chance to prove that to her.

"He took only that which is his." Though the guards might have thought she meant the kiss he knew, as she did, that she had meant her heart.

CHAPTER 28

The wound was but a small cut, made by the edge of the guard's metal bracer instead of the steel he was used to but for some reason Cassian felt the pain more deeply than any wound before, except perhaps his eye. Seeing his blood on her hand crushed him. He felt no glory, no triumph. He was no longer the master of the sands, defeater of death, undefeated by all challengers. With his woman coming to his defence as the guards argued his worth, he felt as though he were suddenly nothing more than a common slave. It did not matter that for years his body had been a prize to his master, maintained and protected with the greatest of care, not anymore.

Here in this house, this night had all but destroyed him. He felt weak and enraged with no hope of victory. Perhaps this fight was over, had Vitus won? Was this what he had intended? To see the woman that he loved so broken and yet trying hard to lift his spirits, crushed him. He had meant to be her strength and yet she was showing that she was his. "We should go now." He said quietly, holding out a hand to her as his gaze fell to the floor. "I would not have him return to look for us."

She might have protested the sudden change in his tone, but when the guards gave a harsh glare Violetta sighed, and rose from the floor to join him in the return to the party.

"Hold head high. Do not let Vitus see your spirit broken by such a simple wound. Seek words with Tertius about the attack." She took a deep breath and looked down. "He may be grieved by it and see you taken to safety, far from here. You stand champion still, my dearest love." The final endearment was whispered softly in his ear as they arrived in the doorway and all eyes turned to observe them.

He squeezed her hand gently. She was so hopeful he could hear it in her words. He tried as hard as possible but as much as he wanted to fulfill her request, but he found it impossible to climb from the pit of despair he had found himself in. He could not explain it, but something had happened when the guard's blow had hit its mark, he had never felt this worthless and small before. Even when he had been the houseboy of Tertius' father and fawned over by his mother he had still managed to hold onto his pride.

He kept his eyes down to the floor. "How can I hold my head high as champion when I stand with blackened eye, a fractured socket, my head bleeding from an errant blow and…" His voice dropped to a whisper. "And my love raped in my presence, forced to submission by my hands. This is not me. This is not who I am."

Pausing in the doorway Violetta pulled his hand to stop him from entering the grand room. "There is no fault in your actions. The one who bares blame in this is Vitus, his perversion is deep to the core. He seeks to break heart and spirit. I beg that you do not let him win this." Her eyes pleaded with him to listen, to understand. "You have not lost yourself. You stand my champion and my heart. It is because of you that I can take courage, that I can hope. Without you I would walk as a ghost among the living."

Raising the hand that held hers she placed a tender kiss upon his knuckles in supplication. "You are my heart, my only love and the reason I keep trying, keep hoping, breathing." She offered him a small smile he could not return, just as Vitus crossed the room to embrace his father who glanced towards the doorway as though he sought their appearance already.

Her hand was the only thing he allowed himself to feel. It was as though his entire body was ice, glacially numb. This was how he had always dealt with pain, the withdrawal from feeling, but he could not do that to her when she was so fragile. Even if he knew he could endure worse, mentally withdraw from physical agony, that stood impossible tonight. The pain was beyond his experience or understanding. He felt strangely vulnerable and though he had barely been touched he felt as though he had been violated as well as Violetta. The hope in her voice reached him and he finally raised his eyes to meet hers. "You, Violetta, are my strength and my reason. I love you like nothing else in my life." He reached a hand to her cheek, but she was torn away by Meridius before the contact.

Her eyes lifted to his and she silently mouthed the words 'I love you' as she returned to her task. She retrieved the jug of Falerian wine that was favored by the guest held in the highest honor of her Dominus and stepped towards them, ready to serve at their whim. She was the picture of demure servitude in the sheer dress that displayed not only her femininity, but the healing lash marks upon her back and the darkening bruises on her arms and face. There was no doubt that she would be questioned regarding the new marks but with Vitus so near Cassian was not sure how she would be able to answer without displeasing one man or the other. He hoped that she could stay calm, focused, while he watched her with the stillness of a statue.

Titus Claudius watched her pour the wine and it was obvious that he wondered how she came by the fresh marks upon her ivory flesh, but she was not his slave and so not his concern. "The rumors of your hospitality do not lie Felix and this wine is splendid." He nodded to the merchant. "Your ability to bring together those in search of something has not disappointed either. The ability to know what a man wants before he knows it himself seems to be yours. Guiding hands touched by the Gods themselves."

He meant of course that the merchant had connected him to the lanista that had exactly what he wanted; a challenger for the arena. "I think that, for all of us, this will prove to be a most profitable endeavor." His eyes narrowed when they moved towards the gladiator and Cassian wondered what the Roman was plotting behind the bright blue eyes.

"Titus, you are too kind, but you do not lie." Felix laughed aloud and toasted the man while clapping the other hand to Tertius' back. "I have thought for some time that you and good Tiberius here would have much to say to each other. Your mutual interest in the games and the men that compete in them is just the beginning of things I think." He said with a gleam in his eye as he looked at Violetta while she served them.

"Titus, you have the influence to access the greatest arena, Tiberius owns the man the crowds want to see, and I possess the woman who inspires his blades to victory. What a trio we could make, no?"

The men laughed and toasted each other as though Violetta and Cassian did not stand before them or have feelings besides those which they were instructed to have. He was broken and bleeding while she stood in agony after the assault by Vitus and yet not a man, or woman, in the room thought to ask what had happened. He had thought that perhaps Titus would have inquired, his eyes were kinder than the men she served.

"Do you desire more wine Dominus?" She asked the man in question, filling his cup when he held it out then filling that of the lanista and her own dominus before she dared to raise her eyes to meet Titus's gaze. Cassian was surprised to find him smiling at her somewhat kindly.

"Gratitude." He said simply before returning his attention back to the merchant and lanista. Titus watched the girls' surprised reaction to the simple kindness of a little gratitude. If only he knew how hard on her Felix and his son were that such a small thing would surprise her. Could he see the bruises on her arms and the mark on her face that would have been hard to hide earlier? He likely thought they must have come either at his hand or someone else, but did he care?

"Tertius? What are your plans for the gladiator now? His training and such?" He smiled at the lanista, but it was not the type of smile that turned Cassian's stomach, there seemed a genuine interest in it and so the gladiator relaxed slightly. "How soon can you have him ready for Rome?" Titus pointed at him with his cup in hand. "The recovery will not take long I hope?" Cassian was rewarded with the look of shocked horror on Tertius' face when he spun to look him in the face for the first time since he re-entered the room.

"Jupiter Maximus!" Tertius said, his smile falling when he saw the swelling and discoloration on Cassian's face. "Excuse me Claudius, I must see to this but trust that you will have your match for the Volturnalia, this Sextilis will be one that all of Rome shall have cause to celebrate. Which is more than I can say for whoever is responsible for the injuries done to my champion."

Rushing towards Cassian he exclaimed again, louder, when he saw the blood dripping down his neck from the blow to his head. Cassian remained still and silent until he was ushered from the room by the lanista who would attempt to glean the truth from him regarding the sudden injuries. He shared a look with Violetta, hoping that she would not worry and would not risk Vitus' wrath by breaking words before he returned.

Violetta watched them go while Felix shook his head and looked at his companion. "That is a most troubling turn of events." His eyes moved to her and she stilled under his stare. "What do you know of this? What happened while you attended to his needs?"

She could tell he was attempting to stay calm, but it was obvious that this could ruin all that he had planned. Since the morning Violetta had first returned from the ludus he had been hoping for this kind of attachment. Cassian was the only man with the skill to interest the great Titus Claudius and if this transaction was to be completed then Felix would have to ensure that the lanista and his man were satisfied even if it was to his own loss of pride.

"Loosen tongue and give answer girl. I would not be kept waiting."

Violetta shook her head, terrifyingly aware that the eyes of Vitus were upon her. "I have no answers Dominus. There is nothing I can say on the matter, apologies." She was trembling, Vitus was so close, but she longed to tell Felix and the man next to him the barbarity of what he had done and how he did not care that it might ruin the plans that his father had in place to rise to the level of his esteemed guest. "I wish that I could give you what you desire but I cannot." Her eyes fell to the floor, fearful of the merchant's wrath at her lack of ability to fulfill his desire but to face the anger of Vitus was something she feared even more.

When the merchant began to sputter in anger Titus put a hand to his host's arm. "I am sure that Tertius will explain all when he returns to us." He smiled with a small pull to bring the man away from her. She knew it was obvious that she knew the answers he sought, but she had no more that she could say if she wanted to stay safe.

"Why do we not speak of more pleasant things hmm? The games in which the man is to fight will be a wondrous thing. All of Rome shall come to see him fight with Finnicius. You have done a thing for which I will surely have to make gratitude known. If the fight goes the way I expect it to then there shall be a great deal of personal celebration, for which I may hold you responsible when it comes to recognizing the cause of it."

Violetta sighed in relief at the help offered by the great Roman. Felix would not want his prize ripped from his grasp. She was certain he would find a way to hold his son in check.

"I am certain that the Celt will not let you down Titus. Though I have never seen him fight a Retiarius I have seen him lose only once and that seemed to be by the blind luck of his opponent." Felix paused and looked at Violetta out of the corner of his eyes before continuing. "Perhaps it would be better if I accompanied Tertius on the road to Rome? I feel as though I may make a better impression upon those within your circle than that small-minded little man." The smile they shared confirmed to Violetta that if Tertius was not in possession of the best gladiator in an age they would not even be speaking to him let alone planning for him to join in a visit to the capital.

"I think that would be a most ingenious thought." Titus said with a grin. "Now tell me about his skills against a Retiarius for Finnicius is a true champion with the net and trident." Titus demanded with a curious and yet polite smile as Violetta was joined by Jovian while his master was with the champion.

"You, boy, you attend Tertius like a loyal shadow. Surely you can give insight into the skill of the men that Cassian fights? When was his last match against a net minder?" Titus asked, turning the focus of Felix and Vitus both to the young man who visibly paled beneath his decoratively painted face. "You must see uncounted matches in the arena and ludus so come, loosen tongue and see me entertained with tales of my challenger."

Felix's attention turned to the youth, his bared muscular chest and painted eyes and lips causing his brow to arch in curiosity. "I have not laid eyes upon your face before, have I? It seems to me that your likeness would have lingered in my mind. Tell me why Tiberius hides such a comely face from those that stand as friend?" He cupped the young man's chin to raise his eyes so that they met, the dark pools lined with kohl seemed to draw him into some sort of trance-like spell. "Not even at the games have I seen you." He murmured, dangerously close to Jovian's face until the boy took a step backwards, right into the resolute frame of Meridius. Violetta shuddered at the thought that her new friend might become a shared victim of the older man's desire.

"My Dominus says that I am far too fair of face, despite my Syrian blood, to be brought to the rampant brutality that is the games. He has already assured me tonight that, had he known there was to be such contest, he would not have brought me to attend him." The boy shivered for a moment under the Roman merchant's touch but grew slightly braver when he did not follow the retreating step he had taken.

Given his teasing confidence earlier Violetta wondered what game he was playing at, flirtation? Distraction?

"I am not permitted within the ludus for the same reasons, though it is also his fear that one of the men might have me to their cot before I would be able to accomplish his bidding." He squared his shoulders and looked from one man to the other. "My master needs me at his side, none can see to his needs as I can."

Both Romans chuckled at the pride the boy had in his position. It was a common one held by exclusive body slaves, especially young men. They would preen like peacocks and give themselves airs to their fellow slaves. They were seldom popular and usually came to depend upon the master as much as he depended upon the slave.

Titus was so powerful that he likely cared little for the pride of Jovian, except that he could provide him with the information he sought. "Your master does not bring you as his shadow to the games and does not permit you unaccompanied within the ludus, but you surely have seen the men at training. How fairs Cassian against a net and trident? As well as any other or does the trident provide a challenge to his dual blades that will lead to a fight of equal ground upon the sands of Rome?"

Jovian took a deep breath and returned to his confident self. "I may not be permitted to the arena but the hours I have spent beside my Dominus watching the beasts train are without count. Cassian stands champion of all for good reason. There are few with the skill to face him and even fewer can best him." He smirked at Felix and Vitus as he continued. "Roman or slave, it makes no difference. He is as blessed by the gods in the ways of death as he is with a form so appealing it turns the head of every citizen of Velletri." When his eloquent bragging lost the attention of the valued guest he smiled beautifully. "No matter what he faces I can promise that the champion always delivers a performance that will send the heart of every man, woman and child racing with anticipatory delight."

Titus looked from the smug Syrian to Violetta who could not hide the expression that spoke of her agreement with what he had just been told and nodded, taking a drink of the rich wine in his cup. "Then I stand convinced. I shall need to break words with the lanista upon his return and see what closer inspection to the fighter has revealed." He shared a swift nod with Felix. "It will not do if these new injuries kept him from achieving fighting form by the times of the intended games." He looked suspiciously at Vitus who watched Violetta like a cat watched a wounded mouse.

"Surely, he will not be long, Felix?" He asked the host, implying that he should go and bring those in question back to the public company.

Before he could do as asked, a slave approached and whispered in Felix's ear which caused him to snap to awareness. He beckoned Violetta to follow him with the curl of a finger before bowing apologetically to his honored guest.

"Or perhaps there is more to this than there seems, Vitus?" Titus asked, though everyone knew that there would be no truthful answer from the son.

CHAPTER 29

In the same room that had seen use for his changing to and from armor Cassian stood still as Tertius circled him, inspecting the wound on the back of his head and his eye carefully to gauge the seriousness of the injuries. He could feel the swelling increase and pull the skin of his cheek tight while the blood dried, congealing on his scalp and neck. He could see the anger building each time the lanista crossed in front of him, pausing as if to speak and then remaining silent to circle him again. He grimaced when his hair was grabbed at the roots and his face pulled to look downwards so he could face his Dominus who was at last ready to break words.

"What in Hades happened? You were sent to remove armor and enjoy the woman, which was not an easy thing to arrange from Felix after your previous behavior." It did not matter that he was lying, his indignation that the merchant had broken his word would be justified to his mind and he was tempted to take his man and leave that very second. If it were not for the interest of Titus Claudius, he would not have even paused to give it thought. "Who struck you and for what cause? Is your eye a result of the match with Vitus? I did not see him land such a severe blow that would have caused that damage. Loosen tongue, I would have answers. Now."

The grimace stayed in place after his jaw had been released, the man could not know that already the answer stood impossible to give in truth. He had no fear for his own safety, he would be lucky if he could piss unwatched for some time now that he was to fight in Rome itself. It was Violetta that was still in danger from the madman and he was not so foolish to think that his departure from the house would make her life easier to survive. He would not leave here without her at his side. It did not matter if that meant he never saw the sands again. She would be kept safe. "I cannot say what you wish to hear Dominus, there are others at risk who I would not see brought to further pain. No matter the consequence to self I will not be the cause of her death." He swallowed hard, the pain of his injuries growing with his apprehension. "If the merchant could be brought to hear then it might be easier to speak truth to your satisfaction."

Tertius rested his fists upon his hips, anger flowing through him with the wine. "You find it impossible to break words of truth to your own Dominus but not with the merchant present? Is it that you have tired of the sands and wish to be his trophy piece alongside Meridius? Cassian that is no life for a man such as you. To be polished and praised in the day and taken to the man's bed at night? You would die inside if faced with such reality." When the gladiator remained silent and stoic despite his words Tiberius stopped a servant passing down the hall and told him to request that his Dominus attend him right away, bringing Violetta but not his son or Titus Claudius. Cassian knew there was to be no hiding things now.

Felix arrived shortly after, with Violetta at his side, the Roman made no effort to disguise his annoyance at being summoned away from his important guest. "Finish seeing this room lit Violetta. I would make sure that all is laid bare to the naked eye and have reason for it immediately." He nodded to the lanista and glared at Cassian "There are marks upon her that were not present when she was left to attend you. How did she come to them? Did you lose your head or take out rage at Vitus on the girl you would claim no affection for and yet have defended more than once? Your own master is here and tonight, now, we will have the truth as it stands. No more games or lies from you."

He circled Violetta as she came to stand beside the gladiator after lighting the room to a brightness that matched the hour of noon. "The dampness upon her thighs tells of your bedding her so explain further marks, are you the brute some would call you for there is blood there as well."

Concern for his woman flooding his mind Cassian had to fight the urge to take her hand before the Romans but instead he met the merchant's eye. "I had requested her, and it was my understanding that she was sent to fulfill my needs. She did no wrong here and if there is blame to be held for that action, I would bear it alone." He knew that this was not the answer to the question they had put to him, but he would not allow for the chance that she would be guilted for the passionate love they had made before the nightmare that was Vitus had begun. "She but did as I asked of her."

Felix looked from Tertius, who still glared his displeasure, back to the Cassian. He was speaking with more boldness now than he had yet done beneath this roof and Felix responded to him with a calmness that bordered upon respect. "Cassian there has been enough blame placed this day and I would have precious little more of it. I seek now to discover the reason that my slave stands trembling with terror, fresh bruises upon hips and arms. Was it you that brought her to such state or did some other event occur to which you have yet to disclose even though ordered to do so by your Dominus?" Felix glanced at the new wounds that Cassian now stood with that were not there when he had left the room earlier and added. "How did you come to your own injuries? For she does not have the strength to cause such a fracture."

Battling with indecision, Cassian found the weight of Vitus' words heavy on his tongue. He wanted to see the truth laid bare so that consequence could fall upon the proper shoulders. The thought that justice might truly be done, and retribution might be his along with Violetta was tempting. It was the threat by Vitus that he would alter his ability to see his love, to touch and make love to her, to sever them permanently, that still worried him. It would not be a surprise if the man sought to do so by attempting to end her life.

That concern would have been enough to silence any man but when he looked at her; battered and bruised, trembling before the tribunal of their masters, he knew that some answer would have to be given that would see the reign of terror ended. Clearing his throat, his eyes lowered to the ground in shame not entirely false, he said flatly. "The bruises upon her arms were put there by my hands when I was commanded to hold her in restraint for the one whose hands marked her hips with his viciousness. I was struck on the head when I made attempt to comfort her after…" He choked on the words "And the eye injury is the result of shared misconduct that leaves her blameless, innocent of any wrong but obedience to you and your house."

Tertius scoffed at the twisting of words, as though the gladiator would be able to fool the pair of Romans with his half answers. "Explain what you mean by 'shared misconduct'. If she is not to blame, then who is the third party in this violence?" His eyes flashed dangerously with the rage that he had kept simmering while Felix asked his questions. Summoning the guards in the doorway with a gesture he commanded that the chain between his wrists be removed. "And the shackles. I would have the champion of this city standing before as a gladiator and not a common house slave." While they set to work with their keys, he turned his attention to Violetta. "Break true words of this night. We would have a proper understanding."

Violetta glanced at Cassian, she looked as eager as he was to answer with the truth that might see Vitus punished for his actions, but it would be her that bore the weight of the Roman's wrath and he was not a man to forget. The lanista was glaring, Tertius expected her to speak but the words Cassian knew she could not hold back seemed to catch in her throat.

"I…I have no surety as to what to say Dominus." She cast her eyes to the ground to avoid the cold blue-grey glare. Cassian wanted to believe that if she spoke the truth to the man, he might demand something be done to Vitus that would make it impossible for him to raise a hand to her again.

"I have been put to painful and rough use this night Dominus. Cassian did leave marks when he was commanded to enforce the savagery of…" She spoke softly, her voice and courage failed her at the end.

The removal of the chains and shackles was a breath of bliss amid his misery. Cassian rubbed his hands around the flesh that had spent the weeks since he had arrived covered by the offensive metal. He nodded to Tiberius with simple gratitude, turning his eyes to meet those of Violetta briefly before meeting those of Felix. "The savagery of your son's lust and his reprisal that stands nothing more than sadistic."

He returned his focus to Tertius, a smile that bordered on smug stretching his lips as he reported. "The son ordered me to a task I stood opposed to my very core, and my refusal to play the part of his accomplice was met with repeated blows to me person until damage was done. The blow to my head was delivered by a guard when I sought to offer comfort to Violetta absent express permission which any decent man would not have refused."

Felix had been continuing to study Violetta and the marks on her skin, trying to determine what had been there before and what was new. "My son ordered you to this? Vitus? Break words of exactly what hand he had in this and I would have explanation of the task that the refusal of which would bring him to applying fist against my express command." It was obvious to everyone in the room that his concern was that the lanista would withdraw from the agreement he had been working hard on all night. He jerked Violetta's head up hard to meet his eyes. "Find tongue and give voice to further words of explanation."

Violetta flicked her eyes towards Cassian only to find her gaze blocked by Felix as her head turned. "Look not to your lover but give answer where you are directed to." His rage was barely contained though his voice was even as he pressed her for an answer. His frustration was showing as she struggled to find the answer he wanted. He raised his hand as though to strike her but stayed it at the last moment as she cringed, tears springing to her eyes in terror, Cassian flinching with the instinct to protect her. "Speak quickly." Was the barked command.

"Yes Dominus." She whispered, her lips trembling as she shut her eyes tight, a tear sliding down her cheek as she waited for the blow he did not deliver. "My bruises are the effect of the hands of Vitus upon my hips and those of Cassian that were forced to hold me against escape from the most violent of hands." Her cheeks were flaming in fear and shame as a sob broke from her lips. Wrapping her arms around her chest she squeezed herself tight as though to hold back a scream of hysteria from spilling into the silence after her words.

Cassian wished he had the freedom to give her the comfort she needed so badly from him.

"I lose patience with this foolishness." Tertius bellowed, throwing his arms wide in frustration as he stormed to Violetta, coming so close that a slight move from her would press their foreheads together. "Do you mean to say that my champion is the one who made such rough use of you? Is it true what has been claimed then? You share no affections but merely stand newest whore? Was this what he was brought to injury for tonight? Speak plain or it is not Felix you will fear."

Her eyes widened in a panic as she shook her head rapidly. "No Dominus. I make no such claim. He would never do such a thing." Her voice tight and full of fear. Even Cassian could tell that the Roman was about to become violent because she could barely speak. "It was Vitus who brought force in the taking of my body. He gave command for Cassian to hold tight to my arms, restraining me to the point of pain so he could have his way without protest." Closing her eyes against the reality she hung her head.

It was all but certain now that Vitus would find a way to part them. Cassian was sure that Tertius would remove him from the house and seek to end the agreement with Felix that allowed them to be together.

Taking a breath, Violetta continued in a whisper. "The wounding blow was applied by the guard when he sought to give me comfort absent permission to do so."

Cassian grimaced as she spoke, fear of Tertius in that moment overriding her fear of Vitus. He moved to take a stand next to her to show the honesty in her words by his nearness and in hopes of inspiring some strength in her to finish what was now started.

"Vitus had been defeated with blades and sought to find a way to make himself the victor of the night. He made threats intended to silence us both before forcing his body upon one who stood defenceless to stop him. He commanded me to assist in the barbaric act, and, to save her from further pain, I did so without fight. The guards that applied the blow serve the father, not the son. I assumed their actions to be related to his commands, not Vitus." Cassian said, glancing towards the older Roman.

"The guards were under no order of mine." Felix looked from the gladiator to the lanista. "Tertius I swear to you that this was not of my doing. I honored my word." He seemed slightly panicked at the thought that blame for this should fall upon his shoulders and bring slander to his name as a merchant within the city. Word would spread from the gathered company who had already heard the outrage in Tertius's voice at the sight of the wound on his man. Cassian had not missed the number of heads that had turned at the sound, watching the greatest entertainment of the night depart and then their host had left to join him was sure to have sparked conversation.

"I will see that this is dealt with, as soon as the dawn I assure you. There is not need to make rash decisions tonight that could effect other dealings." He added, reassurance in his voice.

Tertius looked from Felix to Cassian and shook his head. "I would see you returned to the ludus tonight and the care of Arturo. Go and see yourself prepared for the journey. We will not delay for the end of tonight's celebration." He turned his attention to the merchant. "It stands as no secret to any and every man of this city that your guards are allowed a free hand to punish your slaves as they see fit. I do not doubt for one moment that this freedom is what saw my champion bloodied at their hands."

He took a deep breath, pursing his lips before he continued. "Since he has stated that he does not hold blame in their account I shall not seek compensation for it. Their actions are not what brings me to concern but your son's viciousness does." Relaxing slightly, Tertius shook his head. "His demands were met, and he still sought further contest? Was the mercy shown by Cassian not something that should have been met with gratitude?"

He noticed that Cassian stood still, unmoving instead of taking leave as was ordered. "Why do you still stand here? Was command unclear or do you have more words to break upon this subject?"

Cassian's voice was a quiet whisper that one might think held shame, but the only shame he felt was his lack of ability to protect his woman. "My only words, Dominus, would be that I love her. If I possessed the freedom to do so I would make her my wife before the law. Her heart is my own."

CHAPTER 30

He raised his head to look at the pair who stood gaping at his declaration. "Since freedom is not mine and since we are not free to make the choice I would ask, beg if needed, that we not be parted." He looked pleadingly at Tertius. "Is it possible that Arturo could come here to tend my injury? Could I not train here for the games of Claudius?"

He turned to Felix Census and spoke with all the emotion that he felt. "Dominus what is your say upon this matter? If there is something you would have of me in exchange for her safety? You have but to name it and I will give whatever I am able."

At first Felix did not hear the gladiator's whisper, he was still speaking to Tertius. "Trust that his actions concern me as well Tiberius and I swear that his actions will not..." The softly spoken words finally registered. "Take her as your wife?" He asked, his voice filled with shock.

He turned his head to look at the lanista in complete surprise and so he did not see Violetta turn her head to stare at him with eyes that shone with love and the silent return of the wish that she could be his alone.

"I admit surprise in light of this confession. That is indeed a grand favor you ask of me gladiator. If I were to keep you here it would, no doubt, cause a constant irritation to my son. Who is it that you would train with? My guards are not available for such a thing." He shook his head, denying the idea without words, looking up he met the gladiator's eye. "However, regarding the girl, while marriage stands impossible, I could promise you that she would no longer serve as body slave. She would be assigned as a simple slave to the household, no longer called upon to attend the personal needs of any man or woman of my house. Does this offer suffice to inspire victory?"

Tertius was staring at Cassian as though he had never seen him before and certainly not in this humble, pleading state. He had never doubted that Cassian had feelings of affection for Violetta, but the revelation of their depth seemed to be shocking to his ears.

"Marriage stands impossible Cassian. That blessing is almost never given and with the actions you have admitted to me I cannot allow such a gift." He saw the slight sink in Cassian's posture then added. "However, if Felix would be willing, we could bring Violetta with us tonight. She could serve my house until things can be settled here regarding her safety and position?"

"I would not presume to ask for the allowance of marriage Dominus." Cassian said, lifting his head so the candles reflected in his eyes, the glow in his eyes the same dangerous hunger as when he stepped upon the sands with the purest intent to kill. "I simply ask that we are not parted. To see her at the balcony rails is a thing I have not dared to hope for. I would find it as inspiring as a vision from the gods themselves."

He turned to lock eyes with her once more before he departed the room as directed. Whatever their decision he would know soon enough but he could not bear to stand in the room and wait while they weighed the worth of his plea. He turned down the hall to avoid the celebration that seemed to have grown louder in their absence. Lost in his thoughts he did not even hear his own footsteps as they fell on the cold marble tiles while the darkness cloaked him from all eyes.

Cassian had not even made it to the stairs before the weight of his emotions stopped him. He leaned his head against the wall and for the first time since his boyhood was stolen by invading Romans he wept. The broad shoulders shook with the force of his pain, the agony he could not deny and the shame that he had perhaps failed the one person who mattered most in his world. For once he did not care if the guards that escorted him saw him as a man, the same as they stood, instead of the champion and god they esteemed him to be.

The strike of the guard had hurt, but it was the memory of this night that would haunt him more than the blemish on his seeming perfection. The bruises on his face and Violetta's body would fade, but he would always remember the night he could not protect her and no matter what happened in the future this would always be with him.

Resting his forehead against the stone the champion considered the day to come. Arturo would attend the injury. He could already feel the swelling that would soon make it difficult to see. It was even likely that his friend would force him to partake of the vile drug he used to dull the senses and the pain. Though he hated the addicting liquid it would not be offered but commanded. Violetta might be there, in what capacity she might serve the lanista he had not even begun to speculate, but at least with her in the villa she would be safe from Vitus and he might at times see her, speak with her and if he were blessed they might even be granted nights together.

He was not surprised that his request for marriage had been denied though that did not make the sorrow at the swift dismissal any less. He did not know if it was the greed of Felix or Tertius' memory of his dalliance with the wife of his former champion but that they had agreed without so much as a discussion of the chance told him that his newest and sweetest dream would likely never be his. They all seemed determined that his soul would never know its completion and that he would always remain a tool of Roman greed until the day he failed completely.

They all watched him depart with an air of near defeat that was an unfamiliar sight to any of them. "I agree with your thoughts Tiberius. Violetta can and perhaps should be where Cassian is, at least until the games in Rome. If he stands victorious then we can discuss further events, then but if he loses…well there will hardly be anything to discuss then will there?" He chuckled and stepped closer to the lanista, placing a hand to his shoulder with a tight grip. "I hold to trust that she will not be put upon the sands as a gladiator within your ludus?"

Violetta was watching both the lanista and her Dominus, barely able to hope that it might be allowed. She was still in shock that Cassian wanted to marry her, but the refusal was no surprise. She had to admit that the lanista seemed eager to please his champion and inspire him to his most impressive fighting fire, but he had left the room as though he had been sentenced to the mines. He had not even lingered to see if she would be permitted to depart with him that night or kept here in his villa. Vitus would surely rage at his father's permission but if it kept their house tied to the lanista and his gladiators, at least until the games in Rome, then Felix was likely to endure his son's displeasure.

"Hopefully this rekindles your champion's spark so that he will take to the sands with renewed vigor and drive. Great reward should be his if he manages the victory, but there will be certain death and misery if he fails. Inspire him Violetta and find me much pleased upon your return." He said with a nod for her to depart and gather what few things she possessed.

Violetta could hardly contain her joy that she would, at least for a time, no longer be subjected to Vitus' cruelty or the lechery of his father. She would be in the same house as Cassian. She did not dare to hope that she would be near to him daily but even to be near him was enough after all of this.

She longed to break words with him regarding his request or statement that he would take her to wife if he were allowed. They had never said such things to each other and that his emotions ran as deep as her own sent her heart soaring. Her feet all but ran towards the door to the lower cells. When she rounded the corner and saw him with his head against the wall, the shoulders where she had taken refuge shaking with the power of his emotions, she was shocked. Her steps were utterly silent, moving past the guards as though they were statues so that she could wrap her arms gently around his waist and press a kiss to the shaking shoulders.

She wanted to give him solace but how was that possible after the night that they had just shared? Her only hope rested in the thought that perhaps knowing he had saved her, that the request that they not be parted had been granted, would ease him if only a little. "Dominus grants request." She whispered against his skin.

"No, it was denied." He murmured, shaking his head, not turning to face her. "They said the marriage stands impossible. I should have known that. Apologies for ever breaking word upon the subject." He stood up from the wall and sighed heavily. "We should go and take what moments we can before we are parted once again. I do not know if they will allow us to break words or hold each other ever again, but I would have you know that there will never be another. You alone hold my heart in this life Violetta, I pray you hold to those words in times to come."

Violetta clasped his hand and forced him to turn slowly to face her. Raising his palm to her cheek and holding it there, she shook her head. "The request that we not be parted was granted. I leave with you this night." She dared a brief smile. "To be returned upon victory in Rome if Dominus commands it, but not until then." She could not help the joyful hope in her voice now in her excitement. "Weeks Cassian. They give us weeks together there."

She searched his face for understanding of her words. Hoping they would break through the despair he was drowning in. The tears in his eyes and on his cheeks gave her no pause, except to marvel at his strength that for all she had seen him dealt. This was the first time she had seen such raw emotion from him. "Come, we must gather belongings so that we can leave this place at last, putting its horrors far from our minds."

Cassian followed her guidance as though in a daze. Down the stairs and through the corridor until they entered the cell where they had spent so many nights together locked in passionate embrace. He kept his hold on her, as though her very presence was a gift from the gods without the promise of staying. He seemed worried that any moment the guards would come to pull her from his arms for the last time or maybe that Vitus had convinced his father to change his mind.

"Will you not miss those dear to you here?" He asked in a soft voice. "The ludus is not a grand place, you may well be in danger there. Do you stand certain this is what you want?"

Violetta stopped the gathering of her few belongings when she heard the doubt in his words. "Cassian? No matter the house or standing I will be with you, near you. That is all I can ask of the gods after this night." Tears of her own started to form in her eyes and she stepped near to wrap her arms around him once more. The true depth of the torture they had been put to that night sinking in at last, the physical pain beginning to throb through her entire body. "I pray thanks to the gods for the suggestion that I depart with you and your Dominus for I fear, with the mood Vitus keeps, that I would not live to see the dawn."

Cassian pulled her into his arms, every touch one of utter tenderness, passionate silence conveyed in the brush of his fingers along her skin. He lay his head upon her shoulder, leaning into her strength of heart if not that of her body. She worried that the other gladiators might see her as a whore or that they might make attempts to steal her from his arms, but they would be together and soon all would learn, understand, that she was as much his as he was hers alone.

"Let us go from this place at last." He finally whispered, lifting his head to look into her eyes.

Violetta nodded slowly, forcing the tears back so that she could quickly gather the few belongings she had into the center of the thin blanket from her bed. Though there might be coverings available in the ludus or the villa, wherever it was that she was to serve, she would not hold to trust that she would be able to keep what was given her. More senior slaves were well known to simply take the issued belongings of newer or weaker slaves, and she did not doubt that those in his house would be any different. Picking up the faded linen dress she had worn earlier that day she ripped the sheer fabric mockery of a dress from her body and threw it across the room.

"If I never see such material again, I shall be a happier woman." She declared in a rare burst of anger before returning to his side. "I stand ready to make the journey at your side Cassian."

"I can only hope that the journey will see us to closer stations at its end. I should have known better than to ask for it." He winced and gnashed his teeth making Violetta wonder if the pain of the act was too much, stopping further words. She could not help but place a hand to his cheek below the injury. There would be little ability to see in just a few hours and already he had to feel the ache. Would the 'Arturo' mentioned be able to help? With a sigh he jerked his head towards the door and squeezed her hand as she led him from the damp dark and up towards the clearer air of the villa hall.

"You took the blame for the blows as though they were deserved when that is not the truth. Why would you do that?" She wanted to drop the small bundle of her belongings to cradle him in her arms, to sooth him as he had soothed her so often with his touch.

"Do you fear for my safety in the house of Tertius? Or is it just the worry that we will be within the same walls but never together that causes concern to darken your eyes?" She watched him for a sign that would give an indication of the answer to her question.

He brought the hand in his hold up to his lips, pressing a tender kiss to the tips of her fingers and tried to smile through the pain. "The fault stood as much mine as Vitus. I should have submitted to his command, perhaps if I had he would not have taken his rage out upon that which I hold most dear to my heart."

Cassian released her hand and stroked his fingers down the curve of her cheek. "I would have rather been commanded to end my own life than to do what I was commanded this night Violetta. Please know, that to stand idle during your assault was the hardest thing I have ever done and one I will never forgive myself for my part."

Waking down the hall towards the door that would lead them outside to where Tertius and Jovian waited to take them to the ludus Violetta took a deep breath when he continued.

"As to the ludus, it may yet prove that I was the fool to ask for what I cannot hope to possess. I will do all that I can to keep you safe there and as close to my side as can be arranged."

CHAPTER 31

"A fool to ask for me?" Violetta did not understand him. The sadness covering him was beginning to worry her more than his injured eye. Had the strike of the guard marked more than just his flesh? Had it wounded his spirit as well? As they walked down the cool marble floor, she let out a sigh and leaned her head against his arm. "You defied Vitus in attempt to save me from his wrath. It stands no fault of yours that his anger was unquenchable."

His voice hardened for a moment, his body tightening with the flash of a returning rage. "I would kill him to keep you safe from his sadistic games. Had I thought I held a chance of doing so and getting you from that room before he was discovered I would have done so with my bare hands." He shook his head. "I would give my life to make sure that he never touched you again. His abuse is done." Cassian was firm, but he still smiled at her as the moonlight from one of the windows crossed her face washing it the unearthly beam.

"Only for tonight. If you believe his fanciful lies Violetta, then you are more foolish than I supposed." Vitus stepped out from the shadow of an archway to approach the pair. His steps unsteady from the alcohol he had consumed since returning to the celebration. He licked his lips, raking his eyes first over the gladiator who was tense and, despite his injuries, looked as if he would follow through on the threat to end his life, then to Violetta.

It was a moment before he realized that her dress had changed and that she carried a bundle with her that was obviously containing the few things she possessed. "You think to leave Violetta? To run away to his ludus where he has promised to protect you from his brothers?" The Roman laughed drunkenly and shook his head, frightening Violetta enough to make her press closer to Cassian.

"If my father does not command you to the cross for attempting to escape, the gladiators of the ludus will treat you as more than a whore. You will soon wish to return and when you do you will beg for my attentions." He sneered, watching her tremble with fear as he gave voice to what she only just considered.

She forced the terror back. Cassian was beside her and with the command that she attend his master as Dominus now, he would not allow Vitus to hurt her again. "I but seek to follow the command of my Dominus, your father." She leaned closer to Cassian as he hurried her towards the exit. "It is he alone that sends me to whatever fate awaits me. I hold to trust that the man who cares for me will see me kept safer there than ever I was kept here."

"You would speak so to me? Insolent bitch!" Vitus snarled as the pair hurried away to answer the summons of the lanista's guards. Following them to the doorway he spat his parting words. "You cannot hide in the ludus forever Violetta! I shall be waiting upon your return, make no mistake."

A solitary glance over her shoulder revealed Meridius standing in the doorway of the celebration. His eyes locked to Violetta's, full of questions he would not get to ask, farewells he would not get to convey and for a moment she wanted to run to him for a final embrace that would have to last until the Romans brought them together again, if they ever did. When he blinked it broke the connection, as did Cassian's voice. With a brief nod he gave Violetta's care over to the man at her side, for better or worse.

"Wait as long as you like, Dominus." Cassian said, a mirth in his voice that had not been there moments before. "May your hand chafe your cock for she will never again be yours to touch." He released Violetta's hand as soon as they stepped clear of the threshold, instead looping his arm around her waist to hold her close. There was no longer a concern about the Romans knowing the depth of their feelings for each other.

She spotted Julius Lucius, one of the guards that had been with Cassian when she had seen him in the care of Tertius, waiting for them beside the wagon where Tertius and Jovian already sat waiting for them with barely contained impatience.

Taking in his appearance for the first time she noted that he, like Cassian, kept his hair longer than the normal Roman soldier. That was where the similarity ended. The Centurion had a longer, handsomely angled face and dark, piercing eyes that made Violetta nervous when she caught his gaze watching her steps. He was taller than her champion by more than the span of a hand, but his presence could not compare to that of the man holding her close.

She smiled as he embraced her, warming her with his body before lifting her to the wagon's confines. He climbed in to sit beside her with Jovian on her right and Tertius with Lucius sitting opposite as they departed the villa's courtyard. The last sight they had of the house was Vitus glaring before he spun back inside. He slammed the door behind him as if it would shut them out instead of shutting him inside with his losses.

The wagon left the noise of Felix' villa behind quickly, rolling through the streets of the city that were all but deserted at the late hour. Beggars and street urchins ran from shadow to shadow not wanting to be seen but unable to stop themselves from pausing to watch the champion of the city roll by. He had not been seen or heard of for weeks. It was likely that some citizens had speculated that he had died. The news that he lived and was returned to the ludus would surely be worth its weight in bread come the morning. A few of the bolder among them even ran after the wagon until Julius expertly tossed a few stones in their direction to deter the attempt. He could not be sure, but he thought that he saw a few coins tossed by the guard as well.

Exiting the city through a lesser gate the solemn company made their way across the back of the perimeter wall towards the hill the ludus rested atop of; the few lights lit, waiting the master of the house's return, were the only way to tell that anyone lived at the lonely peak.

Beside him Violetta stared above her in amazement at the brightness of the stars, a look of wonder on her face that brought a unified chuckle from the men in the wagon and a blush to her cheeks.

"It is beautiful, I have never seen such a sky." She said softly, nervous in the unfamiliar company. A rumble of thunder from beyond the hill caused her to sigh. "Though, like all things of beauty, perhaps it is not meant to last." She looked up at him, jumping slightly as lightning flashed over the ludus. "Do the gods send a message with the storm? Have we displeased them?"

The worry in her voice was unmistakable and Cassian was about to answer her, attempt to calm her nerves, when Tertius laughed aloud and shook his head.

"You ask him about the favor of the gods? Violetta, the only god he holds faith in is the god of death. That is only because one day, many years from now, the champion will fall in the arena and come face to face at last with Pluto. Any man that denies his existence would be a fool but the others he holds no faith in."

The lanista chuckled again, "He does not pray even to the pagan ones of his own people. If it is knowledge of the gods you seek then Arturo, my medicus, would be the one to break words with." He leaned back against the walls of the wagon, trying to maneuver some cover from the rain that would not take long to fall. "Perhaps you will find the chance during your sojourn."

His words were stopped by a sudden crack of thunder above them and a downpour of cold rain that brought the wagon to a halt and the driver calling for aid in seeing it covered with the poles and planks stored beneath the flooring. The guard and trio of slaves quickly moved to the task. Violetta handed the pieces to Cassian and Julius who were able to get them in place to cover the wagon while Jovian held a tarp over Tertius so that he was not soaked in the process. The water was frigid and falling in what felt like buckets. Cassian watched, unable to react when Violetta's hands slipped while gripping the wooden coverings, but she did not flinch when the beams knocked her to the ground.

"Violetta!" Cassian called, concern in his voice. He wanted to rush to her side and pull her from the ground, covering and protecting her from cold and pain but there was no choice if the wagon was to be covered enough to provide the sanctuary that was needed. When she rose to her feet, blinking back tears from either pain or shock from the cold, he locked eyes with her. Offering a quick flash of smile he nodded encouragingly. "Just a little bit more, then we can get back inside. Hand me that piece." He jerked his head towards the board that had caused her fall and grinned broadly when she moved quickly, without complaint, to do what was needed so they could finish the journey. She might do better in the house of Tertius than he, or anyone, suspected.

"Back inside, both of you." The Centurion said with a friendly smile as the water ran down his face. "Before you catch your deaths of cold." He climbed in behind them and looked at the lanista. "Warm bathes should be had before the medicus do you not agree?" He noticed the woman at Cassian's side was shivering and reached beneath the bench to grab the rough woven blanket stored there. Handing it to Cassian he bent his head towards the woman. "Keep her warm. You did not go through all this to have her die of cold."

Cassian took the blanket and carefully wrapped it around Violetta's shoulders, pulling it tight. "Does this help?" He whispered, leaning close enough for their foreheads to touch. "Do you hurt? From the fall?" There was no doubt that her body was in pain from the assault, but the worry that the fall had added to it weighed on his mind. The instinct to protect and shelter was raging in his mind as it never had before. When she nodded, teeth chattering, he pressed a kiss to her forehead without notice or care that Tertius watched his every move, calculating its meaning and the significance of the woman in his arms.

Pg 294

Now that the roof of the wagon was in place and he was not being assaulted by the cold rain Cassian could study his master and consider his part in this unexpected night. Tertius had come to the house of Census with the obvious intent of bringing his champion back to the ludus. Had he been informed of his confronting the son of the merchant? No matter what he heard the lanista had likely never even considered bringing Violetta back with them. Cassian's mind spun with the ways in which she could be used against him under the guise of 'inspiration' for victory.

Cassian knew he loved her with his entire soul. The denial of the unspoken request to marry her was not a surprise. It was the greatest reward an enslaved man could have. It would mean that the woman who stood his wife would not be used for the pleasure of any Roman, man or woman, and it would see her protected by the same status that her husband held. These were not things he could give without Tertius holding the title of her Dominus by law. She could not be his wife and serve another household, certainly not one where the sanctity of the marriage would mean nothing to at least one man beneath the roof. As things stood it would cause more harm than good to have allowed even the thought of it.

Violetta pressed against his chest, attempting to find some warmth after the soaking they received, bringing a smile to his face despite his pain. What was the lanista going to do with her? He was hardly in need of another house slave and she was too lovely to serve Lycithia as body slave. His wife's jealousy would be a danger to her and so put the Roman's entire endeavor at risk. He could not have her sit idle though and so the only options that he could see possible would be to have her stationed in the kitchen, far from his wife's eyes and yet useful, or with the medicus.

The former druid was considered a strange and difficult man to understand but to Cassian he was like a brother. The closeness they shared, due to their shared homeland and how he had come to be in the ludus, made Arturo a man that the champion could not protest having the care of his woman. If Tertius allowed it, then Violetta would be near to him even if they could not share a bed nightly.

Violetta shivered as though she were chilled to the very bone. He hoped the rough blanket handed from the guard was beginning to warm her, as well as his arm around her, pressing her against his chest. Once her shivering had subsided, he began to wonder what it was that she would do at the ludus. Did Tertius know himself? His offer was so surprising that it did not seem likely that he had a plan for her, unless it was as Vitus had said, to use her as a whore to satisfy his men. He shook his head, refusing to give in to the fear planted by that monster.

It would likely be some menial task such as assisting the cook or taking care of bedding and clothing since she came from the house of a cloth merchant. It did not matter. She was to be beneath the same roof as him and they were likely to be afforded at least a shared smile and some words daily. Anything was better than the Hades she was leaving behind. Her entire body must ache from pain after pain being poured down upon her, but he would see her comforted, as soon as he was able. The joy he would bring her as soon as he was able would outweigh the pain a hundred times over.

His mind was as dark as the night sky had become and as full of turmoil. Now that he and Violetta were safe, he could reflect on the day and even the weeks leading up to it. The shame he felt at his failure to protect his woman was equaled only by his self-berating for losing his self control to the point where he engaged Vitus. His face throbbed and from the way it hurt when Violetta had reached her hand to touch it, he knew that Arturo would see a need for it to be mended with surgery, this would not heal on its own like so many other injuries.

Aside from the pain of the operation he would likely face and the recovery time before his friend would allow him to set foot upon the sands there was the damned drug that he would be forced to down to make mending the break possible. Above all things he hated opium, though he knew that it was likely the only thing strong enough to render him unconscious he still intended to protest its use. He would rather take the pain than the drug that stopped it. The wagon wheel rolled over a stone causing the cart to jar and she let out a soft whimper of pain that the jolt had caused making him tighten his arms instinctively.

The sound Violetta made, combined with hot tears on his chest brought him back to the present and he looked down at her with an expression of concern. "Are you well? Did the fall cause you injury of which you do not speak?" He gripped her arms to push her back so that he could look her over for injuries, cursing himself when she winced. He had taken hold upon the very bruises he had put upon her arms earlier that night. "Fuck the gods. Apologies, I did not mean to…" He released his hold and pulled her tight against his heart once again. His memory of those marks would not fade when her skin was once again milky white, and neither would his hatred of the man that had caused them to be placed upon her.

She clung to him, flinching at the new ache from his grip upon the bruises. Tears stained her cheeks and she buried her face in his bare chest as they fell like drops of burning rain against his flesh. "I will be. He cannot hurt me anymore, cannot hurt you either."

He was glad she did not see the pity on Jovian's face or the conflicted discomfort as Lucius turned to face the back of the wagon. All he wanted her to know was that his arms were around her and for the first time in six years she would go to sleep that night and not fear waking at the rise of the sun. Whatever fate awaited her in his home could not be more horrifying and damaging as the one she had left behind.

"Soon that nightmare will be just that. You will not be abused like that again while I live." Cassian whispered softly, his voice in a soothing tone that was so foreign to him that it raised the brow of both the Centurion opposite him and the boy sitting on the other side of Violetta.

"Whatever task it is that I am to be put to in the villa or ludus I will be safer than if I was in the villa of Census." She murmured against his skin. It was meant for his ears alone but the lanista was close enough to hear it as well.

Tertius studied Cassian's swelling face as much as he could in the flashes of lightning. The bruising was dark enough now to be seen even in this low light. It was only when the girl raised her hand to the mark that he realized that it was the time to speak of his decision in her regard. It would give them some peace and allow the trust to be rebuilt between Cassian and himself after the damage done by handing him wordlessly to the merchant. "You need have no fear of your duties Violetta." Tiberius said with a warm smile that brightened Jovian's eyes to see for he knew that it meant the man was in a warm and giving mood for all involved in the night.

"Apologies for not breaking word sooner, the rain had washed it from my mind for a time." He attempted the joke but neither girl nor gladiator seemed to appreciate the humor of it. "As you can well expect my household has no need of yet another slave to wash and serve the tables. Recent victories have provided more than sufficient means for that, but it also sees the number of men within the ludus grow." He saw them both tense slightly but continued as though he had not. "This puts a great strain upon the time and resources of my medicus. As good at his craft as he may be, he is but one man."

He leaned forward in his seat to take Violetta's trembling hand into his own. "I would like to station you as his aid, temporarily at first, but if he does not protest a lack of skill on your part then I shall make the position as permanent as our arrangement allows." A small smile lit his eyes as he squeezed her hand tight. "There is a small room between the cells of the gladiators and the medicus's infirmary. It will serve you well as your own during your stay."

Violetta flinched slightly at the touch of his hand on hers, as though her instinct was to recoil from him, but she did as she had been trained to do; she bowed her head and gave him the answer he anticipated. "My deepest gratitude Dominus, it is indeed more than I could have prayed for."

When he nodded his acceptance of her gratitude and sat back, smug in his own indulgence and generosity, she leaned back against his gladiator. He wondered if she was feeling joy in the fact that there would be no bars between her and Cassian, no need to steal moments together. There was a strategy in placing her where he did. It had less to do with her assisting the medicus and more with dangling her in front of her lover's reach. It was intended to inspire his efforts to reach further and pull his prize close to his heart. Tertius could only hope that her meager experience did not disappoint the ever-agitating medic and make more problems for him than he already had.

CHAPTER 32

"Cassian? Is there anything I might do to ease your pain?"

He had felt her eyes upon him while she spoke with the lanista. He had kept his eyes closed so that neither she, nor the other occupants of the cart would see the passion burning inside his eyes when he realized how close she would be to him daily. Cassian was in physical agony and yet all he could think of was the woman pressed against him. He wanted to hold her, his skin pressed to hers, and wipe the memory of tonight from both their minds. Their passion would build as hands touched and teased to the very edge of explosive desire. He needed to feel the weight of her body atop of his, to hear her breathing as she slept in his arms. The memory of waking to her passion sent blood thundering to his loins, hardening him with a painful suddenness and bursting his eyes open.

"There stands but one thing that could distract or ease me from my pain." His lips spread in as wide a grin as his agony would allow and he moved his hand to rest upon her thigh, drawing her legs up to rest across his own. "One thing alone."

A flush lit her cheeks at his implication and the press of him against her thigh, but after the horrifying night he had no desire to pursue thoughts of passion, only to tease in the hopes of bringing a smile to her lips. Though his desire for her had not been lessened by bearing witness to the assault, he did not want to frighten her with an advance until he knew she was healed, body and soul. The hope brought by the blush might have warmed his heart, but the heat was halted by way her eyes protested even the suggestion of physical intimacy. Her gaze fell to his hand upon her thigh, where his thumb was idly stroking her skin where the dress was open. He had not realized his touch was slowly inching upwards towards hip until a panic flashed in her beautiful eyes.

With a gasp on her lips, and her body trembling beyond her control, her hand flew to his. Her fingertips touched his wrist, brushing the skin that had been so recently locked behind the shackles, and she gave a slight shake of her head. It was almost imperceptible but with the expression on her face there could be no mistaking her response in that moment. She opened her mouth to speak but the voice of the lanista cut the silence before she was able to form the words that would freeze his heart.

"Cassian? What do you think to do?" Tertius shook his head with a small laugh, sharing a glance with Lucius and Jovian. He frowned slightly when he saw how intently his body slave watched them. "Stay your hand." He shook his head and jerked his chin to direct Jovian to rub the stress from his shoulders.

Cassian stared at the lanista as though he had lost his mind. He would never hurt her. It was true that he could not deny the flashes of fear in her eyes, but she trusted him, trusted their affection for each other. If the bold passion he had seen in her eyes that morning was to be cultivated, nurtured back to life, then he had to remind her that not all men were monsters thinking only with their cocks. He could not let her become afraid of his touch.

Locking his eyes to hers, pleading for her trust, he raised her hand and pressed his lips to her wrist. There was little he could do in the time remaining on their return, now slowed due to the rain, but he was determined to try and use it to start to teach Violetta to trust his hands once again. Slowly, with as much gentleness as he could muster, Cassian traced up the line of her cheek with the tip of his finger. Violetta's eyes flicked up to his and he could see her fear was turning to calm. He was begging for her trust, hoping that the flashes of lightning showed the warmth of his feeling in the dark of the storm.

She looked unsure if she would stop the progress of his touch or allow it. He would not force her, if she wanted him to stop, but would try to sooth her frayed nerves as much as he could. She leaned her head into his touch, the tease of a smile in the corner of her lips and that small gesture made it near impossible to stop his daring. His fingers threaded into her hair, combing the length of the dark tresses until he was running his hand down her arm. The way she looked at him, trusting adoration, made him want to take the chance on a kiss but the voice of his Dominus stopped him before he could act on the wish.

"Cassian!" Tertius opened his eyes, Jovian's distraction at the action of the gladiator had caused his hands to cease their soothing rhythm. "The girl has been through enough his night and does not need to stand required to satisfy you. If you cannot control yourself after express command and your own consideration for the woman you care for, then I shall command Jovian to see your cock satisfied." Even though the lanista had a grin on his face, as did the other men at his threat, his tone and the look in his eyes were firmly stating that he was not making a jest this time.

Cassian's frown was one of deep displeasure. It was not of physical pain, as one might think, but of pained thought that his attentions to Violetta could be thought of as continued abuse such as Vitus had put her to. He had fought for her, would fight for her all their lives if he had to. For Tertius to say or imply that he would cause her harm, when he sought to sooth her fear ravaged nerves, angered him to the point of violence surging through him.

He looked over at Jovian who was so obviously delighted at the thought of being involved with the lovers that it brought an unexpected burst of laughter from Cassian's lips. The sound carried out of the wagon into the night until the gladiator wiped mirthful tears from his cheeks at the idea that he could ever be satisfied by the touch of the feminine youth beside his Dominus. "I stand chastised Dominus. No further advances this night. I give my word." He turned his attention back to Violetta and winked playfully for the sole purpose of making her smile at him.

His laughter was so unexpected that the other occupants of the wagon paused with uncertainty before joining in. Jovian did his best to hide his disappointment that he found the thought of him being able to pleasure him a laughable thing. Cassian had been the one who had taught him what he knew about passion, though he thought the Celt had no knowledge that he had been his tutor. He knew that Jovian had, whenever possible, snuck to the doors of the rooms that Cassian had been sent to when the women of the city's elite had paid for his time and skill to pleasure them.

The boy must have studied each caress and thrust as though his life could depend upon it. When their Dominus had noticed the growth in his sensuality it had come to be how Jovian lived his life to the disgust of Cassian and Arturo both who saw it as an abuse towards the young boy. It was well known that he had been eager for years to show his teacher, known as the most passionate and skilled lover in Velletri, that he was, possibly, now the second best.

Violetta had startled at his laughter, her own quiet laugh blended with the rest of those in the wagon though she could not understand the joke. It was as though she felt pleasure just to be able to laugh without fear of punishment. "Gratitude, Dominus, for the opportunity. I will do my best to see the medicus' requirements satisfied and ensure that your faith in me is not displaced." She managed to say after stifling her laughter, making Cassian instantly miss the sound of it.

Tertius preened at her words. Even he had to see that, though a slave, Violetta was uncommonly beautiful and to have her adoration was more than just her simple obedience to his commands.

"I stand confident that you will live up to all expectations Violetta. See the medicus pleased with your work and I shall be as well, which will speak well for your future in my house." He adjusted his robes and leaned back, signalling for Jovian to continue his work with his hands so that when they arrived at the villa he would be calmer that he had been after meeting with both the men of the house of Census.

Cassian knew Tertius would have to be at his best when he explained to Lycithia how it was that he brought back not only their own man, who had an injury that could very well prove to be dangerous to his health, but a beautiful young female that would be down among the men of the ludus.

The gladiators would flock to her like flies to honey and the lanista's wife could be a jealous woman. He did not envy the man the attempted explanation, but Cassian imagined that Jovian's hands would make it a little easier to bear.

"Arturo will begin your assessment at once when we reach the ludus. Be prepared to do as you are told and to do it quickly, he will not be forgiving of foolishness or errors."

Cassian frowned slightly at the way the lanista described his friend who stood as his dearest brother. There was not a soul that was gentler and more understanding of the plight of those in slavery. His compassion for the horrors that Violetta had survived would have been great no matter what but knowing that Cassian loved her would cause him to see her as a sister or perhaps a daughter-in-law. If he could have had his choice of any man to oversee her safety while he trained and in the event of his death see her cared for it would be Arturo.

The man was devout in his faith but had been a leader in the army of their people with the skill to fight in the arena for hours if he was of the mind. Often the pair of them trained under the moonlight simply for the love of combat. He leaned over to whisper softly into Violetta's ear. "Do not fear the man. He is one I hold close to heart and I trust he will hold you close to his as well. For my sake at first, then for your own. Who could help but hold one so sweet with anything but affection, unless he stood a mad man and sadist?"

"I will hold to that trust and believe that he and I will find our footing." When he smiled with a brief nod in answer, she would know that his head was causing him more pain than he was willing to let anyone else within the wagon know. It would have been so simple if the childhood belief that a simple kiss could make all things better was true, but the agony that he was in would only be increased with the touch he longed for her to bestow upon him.

As if she could read his thoughts she sighed and rested her head against his chest to take comfort in the steady beating of his heart. "I will not fail at this."

The thunder rumbled above them, and the rain poured down, cooling the night air while those within the wagon made the final leg of the journey in silence. Winding up the hill soon the distant sounds of men still at their training could soon be heard. Wood upon wood followed by the crack of a whip and the deep bellow of the man who trained them became clearer with each turn of the road. Cassian wondered if Violetta was beginning to feel the return of nervousness. Gladiators were often more criminal than slave. She would be at risk living among them and even he wondered if the fear and respect of their champion would keep her safe behind her door at night. The wagon paused as a gate opened to allow them entry to the training yard, closing tight behind them so that no man could escape.

Cassian peered out into the rain-soaked yard and saw nearly a dozen mostly naked men with weapons in hand. A flash of lightning revealed them to be wood but that did not make them any less intimidating to one such as Violetta who peeked out beside him. All eyes were upon the wagon as Lucius stepped down into the mud, followed by Jovian and the lanista who quickly rushed to the shelter provided by a large balcony overlooking the yard.

She seemed frozen, perhaps scared to move, before she turned her head to look at him. He could not stop himself from smiling as she asked; "This is…this is it is it not? The time to move forward and start something new?" She looked back to the yard and whispered, "I admit, now that I am here, and it is real, I am afraid."

Taking her hand, he brought it to his lips. She was right to fear the men that now stared boldly at the wagon with eyes full of curiosity. They had likely been wondering where he had been for the last weeks and once a flash illuminated that it was a woman who sat beside him, they would be curious about her as well.

He stared back at them with equal boldness knowing that any one of them could be commanded to face him when next he took the sands, they would die with honor, but they would die just the same.

He could see Argus, who easily stood half a head above even the tallest man, there was also the Thracian Tarcarus and Proximus who had been allowed a single victory over the champion of the house and so had thought himself his better ever since. Finally, his eyes fell upon Cirandon who had trained him to rise above all others. Despite all the shadows between them with his wife's death the two remained as close as brothers when they stood upon the sands. He turned his head towards the lighted doorway of the ludus and saw the familiar form of Auctus, the captain of the guard and the other man who usually shared his personal watch and behind him the druid, Arturo, waited in silhouette for his arrival.

"Hold no fear, you are with me." He whispered, moving to the entry of the wagon so that his brothers in arms could that their champion had truly returned.

Leaping to the wet ground Cassian squared his shoulders and took a deep breath. How could he describe this feeling? The feeling of coming home, of knowing once again what his purpose in this life was and having his heart lifted high by the knowledge that the woman that he loved was beside him, safe from the treachery of Romans for a time. He was, in that moment, truly content despite his physical pain. The rain was a relentless downpour and yet the nod of each man upon the sands when their eyes met lifted his spirits higher and higher.

He shielded his eyes to look at the men in the door; the lanista whispering to both guard and medicus while the boy stared out at the sands. He raised a hand to acknowledge the pair that waited for him when Tertius and Jovian departed into the dry warmth that would welcome their arrival home then turned his attention to his woman, crouching at the edge of the wagon with the blanket still wrapped about her slender shoulders. Holding out his hand he eased her down gently and threw a protective arm around her before guiding her towards the shelter that beckoned with its light in the dark of the storm.

The security of his touch calmed her nerves enough that she did not slip in the mud, but the stares of the men sent shivers down her spine. She had not thought that they would take such interest in her arrival, nor had she considered that she might be unwanted in a place reserved for men alone. It was his utter surety and confidence, the way he held her protectively despite the curiosity of others that settled her unease. Blinking as the rain pelted her face Violetta looked up at the medicus, silhouetted in the doorway while he waited for his patient and now his assistant. What had Tertius told him? Had he been commanded to deal with her in a certain manner or was her presence left without explanation at all?

Drawing closer she could see that he was not a tall man though he was handsome in a way that made her think of warriors and fire. He had warm brown eyes that sparked beneath thick brows and a gentle, teasing smile on a broad face with a chiseled jaw. His hair, as black as the night, fell, like Cassian's, to his shoulders, which made her wonder if it was the way of the Celt's as no other man upon the sands wore their hair in such a way. "Medicus?" She called when they arrived "I bring your patient and he brings me to aid you."

Arturo stayed out of the worst of the rain. The archway was designed to shield its occupants from the worst of the weather that would strike the hilltop. He was happy to see his friend return, there had been much speculation as to if he would come back to the ludus alive. A smile lit his face at the approach of the couple. He was glad to have the lanista gone from what he considered to be his own domain, far from Roman control.

"It is good to see you once again brother." He said to greet the man who was obviously injured beyond the point where he should be speaking, not that it would stop him.

Turning to the young woman he welcomed her into the infirmary with a gentle sweep of his arm. "Welcome Violetta. All has been prepared for whatever need we have. Are you prepared to fight the fates in a way unlike the man beside you? We are all warriors here, in our way."

When she nodded slowly, from either fear or awe, he softened his smile and drew the pair down the lit hallway. "Come, let me show you the way."

Continued in The Champion's Test...

About the Author

Born in Hardisty, Alberta Monica developed an undeniable love of reading at an early age. Homeschooled during her primary years, her mother not only taught the basics to her five children, but she also read to them at least twice a day. From Anne of Green Gables to Tolkien's Lord of the Rings the stories and the people behind them instilled a love of the written word.

As soon as she could hold a pencil Monica began to write her own stories. Her first complete work was 'Monkey Millionaires' in which a pair of monkeys became millionaires by selling ice cream. While it was a huge hit among the kids in the neighborhood it was just the beginning. After discovering the TV show Spartacus, and full immersion into that fandom, Monica was disappointed to find there was very little fiction to satisfy her desire to indulge a love of Roman era romance. The spark was then lit to write the stories she wanted to read herself.

Despite some eye-opening experiences (it's not as glamorous a profession as the movies would have you believe) she would not change her journey in the slightest. When she is not working or writing, Monica is a single parent to a little girl. Nothing makes her happier than when her daughter tells her that she wants to be a writer, "Just like you, Mommy." So, to keep inspiring a very special little girl, and to bring some elements of romantic Rome and the romance of real life to some not-so-little girls, she is pleased to be writing as M. Francis Lamont and brings you "The Champion's Torment," the second book of her centurion saga, and many more stories to come. She encourages everyone to "Live with Passion. Live with Purpose. And most important of all, Never Lose." Welcome to the beginning of something wonderful.

Book 3 of The Champions, "The Champion's Test,"
Coming Soon!